JOSHUA'S TREE

Joshua's Tree

LEAH MARTIN

DEDICATION

This book is dedicated to my parents, Roy and Janice Martin, who gave me a magical childhood. And to my siblings, Niels, Eric and Karen, who shared it with me.

"A sibling may be the keeper of one's identity, the only person with the keys to one's unfettered, more fundamental self."

— *Marian Sandmaier*

ACKNOWLEDGMENTS

I want to offer my sincere appreciation and thanks to my dear friend, Robin Zaborek. Her belief in me, her encouragement, and the hours she imparted reviewing and editing this book all contributed to its realization. Most of all, I am honored by her loyal and enduring friendship, which I cherish.

1

My eyelids were so heavy, I felt like I was coming out of the dense fog of anesthesia. I was awake enough to appreciate the irony, though; I was in the hospital, but I wasn't the patient. I was just suffering from debilitating exhaustion, and my body was fighting the urge to rejoin the conscious world around me. My sluggish state wasn't just rebellion against the fatigue, or against my grouchy bones complaining of their rusty joints each time I shifted my position; my heart was also desperately trying to deny the despair that was patiently waiting for me to wake up.

Despite my attempts to keep lingering in the land of my dreams, my eyes opened to see Joshua lying in the hospital bed, same as I left him when I slipped into my brief slumber just two hours before. My arm had fallen asleep, and I had to swing it around like a lumbering log to get it to follow my weary frame to an upright position in the chair that doubled as a "bed" for anyone wanting to stay the night. I cradled the dead arm in my other good one and tried to hold it as still as possible. I knew the pins and needles would be coming when the blood started to flow freely to my arm again. Any movement would just cause my nerve-endings to go crazy, and if I could minimize that weird pain sensation, I'd be happy. Well – not happy. How could I be happy ever again unless Josh opened his eyes and talked to me?

He had been this way for two days now, his limbs limp and lifeless, refusing to answer me when I talked to him, pleading for him to respond. I wanted to join him in his peaceful oblivion and put away my own aches and bruises. It seemed my body got sorer as the hours dragged on, the sinews of every muscle group murmuring their objections to any movement.

I was all at once angry with Josh for ignoring me and scared that he was leaving me. Tears started their well-known course down my face with that thought, and I tried to bury it deep into the fissures of my broken heart. If I ignored it, maybe it wouldn't happen. Truth be told, if he didn't open his eyes again, I felt there was nothing in this world worth me seeing. If he didn't walk again, then why should I have to take one more step on my own?

Hospitals can't help but corner the market on sorrow and melancholy. It's not their fault – it's just that way. Kind of like airports – they're both places where you have to say goodbye. I mean, they can also be happy places where you welcome people home, but my experiences at airports were mostly saying goodbye to Josh. I'd sent him off to war more times than I care to remember, not knowing for sure if he'd really come home. So, when he did come home after his deployments, the airport turned into a happy place of joyful reunion. Would that happen here, too? Would I get to welcome him back to a full awareness of his surroundings, and would he open those piercing blue eyes and let me see the sparkle of recognition in them when he looks at me again?

At the airport I would always be there, waiting for him to walk off his plane. My calves ached from standing on my tippy-toes in order to see over the heads of the crowd, searching each face as it came off the jet-way, until that one I recognized as my own came into view. Then, pure joy. I'd jump into his arms and wrap myself around him. His fatigues exuded that unique smell of exotic markets in foreign lands, flooding my memory of days gone by. If I held on tight, nobody could take him from me ever again.

Hospitals have been happy places, too. It was probably happy in the nursery, because parents were all welcoming a new life into their families, and none of them had any clue that Josh was fighting for his life up here in the ICU. Right now, I couldn't really remember any happy hospital times – all I could feel is anxiety and panic, hoping against all hope that I wouldn't have to live my life without my beloved brother Joshua. Please, God – let him live.

I managed to get my eyes open long enough to look at the machine that monitored his pulse. I could hear it beeping, but I just needed the double sureness of seeing it with my own eyes, in case I was just imagining the incessant and unbroken procession of beeps in my restless dreaming. Those patterns of sinusoidal P and T waves, a parenthetical bracket to the beeping spike of the QRS Complex on the heart monitor, were the notes of my lullaby, singing me softly and securely into siesta.

A couple of visitors had come by in the past two days. Only two people were allowed in Josh's room at once, and even then, visitors to the ICU were tightly controlled. But these were people who wanted to come by to thank Josh – even if he wasn't awake to hear their tearful whispers of gratitude. I wouldn't leave Josh's side, so I was there to see each person as they called on him. They would all do the same thing – pull up a chair to his bedside, take his lifeless hand in theirs, and then the tears would start to come. They didn't know what to say, so they would just murmur "thank you" over and over again as they touched their foreheads to Josh's hand that was clasped tightly in theirs, anointing him with their tears. As they left the room, they would tell me what a hero Joshua was to them. I smiled at them as best I could, wondering to myself how I could be the only one who seemed to have been born knowing that about him.

I knew I had to emerge from my cocoon at some point. My chrysalis was a comforting protection, but it was time to transform from this sheltered existence and face the realities around me. I owed that much to Josh and to his visitors, so I deliberately shook off my personal shackles of worry and grief for those times when people came to visit.

In those moments I could certainly feel their emotions and compassion for Josh and me. In a very real way, I completely empathized with their gratitude for him. I owed my own life to Josh, and I had spent my own time at his side thanking him for what he had done. The internal struggle I was having, though, was that I didn't want to survive without him. I didn't want him to leave me here by myself in this world that would be utter desolation and loneliness without him in it. So, while I was grateful to him for such a selfless act of heroism, I was also reprimanding him for letting me live. An absurdity to anyone else – but to me, perfect sense.

There were still two others that were struggling for their lives down the hall from us. Not everyone had survived, and perhaps there would be more that would not live. At that thought, my heart constricted with dread and anxiety – maybe one of those who wouldn't live would be this kind and tender man lying in front of me. But the tragedy would have been so much worse if it hadn't been for my sweet Joshua. I had to keep reminding myself of this fact, because if it weren't true, then losing him would be for nothing, and I couldn't bear to consider that notion, let alone the thought of losing him for the sake of others – even for my sake.

If Josh could hear my thoughts, he would reprove me in his unique way – eyebrows raised, and the right corner of his mouth turned up in the tiniest semblance of a smile. He wouldn't want me to begrudge him doing the right thing. He wouldn't have changed anything – I was being selfish for wishing he wouldn't have risked his life in that bitter and icy river, its twisted currents and dark abysses pulling at our feet as we fought and kicked for the surface. He would have softly scolded me for bidding time backward to undo the events that seemed to have derailed the course of my life.

I knew I couldn't change the unchangeable, or wish time in reverse. And I knew I was being uncharitable in wishing his life for theirs. Truthfully, I wouldn't alter the outcome, or even trade his life for any other. He wouldn't want it that way, and I knew it wouldn't be right. Things happen for a reason, and Josh would probably tell me that this was all part of the plan for his life, and this is what was meant to be. But I couldn't help those natural and innate emotions from occasionally surpassing the more spiritual understanding that pierced my soul as I looked upon him. I knew in my heart, of course, that he had done such a noble and good thing. I just didn't want to admit that it might have cost him his life – or should I say, it might have cost *me* his life.

2

Two days ago, Josh and I were driving along the county road, taking our time, not just because the roads were icy, but also because we were enjoying our time together and it didn't matter to either of us how long it took to get from one place to another. We were on an actual drive down Memory Lane, on our way to visit the little town we knew so well but hadn't seen in quite some time. We wanted to see the old house where we lived and take a look at the school to see what had changed since we'd been there last. My memories were full of poignant images of summer parades, town festivals at the City Park with contests of every kind throughout the day, and outdoor movies in the park at night. Pie eating contests and kids chasing around a greased pig, the first to capture it winning five dollars – these images were swirling around in my mind as Josh slowed the car, having caught up to a school bus ahead of us on the road.

The county road followed the river's meandering path, and we saw the tail of the bus slip a little each time it rounded a bend. The red brake lights fluttered and flashed, revealing the nervous hesitation of the bus driver in the slippery conditions. I wasn't sure if the driver was new to the area and not used to the winter driving conditions, or if it was just particularly problematic to maneuver the bus that day. It really was cold outside – the temperature had dropped drastically in just a matter of a day or two. The hair in my nostrils froze just from inhaling a breath of the wintry air.

The school bus started over a small bridge that spanned the river, and that's when time seemed to come grinding to a near halt, moving forward by incremental frames of a film that I could replay in my mind's eye over and over again in the days to come. The driver hit some ice on the bridge, and the back of the bus slid to the left and kept gliding gracefully like a puck on a hockey rink, nothing to stop it. The bus driver turned the wheel into the sliding rear end, attempting to correct the movement. Not even that helped, though, and Josh and I just sat there in our car watching helplessly as the back of the bus hit the guard rail, ripping it from its place on the edge of the bridge. The point of the bus's equilibrium was still on the bridge, so it kept turning, coming to 180 degrees from its original bearing and turning still, like a massive yellow ice ballerina, awkward on her skates. I saw the look of horror and panic on the bus driver's face, and our eyes locked for just a brief moment before the front of the bus was carried over the edge of the bridge, only air beneath the front bumper.

The bus still had some forward momentum, skidding across the bridge as it turned. But as soon as the front wheels dropped over the side of the concrete, the undercarriage scraped along the hard road surface and shaved the stubbly guardrail off the face of the bridge.

The driver held his eyes on mine as long as he could, craning his neck to see me, powerless to do anything but hold on and pray for the souls he had onboard. Then he was gone.

The bus careened over the edge of the bridge and plunged nose-first into the frigid water just twenty feet below. The water wasn't exactly shallow in that part the river; it might be two or three people deep, standing on each other's shoulders. But even that was deep enough for a bus to be submerged, and for the kids to be in serious danger.

I couldn't see the bus from our vantage point anymore, and I was in shock and complete horror – tears flowed automatically from my eyes because my body didn't know how else to react. Josh was already springing into action as soon as he put the car into park. I followed him as the hot breath from our lungs puffed into the cold air; we were fire-breathing dragons, our vapors trailing after us as we ran to the bridge and looked over. The rear emergency door of the bus was peering out of the surface of the water like a drowning face reaching its mouth for life-saving air. Before I knew it, Josh had lunged himself from the bridge into the water below. Without a thought, I followed.

When I was a teenager at girls' camp, we would jump into the cold river every morning. We called it the "Polar Bear Plunge." Everyone thought it was so cold, and only the bravest and most daring girls would face the freezing dip in the stream. Of course, I was first in line – anything that took intestinal fortitude drew me in like a bee to honey. All we got from it was bragging rights – worth every frigid moment. Girls' camp was in the summertime, though, so even if the mountain streams were cold with glacial run-off, that ritual in no way prepared me for the paralyzing bone-chilling arctic cold that I experienced as I followed Josh into the river.

The shock of the water temperature almost made me lose my breath when I plunged into the river. I swam toward the light of day, breaking the surface with a forceful splash, and filling my lungs with a shrieking inhale of air. Josh had already reached the back of the bus, and was working the latch on the back door, pushing it upward and open. I swam over to him, and he was already climbing into the hatch. The bus was quickly filling with water, row after row of seats being submerged. Kids were climbing furiously up the aisle and across the backs of the seats, scrambling for the back door to their salvation. All I could imagine were rats on the Titanic, trying to outrun the water, scurrying for safety.

The bus was at a sharp angle, and it was hard for them to climb. I peered over the edge of the door opening and saw one little girl who couldn't have been more than seven years old holding onto the back of a seat, struggling to climb up the aisle. Her tennis shoes were slipping on the black grooves of the rubber mat that lined the aisle way, and she stumbled to her knees. Her panicked almond-shaped eyes found mine; her screaming filled my ears and pierced my heart.

The shock was starting to set in; I suddenly found myself strangely concerned that these kids would never want to be around water again. This experience would traumatize them, and they would probably never want to splash in the river like I did when I was their age, diving for treasure, or floating on my back with the warm sun tanning my face. Time was frozen, like all of my fingers and every muscle on my face. In that fraction of a minute, I could see my seven-year-old self, frolicking in this very river so many summers ago, carefree and happy. My heart broke to think that this girl looking at me now through her tears may never want to swim again because of this moment.

Time snapped back into motion, and I saw Josh grab the little girl's hand, pulling her toward the back of the bus, delivering her into my arms. She clung to me for dear life, her whimpering cries filling my ear, and her petite arms wrapped tightly around my neck. I looked again at her distinctively shaped eyes and realized suddenly that this girl had Down syndrome. This altered everything in my muddled mind. With all the confusion and panic around me, I wasn't thinking through anything rationally; my wit was dimming in the numbing cold as swiftly as my extremities became callous to my commands. But this piqued my level of awareness and brought clarity for just a moment.

Certain experiences in my life had molded and formed my convictions long ago. One glance at her precious little face brought those experiences to the surface and hit my heart with an almost magical epiphany, and I almost broke down right there with her in my arms. The genuine compassion and love I felt for this unknown child was both consuming and undeniable, as if God Himself brought me purposely to her. It happened in a few fleeting moments, and I wondered how I could feel such affection for someone who wasn't even mine. I wanted to take her safely home with me, and I felt a twinge of illogical loss when I knew I couldn't; she was someone else's treasure.

I couldn't fathom the trepidation and turmoil she must have suffered as her bus ride home went so horribly wrong, and I thought my heart would burst with this strange sense of sudden attachment. Every life in that bus was just as valid and significant as the rest, but for whatever irreconcilable reason, I instantly promised God that I would protect this child as if she were my own.

I murmured in her ear that everything would be ok, and that she was alright now. "I want my Daddy," she whimpered. I prayed silently that I could impart some love and comfort to her - that God would take her fear away. I looked toward the bank of the river and saw that it was just a short distance from us - maybe just fifteen feet away. I looked up to the bridge and saw some peering faces standing above us. "Help!" I screamed. "Call 9-1-1! Help us!"

"What's your name?" I asked, turning back to the little girl. She just kept crying, though, so I told her I was going to give her a piggy back ride, and that she should hold on to me. It was like ripping Velcro apart to get her to adjust her position from in front of me to my back, but I finally managed to get her shifted around. I slid into the river and paddled toward shore. Luckily, she hardly weighed anything, and it was easy to swim with her on my back. We kept our heads above water, and I mindlessly kept moving my arms, hoping they were obeying my directives to stroke, stroke, stroke. My neck was getting squeezed by her delicate arms - she was a strong little girl for her age, and my windpipe felt like a vacuum hose getting pinched off so that it had hardly any suction.

We made it to the riverbank, and I breathed freely again as a woman grabbed the little bundle from my back and wrapped a blanket around her that she had brought from her car. I looked at my sweet little friend, and I saw right away in those exquisite eyes that she didn't want me to leave her. I didn't want to leave her, either, and fresh hot tears fell down my chilly cheeks at having to abandon her here on the bank of the river, even though this kind woman was there to take over. But I had to help Josh.

"I'll be back, ok sweetheart?" I told the little girl. It hurt me to the bones to have to walk away from her – I cried harder as I turned away and started walking. The woman told me an ambulance was on its way, but I was already heading back to the bus and I didn't hear anything else she was saying.

Two more kids had climbed to safety outside and were huddling together for warmth. When I poked my head back into the end of the bus, I could see that Josh had positioned more kids toward the rear of the bus on top of the seats near the door. The water had stopped filling the cavity of the school bus, and I saw Josh take a deep breath, and dive back down into the water toward the front, which had been fully submerged for several minutes now. I could see a little body floating just next to the shell of the rooftop, and I dropped into the water and grabbed his coat, pulling him toward me. I turned him over, and his face and mouth were blue, his eyes lifeless. A lump in my throat suddenly grew the size of a boulder. I tried to cry out loud, and to call for Josh, my lips hardly willing to move and my throat not wanting to give way to sound. Josh's head came up out of the water, and when he saw the boy in my arms, he told me to rest his body on one of the seats that was still out of the water's reach.

"The bus driver's seat belt is stuck. I can't get it unbuckled," Josh said, and he reached inside his pocket to pull out his knife. I was just staring at him, mesmerized by the white puffs of water vapor coming out of his mouth every time he breathed. The scene was surreal, and I wasn't reacting the way I knew I should. Instead, I was recalling my dad explaining to me why I could see my breath on cold mornings. He explained that water vapor would be an invisible gas when it was warm, the molecules moving freely and uninhibited. But when the air moved from our nice warm bodies out into the cold air, the molecules slowed down and packed together, and could no longer remain invisible gas - rather they turned to a liquid state and condensed into puffs of air that we could see. Josh's puffs of air kept coming short and fast, and he was saying something to me that wasn't registering.

He took another lung-full of air and was gone again. I could hear someone yelling from outside, and I climbed through the back door to see a man with a rope, yelling for me to catch the end as he threw it to me. I climbed up and held out my arms, hoping I could catch the rope with my lethargic appendages that no longer seemed to belong to my body. The rope fell short in the water the first time, but on the second throw, it landed near the opening of the door, and I fell against it to keep it from slithering away.

I tried to tie the rope to the bus, threading it around the hinge of the open door. Tying it in a knot seemed impossible with my uncooperative hands. I couldn't feel them; they were so numb, and slow to submit to my dictates. When Josh came up for air again, I tried to talk to him, but my mouth wouldn't move, and whatever I was saying didn't make sense even to me. He pulled the bus driver out of the water with him, and I saw his eyes - the same ones I had seen just minutes before as the bus was sliding on the ice. But now, those eyes were glassy and fixed open. He had been trapped in his seat too long, and he was dead.

The rope was tied crudely, the best I could do with hands that seemed to be just useless clubs with no dexterity left to speak of. The man on the bank was holding it taut, ready for me to send the kids over to him. I asked the boys if they thought they could hold onto the rope and pull themselves over to the river bank. They nodded, and shimmied over to the edge of the bus, held on for their lives, and started pulling their way to safety. Josh pushed the next girl up out of the doorway, and she followed the boys without a word. Josh took over from there, and he shepherded the four remaining survivors out from the back seats, and onto the rope. I sat there shivering and looked through the back window at the little boy who had been floating on his face just a few minutes ago. Josh cradled the boy in his arms and handed him to me through the open door. I knew in my brain that he was dead, but still, I mechanically tipped his head back, placed my blue lips over his, pinched his nose with my quivering shivering fingers, and tried to breathe air into his little lungs. More tears streamed down my face, mixing with the icy water that drenched my entire being.

"He's gone," Josh said to me. "You can let him rest, and we'll be sure to get him back to his mom and dad." I looked into Josh's eyes, my brow lifted high, and then reluctantly laid the boy on the back of the bus.

The ambulance was here now, and rescuers were starting to get suited up in wetsuits and protective gear. That's when we felt the bus shift and give way. The mass of metal slipped further into the water, completely submersed now, the pockets of air filling with the river's liquid fingers, reaching into every crevice until she relinquished herself to her watery grave.

I went under, too, and could see the surface maybe five feet above me. I let my body droop, unable to move anymore, my energy sapped and my regard for all around me waning by the second. The current started to carry me, drifting slowly away from the bus. I stared at the little boy as he floated away from me on the surface, and I hung there in the water, weightless and still. The mass of liquid encased me all about, and I was floating almost as if suspended in outer space, the sounds around me muffled because the river filled my ears, creating an odd sense of peace and quiet, only the sound of my beating heart echoing in my head.

My body jolted abruptly, realizing a basic need for air, and I kicked toward the surface. I was so stiff and my senses so dull, though, that I hardly moved. I couldn't hold my breath any longer, and I envisioned my seven-year-old self at the shallow end of the City Pool, trying to hold my breath for an entire minute. Those were sixty very long seconds for a little girl, and I was so proud of myself when I made it the entire minute. But now in the river, I didn't think I could last even five more seconds, and bubbles from my lungs started seeping from my nose and mouth. I reached my neck and chin upward, straining for the surface where I knew I would find that glorious air. I panicked and sluggishly flung my arms and legs, no rival for the endless gallons of water surrounding me. It was the most horrific feeling I'd ever experienced, and when I realized I was going to die and that I had no choice but to succumb to the liquid enemy enveloping me, I breathed in.

My lungs felt fire, and I choked and coughed, if that's what it could be called. After what seemed like eons of time, but was probably just an instant, I felt the peace of unconsciousness begin to actually warm my body and overcome my fears. I was almost transformed from the petrifying panic to a serene oblivion when I felt a hand grasping my wrist, tugging me upward, jolting me from my near slumber with regular interval. Pull, glide – pull, glide. And then my mind went mercifully blank.

I found out later, even though I somehow already knew, that it was Josh who saved me. He was so strong and so skilled – his body kept going so much longer than mine ever could. And he was brave. And willing. And selfless. He pulled me to the surface and dragged me to the shore. He breathed the air of life into my lungs over and over again until it forced the river water out, and I started breathing again on my own.

The slow current had carried us lazily downstream, so the rescuers followed the bank, navigating over the rocks and through the bushes until they reached us. It took them long enough, though, that Josh was barely holding on when they arrived. We rode to the hospital next to each other, talking only briefly, but holding hands and not wanting to let go. The longer we drove, the weaker his grip on my hand became, and by the time we made it to the hospital, Josh was unconscious.

3

And that's how I ended up at this hospital, next to this bed, worrying for this man. I found out that eight children had been saved because Josh had systematically retrieved every single one of them. The bus driver's body was recovered, and so was the little boy who I saw floating away from the bus, having either drowned, or died from the impact of the crash – I wasn't sure which. There were two other kids who were suffering from hypothermia, and they were still fighting for recovery in the hospital, too. Josh was the one who exerted the most energy, who was in the water the longest, and who nobly risked his life over and over again for each of those souls. His body took the most stress, and now it wasn't willing to wake up.

I sat in the convertible chair, looked over at him and started talking – I heard somewhere that people in comas might still be able to hear things you say. So, I closed my eyes and talked out loud, hoping that the familiar timbres of my voice might spark something in his mind and ignite his senses. Maybe a small fire of recognition would be warm enough to awaken him from his two-day hiatus.

"I don't know how you were able to find me in that river, Josh," I started. "I thought I was drowning, and then out of nowhere, you grabbed my wrist." I ran the scene over in my mind again, imagining if he hadn't saved me. I could be dead right now, and maybe I'd be with our mother and father, who had already passed beyond the veil.

"Did you see that little girl with Down syndrome?" I continued. "She broke my heart, and I felt so responsible for her," I paused, contemplating. "I know it sounds crazy, but...I love that little girl and I don't even know her name."

I sat back to get more comfortable, but I kept talking to him. "I tried to swim, but my arms just wouldn't move for me...I was too tired..." My voice started to trail off, and my words became lethargic and slurred. I was falling asleep, starting to dream that I was still swimming, my arms stalwartly displacing the water, stroke by stroke...

1978

I parted the sea of cornstalks in front of me with my small hands, making strong breaststrokes as I made my way through the field, row after never-ending row. The stalks were so tall I was drowning in their waves, and I swam a little faster through their rustling leaves, my lungs starting to feel a small panic of dusty suffocation. Suddenly I reached the edge of the field and broke free to the surface, gasping great gulps of fresh air in the wide-open space of our farm.

Josh and I ran as fast as our bare feet would carry us from the cornfield to the county road. It had been a dirt road until recently when the county had covered it with a layer of gravel, then poured hot tar all over the small stones before adding a second layer of gravel, forming a pseudo-pavement. On especially hot days, I would hunt for little pockets of melted tar that expanded with the heated air and formed bubbles on the road surface, and I'd pop them with my finger. We followed along the edge of the road for a while, so our feet wouldn't get burned on the hot black surface, until we came to our hidden path in the thick of the bushes and saplings lining the shoulder of the road. The soft dirt path led us through the foliage, each running step leaving a shoeless print, our toes flinging the velvety dust into a brief suspension in the air before falling to the ground on the powdery path behind us.

We kept running until we came to a steep bank of shale. The slippery slide of smooth gray rock delivered us to the bottom of the little river valley in a matter of seconds, like a slide at a water park. I skimmed on my backside down the hill, a whoop and holler erupting from my throat in sheer glee. My echoes floated and hung in the air, invisible clouds of sound that filled Josh's ears as he slid through them after me. He couldn't help but join in my cheerful chorus, belting out the best Tarzan jungle call he could muster. We'd spend the afternoon damming up the flow of a small side tributary of the river until we made ourselves a nice little swimming hole that we'd jump into, seeing who could make the highest cannonball splash.

We'd play for hours until we realized the sun was veiling its face behind the lacey leaves of the trees enough to shade our surroundings and make the water too cold for comfort, and we'd head back home to our mother. Life was so innocent and uncomplicated. Summer sun bronzed our limbs and bleached our hair. Mom would send us out for the day with a sack lunch and wouldn't worry about us until dinnertime.

I always thought I was lucky for having been born at the beginning of a decade. It's always so much easier to calculate my age that way. No complicated borrowing or carrying of numbers. My grandma and I shared that fortune; she was born in 1930, and I followed her into this world exactly forty years later.

My brother, though, was even more fortunate. Josh was born a mere thirteen months before I was, which meant he was born in the year of the triumphant lunar landing. It was the year that America won her rightful First Place, edging out the "Commie Russians" in the race to gain the first foothold in space. All time is now measured by this American achievement. "That was fifteen years before Neil Armstrong walked on the moon." Or, "It's already been a decade since the lunar landing." See what I mean? My brother won on that account – even if it would be harder for him to quickly calculate his age when he got to be older, it seemed all time was measured by the year of his birth.

Being the younger one, I would follow Josh around like his shadow. In my eyes, he could do no wrong. That summer, he and I had our sights set on a couple of straw cowboy hats that sat on the tippy-top shelf of City

Market in the next town over. We needed some money to buy those glorious cowboy hats, and for the next few months, we set our minds to earning it. I smiled inside to think that Josh and I would have matching cowboy hats; he never made fun of me once for wanting to be like him, even if I was a skinny little eight-year-old girl.

He was nice that way, though. One time when we were walking to school on our first day back for the year, I dropped all my new crayons on the sidewalk. I was flustered with the other kids walking by, and I started to panic that I would be late to school. Tears threatened to sting my eyes. Josh bent down, picked them all up for me and helped each crayon find its rightful home back in the box. I knew right then that he loved me.

Mom and Dad both taught us to be hard workers – even at our young age. Some of my earliest memories were following my dad out into the fields early in the morning when the frost was still clinging to the blades of grass, crunching under our feet before the rising sun had time to melt them into submission. The irrigation ditches ran along the far side of the fields. Dad would bury the shovel into the ground and pry out a slice of earth that would dam the small ditch enough to divert the life-giving flow of water to the crops.

I tagged along, watching him work. My little legs wouldn't quite stretch far enough to meet my dad's pace, so I would leap and hop from one big boot print to the next, trailing along behind him as we went. His shovel would ride on his shoulder, its spade dancing back and forth with the sway of his stride. I wanted to walk where he walked, not to let my little feet touch unbroken ground, thinking that the frosty dew was a lake of lava that would swallow me up if I missed my dad's footsteps.

Josh always wanted to be just like my dad. He was his carbon copy – not just in his outward appearance, but also his demeanor and personality. They were both kind-hearted, non-confrontational, and forever the peacemakers. My dad knew how to do everything; he was so smart and capable. Later in our lives, after our parents had died, I'd often look at Josh and see the younger version of my dad – the dad of my childhood – and my heart would pull and yearn for those innocent days when I could run and jump into his arms. When I was just a toddler, he would perch me on his right shoulder like I was sitting on a chair, my little legs dangling down to his chest, and his strong hands grasping my ankles. He would count, "One, two, three!" and I would fearlessly jump out into the open air, my arms stretched out in full faith and confidence. He'd swing me by my ankles, down to the floor, past his legs, and then like a pendulum swoop me back up to my perch on his shoulder. I screamed with delight.

I was more like our mother, not just freckled cheeks and bright blue eyes, but also a less disciplined and more rebellious spirit; we were both full of life and adventure, undaunted by challenges, and loyal to a fault. My mom was the most devoted wife and mother I've ever known, following my dad around the world, two kids in tow, and enduring what most women would not – dutifully and without much complaint. I found little wrong with my mother, and if I could just be a portion of who she was, it would be cause for celebration. She made of our childhood an anthology of matchless and marvelous experiences that I couldn't have dreamed up on my own given three wishes from a magic lamp.

4

We had a lone Joshua tree growing on our land. It was somewhat out of place, and really shouldn't be growing this far away from the desert. But there it was, standing with its arms stretched to the sky.

I thought we called it the Joshua tree because it was the place that my brother liked to go to be alone. He would hang around that tree for hours sometimes, lounging on its branches like a leopard with its prey, or like the silhouette of a cowboy lying down for a nap with his hat tipped over his eyes, his legs outstretched, and boots crossed. He made a platform in the crook of the branches where he could perch himself for quiet contemplation. He had me climb up the wooden footholds that he had nailed to the trunk of the tree and help him tie a rope from its branch, so we could swing from the platform and drop to our feet miles from its shadow.

Josh could do most things by himself, but he liked companionship – even if it was just his little sister to watch him while he worked. It was better than doing it alone. Even when we were older, he would call me to help him do odd jobs. I would lend another set of hands to the job to be sure, but I knew in my heart he just wanted my company. Which, of course, I freely gave. But, still, he just wanted to have time alone in that tree.

It was a safe place of retreat for him, because it wasn't exactly built for your typical tree-climbing pastime. Its leaves could be dangerous; they were shaped like bayonets, flat and tapering to a sharp point. Clusters of these leaves grew from the branches and thwarted any invader of Josh's privacy. Nobody wanted to hang out in that awkward and prickly tree – except for my brother. It was his quiet fortress, and he dwelled there from time to time in his secret place, guarded about by its shadows, his refuge and fortress.

One day I couldn't find Josh anywhere. I wanted him to play with me under the trailer house where I had lined up all our Matchbox cars. Well – they were *his* Matchbox cars, but I was tired of playing with dolls and girly things, and he always shared his cars with me. We were tiny land moguls, developing small towns and communities in the dirt where our cars and imaginary people could live out their illusory existence.

We had an elaborate network of roads connecting every part of the community, and even a little river that our cars crossed over on a bridge made from a piece of scrap wood. We would bring a bucket of water under the trailer and feign the flow of the river by pouring water into the little canal we had engineered. As the water ran under the bridge, I pushed a little yellow school bus safely across the rising tide. It only lasted a moment, though, and then our contrived stream was mud. We would push our cars over the roadways throughout our town, from our houses to the school, to the grocery store and home again. It was a glorious way to spend an after-noon, and I went looking for Joshua to see if he would play with me.

"Josh!" I called, as I poked my head into his room. When I found it empty, I ran out to the barn to see if he might be there. "Josh, where are you?" I finally found him sitting out back in his tree.

"I've been looking all over for you," I said, breath-less from running far and wide around the farm.

"Sorry, I didn't hear you. I've just been up here hangin' out," he answered.

"Well, come play with me," I petitioned. "I've got all the cars ready under the trailer." At that, he threw him-self off the edge of his perch, and swung on the rope to the ground. We raced each other back to the trailer house, and clambered underneath it to our Matchbox make-believe.

I just figured that was what our family called it: "Joshua's Tree" – not the *Yucca brevifolia*, whose com-mon name was given by a group of Mormon pioneers crossing the desert. The tree's branches can sometimes look like arms reaching toward heaven, and it reminded them of the Prophet Joshua reaching his arms in prayer and supplication toward heaven. You can't tell how old a Joshua tree is, because they don't have growth rings in their trunks like most trees, but you imagine them as the kings of the desert, towering high above their throngs of adoring high desert brush.

I found out much later that it wasn't my brother's tree specifically – although that one tree on our farm was surely his. "Joshua tree" is just what everyone in the world calls that species. To me, though, those praying plants of mysterious age will always be my brother's trees.

5

Our Bishop asked my parents to do their part in the renovation of the church house by committing to a certain monetary contribution. A large portion of the budget had to come from the congregation, and my parents were happy to do their part. They had also talked to Josh and me about what we could do for the budget. So when my dad turned to Josh and said, "Kids, tell the Bishop what you're willing to commit to," Josh told him that the two of us would raise fifty dollars. As we walked out of that office, Josh and I shouldered a heavy burden for two young kids under the age of ten. My parents had wisely helped us to set a goal that was lofty enough to make it hard to attain, but doable all the same. Josh and I didn't know it yet, but we had just become the youngest corn farmers in the county.

My parents helped us plant our own little field of corn. The plan was to raise a crop of sweet corn and sell it door to door to raise our fifty-dollar promise. Our small bodies bent over the freshly plowed earth and our bare feet softly sunk into the cool clumps of lush and fertile soil that now lined up in a diminutive berm. My toes curled into the richness of the ground with each step I took as we plopped corn seeds here and there. My mother would follow behind to rescue the wayward seeds. Our tiny hands covered the hopeful kernels with the dark soil, and our little feet walked down the length of the rows, carefully putting them to sleep until they would take root. Finally, after much anticipation, bashful sprouts would poke out of the dirt in the nourishing sun. Our little hearts soared!

Josh called to me every day, luring me outside with his warm and inviting pleas. I'd run outside to join him, and we'd judiciously inspect the progress of our crop.

"We've got to make sure the corn seeds get enough water," he said to me, trying to imitate our dad the best he could. "Water is what gives life to plants. That, and the sunshine." Josh was showing me his botanical expertise; our dad was a Botanist by education, and Josh was parroting something he had heard dad say.

We made sure our little seedlings had enough water running down their furrows from the irrigation ditches, and that all the weeds were cleared from around them, ridding them of any herbal competitors for the soil's life-giving nutrients. We witnessed the miracle of seeds giving way to their ultimate fruitful destinies. After many weeks of what seemed like toil, the stalks were taller than we were, and the ears of corn were plump and sweet.

We loaded our wagon with ears of corn to overflowing and walked it down the streets of our small town, selling the corn from door to door. And this is how we eventually raised the fifty dollars that we proudly put into our Bishop's hand. What a sense of satisfaction we

felt – not just because we saw a result from a hard summer's work, but more the warm feeling inside from our
pledge and promise kept. We walked home with our
empty wagon.

"High five," I said. We clapped hands up top, and
then swung our arms down, smacking them together
again as they crossed at the bottom, all in one motion.
This was our usual celebratory routine – an "around the
world" high-five with one thwack of the hands at the
North Pole, and one at the South.

In our free time, we were obsessed with earning
money for our cowboy hats that sat patiently waiting for
us on that top shelf at City Market. Our friend, Jude, said
that his grandpa would pay us all to pick up nails from
his property. I think there was an old house that burned
down on that piece of land, the fire consuming all the or-
ganic material, but leaving all the metal behind. His old
Gramps lived in a trailer on the land now, but he wanted
the nails to be cleaned up. So the three of us picked up
buckets of nails, and Jude's grandpa paid us one cent for
each nail. We'd find coins under the cushions of the
couch sometimes; Gramps' pockets didn't always hold
his coins very well, and they'd fall into the cracks of the
couch to be rescued by us.

Jude would play with us a lot, making us the Three
Musketeers. At least that's how I saw it – most likely the
reality of the situation was that they were best pals, and
they just let Josh's little sister tag along. I kept up with
the boys, though – we played some rough tackle football,
and I wasn't the least bit shy about getting hurt. I played
just as rough as the boys did, and I took my bumps and
bruises right alongside them. I'd get the wind knocked
out of me, or get slammed to the ground running the football – and the pain, in a strange way, made me feel alive

in my young body. I followed those boys off the rope swing into the river; I rode my bike down scary hills, and took my turn sledding down the biggest slope in town when it snowed. I wasn't going to be left behind, and they generously tolerated me most of the time.

Josh and I had been playing out in the sage brush on the farm when we uncovered some old pottery shards. There were ruins of Anasazi Indians in the area, and the pottery we found were the broken remnants and relics of their beautiful handiwork. We found remains of large white clay pots with black painted geometric designs. We uncovered big Metate stones that they used with a smaller Mano stone to grind maize into corn flour. We were fascinated by the arrowheads and other artifacts we discovered there on our farm, and we collected each and every piece of our dig into our wagon, ready to transport it to the Hogan.

The Hogan was a small trading post and tourist shop located on the highway that would sell Indian artifacts, jewelry, clothing, and a myriad of other interesting items that tourists would buy. Mrs. Brimhall was the owner of the Hogan, and the granddaughter of some old-time traders who settled the area. She wore silver and turquoise jewelry, beautiful against her wrinkled skin and greying hair. She would pay us cash per pound for our pottery shards. I envisioned her taking our wagon full of broken pottery and staying up all night gluing all the pieces back together again under a desk lamp in the back of her Hogan, the result being a large ancient pot that she would sell in her store. Little did I know at the time, but Mrs. Brimhall didn't really have any use for our pottery – she just bought it from us because she loved our little entrepreneurial spirits and humored us out of the kindness of her heart.

It took the good part of a day to get our treasure there, make the exchange for cash, and then get ourselves back home again. Mom made us some peanut butter and jelly sandwiches that we carried in the basket on my bike, and we set out down our county road, heading toward the big highway. Once we got that far, we would cross over to the other side, where we would find the Hogan.

I had a pink Huffy girl's bike with a banana seat. Josh's was brown. We loved to play *Chips* – the California Highway Patrol TV show, where one of us would be Ponch, and the other Baker. Our front wheels would have to be aligned perfectly as we rode our bikes down the county road, and we'd pretend to save people from the distresses of the world. Sometimes I'd ride on the handlebars of Josh's bike, if mine had a flat tire, or some other problem that rendered it temporarily useless. I could pump Josh on my bike, too, even though I was just little – I had strong muscles for a girl my age and could even beat some boys in arm wrestling. But most of my strength came from sheer will – the power of the mind over the body. The very notion that I could be like my brother fueled my abilities and gave me strength to rise up to the challenge with wings as eagles.

I sat on Josh's handlebars one day, my bare feet buttressed on each side by the large bolt that kept his front wheel attached to the bike frame. We rode down the street past our grade school, the breeze flowing through our hair, and summer sun kissing our faces. I fit right inside the bottom of his tall ape hangar style handlebars, balancing with no hands.

A bright glint on the road caught my eye, so I told Josh, "Stop! I think I see a quarter!"

I was ready for him to stomp backward on his pedals and slam on the brakes, so as the bike stopped, my momentum continued, launching me forward through the air. I bent my knees and threw out my arms in a surfer stance and landed a few feet in front of Josh's bike. My knees were shock absorbers, taking the weight of my little frame as I landed, and then I scrambled my feet in a Fred Flintstone run until I could come to a stop from the catapult action off the handlebars. I ran back to see if there was money on the ground where I had seen the sun shining on something silver. It was a dime – less than half of the quarter I had hoped to find. But I smiled anyway, shoved it in my pocket and climbed back on my perch. Josh balanced the extra weight as I hopped on, and then shoved off from his left foot as he pedaled us back onto our wandering way.

Just as we were passing in front of the convenience store, my foot slipped off the bolt that it was balancing on, and my big toe got caught in the spokes. We wrecked onto the pavement of the street, and Josh picked himself up to help me hobble over to the curb, where I sat to examine the damage. The thick pad of my big toe was hanging just by a thin flap of skin, and Josh went straight into "rescue boy" mode. He did this whenever there was an emergency. He took total control of the situation and came to the aid of whomever was in distress. As adults, I teased Josh by referring to him by this term of endearment whenever he transformed into this superhero form. "Ok, Rescue Boy, I can probably walk on my ankle, but if you insist on carrying me on your back, go ahead." Or when he overreacted to a knee injury I sustained while playing women's intramural flag football in college and yelled for someone to call an ambulance because he was pretty sure I got hit in the head, I said, "Calm down, Rescue Boy."

In any case, I learned my lesson about riding on the handle bars without shoes.

Yes, Josh was always helping me in one way or another. When we were getting ready to go sell our treasure of Indian pottery pieces, we tied a rope from the back of each of our bicycle sissy bars to the handle of the wagon, and we rode slowly and in parallel so that our wagon wouldn't tip over. Each of us was pulling some of the weight as we rode our bikes down the county road, forming a giant "V."

We stopped to eat our sandwiches, devouring them like ravenous wolves in seconds, realizing too late that we should have brought something to drink. Now the thick peanut butter coated the inside of our throats, with no relief in sight until we could beg for a drink from Mrs. Brimhall.

"Boy, am I glad you two are here! Where's your other partner in crime?" Her eyes were beaming as she saw us walking through the door, its frame knocking into the bell that announced our arrival. She seemed so delighted to have the pottery, as if she had been waiting for this important delivery from us for days.

"Oh, Jude had to stay home today," I explained. "His dad grounded him because he didn't come home in time." I didn't say that he had been slapped across the face, too, and Jude didn't really want to be seen in public with a fat lip and have to make a story up every time someone asked about it.

Mrs. Brimhall weighed the shards on her hanging scale, counterbalancing our pottery with some pre-measured weights, and then paid us for our valuable treasure. We left her shop, free from our laden wagon, free from our self-engineered yoke of rope, and rode home with money in the pockets of our cut-off jean shorts. On the way home, my little legs grew weary, so Josh tied the rope between my bike and his, and he pulled me the rest of the way home.

Mom drove us to City Market the next day in our station wagon. We sat on the fold-down bench in the back of the car that faced the rear, the large window rolled down and open to the outside. We hung our heads out the back window, watching the gray and black as-phalt speed past our faces. We'd climb over the seats and move around the car as our hearts desired.

The station wagon was great, but we really loved to ride in the back of our dad's pickup truck, standing be-hind the cab, cheeks flattened by the airstream and mouths shut tight to avoid any bugs from flying into our teeth. When dad would take us on work trips out into the sage brush country, we'd put down the tailgate and ride with our feet flopping over the edge. When he was going slowly enough, we'd jump off our perch, hold on to the chain that kept the tailgate at a 90-degree angle, and run as fast as our legs would carry us on the dirt trail until we had the chance to jump back up onto the tailgate. It was a thrilling game, and part of the reason we were skinny and fit.

There's a distinct sense of self-determination and even reckless abandon in riding down the highway in the back of a pickup, hands stretched over the cab and bare toes gripping the grooves of the bed. Even sleeping on the floorboards of the car on a road trip, or holding your baby cousin in your lap on the trip to town – these are things of our past now, only to be found in the Third World, where even more dangerous habits are displayed every day with families of five stacked up on one motor-cycle, commuting to school and work. The dad would be driving, his wife behind him holding the baby, one boy squished in between the adults, and one riding in front of his dad.

It was with this feeling of ultimate freedom that Josh and I were riding in the back of dad's truck one day. As we pulled up to a friend's house in town, I was overly anxious to jump out of the bed of the pickup. I slipped on the side of the bed and fell right in between the curb and the tire of the truck, which was still rolling to a stop. I jumped up, unscathed, and acted like nothing was wrong – no need to get the privilege of riding in the back of the truck taken away for having jumped out too soon and al-most gotten myself run over.

On this day, though, mom pulled into the City Mar-ket parking lot in our station wagon, and we jumped out of the back window as soon as she parked. She led us in-side where we gleefully made our big purchase. You didn't see us for the rest of that summer without those cowboy hats on our heads.

Josh was my best friend, and I tried to keep up with him everywhere he went. He led the way, and I willingly followed. Two kids wandering the back fields and rivers, barefoot, grimy and adventurous, sun-tanned faces now shaded by straw cowboy hats. I couldn't have asked for more.

6

Death was just a normal part of animal life on our farm. Some died from the cold temperatures, like the baby rabbits that Josh and I were awaiting with anticipation to welcome into the world. They started out so tiny when they finally were born and didn't look much like rabbits at all – more like seven wiggly, bald babies the size of a mouse, eyes shut tight and ears still closed. I was sure they all nestled together to get warm, because they were so cold from being bald, no coat of fur to keep them warm. When they started to grow a little bigger and were covered in a thin layer of the softest and smoothest fur we'd ever touched, they transformed into tiny rabbits with longer ears and little tails, their eyes peering around with curiosity.

One night they must have been left without the warmth of their mother. Maybe something happened to her, like a fox or another predator may have gotten to her. We never did find out why she wasn't there with her babies. Without her body to keep her little baby rabbits warm, all seven of them died during the cold night.

Other animals died because we ate them for our family's food – something my dad called "The Circle of Life," a phrase that I didn't really get, but figured it meant that it should be ok to eat our farm animals. And then the animals sometimes killed each other, too. Coyotes or foxes would sometimes kill cats or small dogs, and definitely chickens. Of course, cats would kill mice and other rodents. Sheep were always leery of predators, too.

One time our two dogs got into the chicken coop and killed a couple of hens. Sam was a Labrador, and Bernie was a wiener dog – small, but ferocious. My dad taught them a lesson by tying those dead chickens around the dogs' necks – he called it a "chicken necklace" – I learned very quickly that even dogs have shame. They hid under the porch all day and wouldn't come out again until my dad cut the twine that set them free from their dead weight. Those dogs never went after the chickens again.

One of my dad's favorite stories that he told us from when he was a boy was about his own pet chicken. He had a hen that he took care of, and she hatched several broods of little chicks. When only one survived out of her latest brood, his hen would go around guarding that lone survivor under her wing, keeping it safe and warm, hovering over it and chasing it all around the hen house.

Pretty soon, she had another brood, and those little chicks were just miniature puffs of yellow downy fuzz compared to their older sibling fledgling that was already maturing into an adolescent. Just a stiff wind would be all it took to blow those fuzz balls around the coop. The older chick could hardly fit under its mother's wing anymore because it had grown up so much. But my dad said his hen was such a good mother that she didn't

care how big her baby had become – she still put him under one of her wings, warm and snug and safe as any
child should be. He took up all the room under that wing,
so the mother hen gathered her newest brood of chicks
and fit each and every one of them under her other wing.
She had all her chicks safely gathered in, and my dad said
she was the best mother hen he'd ever seen. He said
that's how a mother loves her children – and how our
mom loved Josh and me.

"But Daddy, what about Jude? He doesn't have a
mother, so who is going to love him?" I asked sincerely.
"Who's going to put a wing around Jude?"

He looked at me, eyes softening and replied, "I guess
we'll all need to put our wing around Jude, then, won't
we?" Josh and I felt satisfied with that answer, and our
hearts were full again with hope of a fair and just existence.

Dad acquired two pigs from Mr. Cox, and pretty
soon we were up to our ears in piglets. Little piglets are
also really cute – it's not until they grow bigger that they
turn into huge hogs that terrify you with visions of being
eaten alive after falling into their pen. Josh and I understood well that we would be eating the pigs at some point
– and we were fine with that. We enjoyed bacon and ham,
and we'd rather eat the pigs than have them eat us!

Our parents would sing to us a lot – songs that I still
sing today to any willing ear. My dad didn't really have
much of an aptitude for music, but he loved to sing none-
theless. It seemed like he and mom knew the words to
every song there ever was – I was so impressed with
their repertoire, from nursery rhymes to folk songs, to
their ability to recite long literary verses given by various historical figures, like the *Ride of Paul Revere*, or the
Gettysburg Address. Every Sunday, Dad's discordant

singing could be heard above the swells of the congregation, and I'd peer over from sitting next to him to see his
beaming face and radiant smile. I was so happy he was
my Dad.

There was one that he would sing to us about two
friends named Jack and Joe that sailed off to find their
fortune. Joe loved a girl named Nellie, but Jack ended up
coming home first and marrying her right out from under Joe. We loved joining in with Dad and Mom on the
chorus:

> *Give my love to Nellie, Jack.*
> *Kiss her once for me.*
> *The sweetest girl in all the world,*
> *I'm sure you'll find is she.*
> *Treat her kindly, Jack, oh pal.*
> *Tell her I am well.*
> *His parting words were, "Don't forget*
> *to give my love to Nell."*

Poor Joe. He lost his true love to his friend, Jack. So,
in honor of this favorite song, we named our pigs "Jack"
and "Nellie-Jack"; we didn't realize it was *Give my love to
Nellie*, comma, *Jack*. We thought it was a hyphen.

The day came when Jack and Nellie-Jack were to be
butchered. My mom was really nervous about how we
would take the news of their impending doom, and she
cautioned my dad that maybe we should stay inside
while he did the dirty deed.

"They need to learn about the Circle of Life one of
these days," Dad said. "It may as well be today. I'm sure
they'll be fine."

So off we went, following my dad down to the pigpen
with his rifle in hand. When we got back to the house,

Mom asked Dad how it went, and how Josh and I handled it. He reported back to her that we did just fine. In fact, when he shot Jack, we were perched up on the top rail of the pigpen fence. When he turned to us in order to measure our reaction, we said to him, "Shoot him again, Daddy! Shoot him again!"

Lucky was our beloved milk cow, and one of our chores was to milk her. On our walk home from the barn, I was always in awe when Josh could spin the bucket super-fast, half full of precious milk, around and around in a circle way above his head and down past his feet. His shoulder was the hub of a wheel, and his arm the turning spoke. He didn't spill a drop of that milk, because the centrifugal force kept it all inside the spinning bucket.

When we got it home, my mom would put the milk into big gallon jars to chill in the fridge, and after a while the cream would rise to the top where she could skim it off to use for other things. One time, Lucky stepped in a bucket of milk just before we were done milking her. Josh was exasperated.

"I can't believe after all that time we spent, she had to step in the bucket!" he complained.

"Well, she just barely stepped in it," I said. "Do you think anyone will notice?"

"Maybe not." Josh mulled the idea over in his mind, gauging the acumen of our mother, and wondering if just this once she wouldn't notice. "It'll probably be fine, don't you think? It's not like she soaked her hooves in it."

We were loath to waste all that milking time, so we brought the bucket home, hoping Mom wouldn't notice. We poured the milk into the gallon jars, straining all the liquid through some cheesecloth first, just to be sure Lucky hadn't left some straw in the bucket from her hoof.

We carefully set the jars to cool in the fridge, and promptly forgot about them.

The next day our mom summoned us to the kitchen, where she had the gallon jars sitting out on the counter. The milk was a shade of green, and the cream on top was greener still. Her look was one of, "Really? You thought I wouldn't notice?"

Mom knew how to make butter from the cream, and lots of other dairy products, too. She made "Lucky butter," "Lucky ice cream," "Lucky buttermilk." Eventually we ate "Lucky burgers" and we were truly thankful for that peaceful bovine friend that we once knew.

There were other animals that weren't so nice to us – as if they sensed we might want to put them on our dinner table one day, or something. We would try to avoid the geese at all costs. We were almost more scared of the geese than we were of the big bull all alone in his vast pasture. The geese would deliberately chase us through the fields, honking and hissing, nipping at our barefoot heels so that we danced on our tiptoes, trying desperately to avoid the sticker plants. We'd rather get stickers in our feet, though, than be bitten by the angry geese, so we'd run as fast as we could until we could scurry carefully under the bottom wire of the electric fence, safe from our predators.

We had never named the geese. I thought this was sad, because even angry geese deserve a name. I decided we would call the meanest one Lucifer, and the other one would be called Aunt Rhody – probably just from wishful thinking that it would hasten the "Old Grey Goose's" death.

When our little baby bunny rabbits died, Josh and I decided we would bury them in a Mason quart jar. Jude was over at our house that day playing with us, so the three of us gathered the dead bunny rabbits up in our little hands, their soft bodies limp and lifeless, and laid all seven of them gently to rest inside the jar, all snuggled up together to keep them warm in their glass sepulcher. Maybe if they had been all snuggled up like this during the cold night, they wouldn't have died.

"Let's say a prayer for them," Josh said. Jude looked a little uncomfortable, not used to religion at all, other than when he was around us. I bowed my head obediently, though, and Jude quickly followed. Josh prayed for the souls of the little bunnies, asking God to keep them safe. I dug a shallow hole, and we buried the quart jar.

It wasn't until a week or ten days later that we remembered our little buried treasure, and we ran out back by the rabbit hutch to dig up the time capsule tomb. We just wanted to check on them, and make sure they were still ok. We took them from the quart jar to examine them, touching and handling each one before returning them to their final resting place. My mom wasn't too pleased with the dead rabbit smell on our hands. I started to fear that the three of us would emit a permanent stench of rancid rot and decay that is distinctive to death and decomposition. No amount of scrubbing would get rid of it; only time would eventually wear it from our skin.

7

"Mom, do you think it would be ok for me to marry Jude?" I asked, nonchalantly.   In my eyes, Jude was the next-best boy in the world after my brother, and I wanted to marry him. He didn't have any idea I felt this way about him, but his deep brown eyes and dark locks caught my attention every time I saw him. He was funny, and he was always kind toward me. His smile was bright against his olive skin; I had a crush on this Second Mus-keteer.

"You might want to wait until you get older before you make up your mind," she said wisely. I think she was a little hesitant about this idea. She loved Jude and tried her best to provide a good example to him, but there had been more than one occasion when my parents had needed to sit Jude down for a discussion. He had stolen twenty dollars from my mom's purse once, and he had lied to them several times. But they understood his home life and lack of decent adult supervision and role models, so they did their best to reproach him with gentle kindness, at the same time attempting to teach him honesty, hard work, good character, and love. Even so, as a young girl, I was pretty sure Jude and I would get married someday.

Jude didn't have any brothers or sisters, and that's maybe part of the reason why he loved spending time with us. His parents were divorced, which wasn't very common for the time, and it made him a little different than everyone else at school. He lived with his dad, who drank way too much. He wasn't sure where his mom was, and so he clung to our mother as his own, loving any attention he got from either of our parents.

The three of us sat up in Joshua's tree that summer, and I watched as Josh and Jude took turns cutting the palms of their own hands with Josh's pocket knife that he got for his birthday and always kept in his pocket. Dark blood oozed slowly from their wounds as they clasped their hands and mixed their blood as an oath of brotherhood. I think they saw some Indians doing it on *The Lone Ranger*, and they wanted to make the same promise to each other. They were "blood brothers" after that, and it was amazing to witness the alliance and bond that they formed from that time forward. I stood as a witness that day to two young boys pledging their loyalty to one other – an outward display of solidarity that continued into manhood and was just as real as a bond of true blood.

Josh and I were no strangers to corporal punishment; a spanking now and then would set us straight and keep us honest. But Jude's dad would go a little too far sometimes, and we'd see bruises now and then on Jude's arms and neck. The older he got, the more time he'd spend at our place, and his dad was too drunk to really care.

The first dead person we ever saw was when I was in the third grade. Mrs. Aspromonte was trying to drill the multiplication tables into our brains, our minds so easily distracted by daydreams of summer adventure. I would stare out the window and imagine my bare feet dangling into the cool water of the irrigation ditch. But when I heard her promise an ice cream sundae at the drug store for the first three students to memorize their times tables, I snapped back to reality, suddenly engaged with a challenge. Of course, I was one of the three to enjoy that ice cream sundae a couple of weeks later; my competitive spirit wouldn't have it any other way. Mrs. Aspromonte drove us over to the drug store where we perched ourselves on the bar stools at the counter and ordered ourselves a rare treat. Ice cream, chocolate syrup, caramel, strawberries, nuts and whipped cream with a cherry on top. I was on cloud nine! Who knew that multiplication tables could lead to such a luxuriant award?

The bell rang, and I ran to meet my brother and Jude. We were headed to the store to buy some intensely grape-flavored Bubble Yum. We'd stuff our mouths with several pieces at a time, gluttonous gourmands with no concept of savoring the occasional indulgence. With these visions of sweet pleasures dancing around in our heads, we ran out of the grade school and on to the sidewalk along Grand Avenue. We came to a sudden halt in front of a man who was blocking our path with his sprawling body. His head was in a pool of blood that stained the sidewalk for months after that, and his eyes weren't quite closed. Kids kept coming up beside us, and soon we were all around the man, standing still as statues, and just as quiet, too. The man wasn't very big, but his dark brown skin was leathery with deep wrinkles, and Josh knelt down to close his eyelids. The man's hands were motionless, but well-worn and calloused by years of toil.

The principal was there now, and he sent us all on our way, saying he would take care of things, and this wasn't something we needed to see. We still went to the store and bought our gum, but we weren't running with excitement anymore. We walked quietly, not sure how to process what we had just seen. We stopped at the playground on our way home and pushed each other on the swings. The seats were made from a piece of wood, flat and strong, perfect for pushing each other higher and higher until we launched ourselves from the seat and into the sandy pit. I could propel myself the farthest, and neither one of those boys could beat my distance.

As Josh gained altitude on the swing, I would hitch a ride on the wooden seat by grabbing onto it from behind him, and letting it lift me with his backward momentum. My fingers caught the back edge of the seat and it lifted me briskly off the ground, my weight suspended for a moment at the apex of the backward motion. As we came back down to earth, I would push with all my might in tandem with the downward force of my body, and the swing would go even higher. When he swung high enough, Josh let go, and landed a foot short of my mark. Being small had its advantages.

8

Our small and sheltered world was disrupted when my parents told us we would be moving out of the country. My dad had taken a job in Africa, and we would be moving there for at least a couple of years. When our parents sat us down to break the news to us, Josh looked a little forlorn, and went out to be alone in his tree. He wasn't really sure how to wrap his mind around leaving his best friend. He felt responsible for Jude and was worried who would watch out for him if we weren't there. Where would Jude go if his dad was mean to him, and he needed to get out of the house? Who would put his arm around him and make him feel like things would be ok if Jude got pushed around and treated badly? We were Jude's shelter and safety. We were his comfort and his refuge. We didn't know how to articulate that at the time, but we felt it inside of us – Josh more than anyone.

I was excited for a new adventure, and I found out we would have to learn French. We were moving to a country called Mali in West Africa, and the idea sounded so exotic to me. Before its independence, Mali was a colony of France, and French was still the national language of the country, although many native dialects were spoken throughout the region. Our parents arranged for French lessons right away, hoping to give us a jump-start before the big move to its capital city of Bamako.

I didn't really know what my dad did for his job – not exactly. I knew he was a "plant guy" because that's what my mom called him. He knew the names for every plant we ever saw. Not the normal name, like "sage brush" – he would call it by its scientific name, *Artemesia tridentata*. We thought it was impressive and teased him endlessly about his big brain.

His job in Africa would be working as a contractor for a Range Management project, conducting plant classifications and mapping them for the Ministry of Agriculture, through a USAID contract. I had no idea what that really meant, other than he would be working as a "plant guy," and that Josh and I would get to move to a new place, somewhere over the endless expanses of ocean, and start a new adventure.

A few weeks later, Jude and Josh sat up on the platform in the Joshua tree, dangling their feet over the edge, swinging them back and forth as they took turns trying to spit the farthest. Pretty soon, though, their mouths ran dry and the contest lost its thrill.

The two of them were laughing and joking, subconsciously prolonging the moment they were sharing. Both of them were aware that they'd be separated soon, and they were avoiding that reality. They were silently afraid that there wouldn't be any more of these youthful chapters they'd been living, which had formed and framed the plots thus far woven into the genesis of their life stories.

Eventually, there was nothing left to joke about, and they sat for a few seconds before Josh broke the silence.

"So, are you going to write me letters while I'm gone?" Josh asked, not really knowing how to broach the conversation about his sudden exodus from Jude's life.

"I doubt it," Jude snapped, suddenly and seemingly out of nowhere an edge of bitterness in his tone. "I don't even know if letters can make it that far, Josh, so don't count on it." Josh looked at Jude out of the corner of his eye, trying to gauge what had gotten into him.

"OK...well, just so you know, I'll still try to write letters to you sometimes." Josh was trying to make peace, sensing an uninvited vibe of tension starting to rise between them.

"Don't bother, Josh – seriously. I don't even care." Jude stood up and reached for the rope swing, eager to get out of the tree and out of this conversation. His heart felt weird like it was being squashed, and he didn't like the feeling. His vision was already starting to get a little blurry from the tears that were threatening to develop, and the last thing he wanted to do was cry in front of Josh.

Josh watched him getting ready to swing down to the ground, and he pleaded with him, "Don't leave, Jude. I'm sorry...don't be mad."

"I'm not the one leaving, Josh." Jude's feet were already on firm ground, and he dropped the rope, walking away as it swung lazily back and forth losing its momentum against the friction of the air and against gravity itself, coming to rest again in its usual spot. Josh watched the rope until it was still. He peered down through his eyelashes at his hands, a bit forlorn and not sure what he could do for his friend.

I was on my way out to the tree to get Josh for dinner when I ran right into Jude, who seemed like he was in a hurry. "Hey, Jude!" He looked up to meet my gaze, and I could see the look of hurt on his face, and the tears welling up in his eyes. "What's wrong?" I implored.

I think I caught him right at the moment where he simply couldn't keep up the tough guy routine for one more second, and he surrendered his broken heart to the first person he saw, my skinny little eight-year-old self. He practically ran into my arms, hugging me, crying out loud in thick and throaty sobs as if this was the only time in his almost ten years of life that he'd ever let his raw feelings emerge from within. I just hugged him and told him it was going to be ok, even though I didn't know what "it" was.

Once he calmed down a bit and pulled away from my embrace, we sat on the ground where Josh joined us, having followed Jude toward the house. He let his heart spill over, having reached its emotional capacity, and he told us everything he felt.

"I just don't know why I have to be left behind," he started, trying hard to stop the sobs, taking deep breaths in between his words. Finally, he inhaled slowly from deep inside his chest and let the air out, breathing slower and more regularly until he could talk again.

"You guys are leaving me, and I don't know how I'm going to do my life without you. You're my best friend, Josh, and I don't know why you have to leave." A few lingering tears trickled down his face, leaving pale tracks through the dust on his cheeks. My own eyes welled with tears just from empathy for his, and I reached over to hold his hand – he didn't pull his away.

Josh tried to reassure him. "Jude, we don't want to leave you, either. I wish there was something I could do!"

He tried to help Jude see any sort of silver lining and said, "I'm sure it will go by super-fast, and we'll be back before you know it." He didn't know what else to say, and this seemed like a lame conciliation once he said it out loud.

"It might go by fast for you, but you don't know what it's like living with my dad. I just – I'll miss you guys. And I'll miss your mom and dad, too." With that admission he pulled his hand from mine, and buried his face into both his hands, quiet sobs escaping his throat this time, his shoulders shrugging with each sound.

A thought came to my mind, and I thought I had just come up with the most brilliant idea ever known to mankind. "Jude, maybe our parents will take you with us!" I exclaimed. My eyebrows arched high and my eyes filled with excitement. "Really! You stay with us all the time anyway – and your dad won't care. Right? Let's go ask mom and dad, Josh!"

All three of us felt a nagging aura of skepticism looming around us, but for lack of a better idea, we got up, and headed to the house to pitch our proposal to my parents. If wishing could really make things come true, we had it in the bag. But of course, reason and the rule of law trumped any wishing, and in the end Jude had to stay home while we moved to our new home across the briny deep.

Initially when we approached our parents with the idea, they saw the desperation on our faces and the swollen eyes from Jude's lamentation – so they promised to talk to Jude's dad about the possibility. Of course, he reacted defensively, accusing my parents of wanting to take his son away from him. "He's got a dad!" he yelled at my father, his breath reeking of alcohol and his eyes riddled with broken capillaries.

I think my parents knew all along that it wouldn't be possible, but they wanted Jude to know that someone cared enough about him to at least try. To at least *want* him to come along. I think the effort made a difference to Jude, although later in life he looked back on this time as a dichotomy of possible paths: one that would have opened his world to adventure, a true sense of family – even privilege – and the other an avenue leading directly to his scornful reality. He seemed guarded from then on, never wanting to expose himself to disappointment again, and never allowing his heart the chance for vulnerability, and therefore genuine love.

9

Kéta was crouching down on the backs of his heels
– a stance that seemed to be a special talent that only Africans possessed. I certainly didn't have the balance or
the flexibility in the tendons of my knees to sit for hours,
flat-footed with butt resting on heels. I didn't have much
meat on my bones, and yet I couldn't crouch like that
without balancing my weight on the balls of my feet,
heels in the air. As soon as I put my heels down, I fell over
backward.

Kéta was our *gardien*, the person who sat at the end
of our alley at night to guard our house. Most of the ex-
patriots and wealthier Malians in Bamako hired a *gardien* – it was almost a system of forced employment. If
you didn't hire someone to guard your house, word would
get around and the locals would reciprocate by breaking
into your home.

Even when you did have a *gardien*, people still
broke into your house. At least if your *gardien* was Kéta,
who tended to sleep by his fire at night at the end of our

alley instead of staying awake and vigilant. One night my dad heard an intruder and chased him out of our house. Kéta woke up and ran after him, chasing him with his shoe in hand.

The insult of the shoe is fairly well-known in Muslim culture. Shoes are considered filthy, lower than dirty feet, and hitting someone with a shoe is a way of showing great offense and disdain to the recipient of the blow. So, when Sungalou, our nineteen-year-old houseboy, took off his sandal and chased us around our dining room table with it held high in his hand, we knew our teasing had gone too far.

"I'm sorry! I'm sorry!" Josh yelled, keeping just far enough ahead of Sungalou to keep out of his grasp. I just shrieked and screamed as I ran around the table, full of both fear and fun all at the same time. My screeches were interposed by surges of laughter; my vacillation between the two made Sungalou even more irritated.

He was mad at us for laughing at how he said some English words. His thick African accent, laboring to pronounce our bizarre and awkward lexes, was new and almost whimsical to us; it just tickled our funny bones. But our amusement had gone too far – instead of it being fun, his pride was starting to get hurt, and off came his shoe in disdainful reproach.

When our giggles gathered steam and finally combusted into bursts of laughter, we ran for our lives out the front door and into the yard, Sungalou eventually giving up the chase.

Yes, I learned quickly that *gardien* didn't always mean to actually guard something. Whenever we drove to the open marketplace in downtown Bamako, we would be surrounded by twenty or thirty kids, hardly letting us get out of the parked car because the throng was pressed up against our doors and windows. Each one of them was yelling, *"Gardien! Gardien!"* hoping they would be the kid we would hire to stand guard by our car for the hour that we would be gone doing our shopping.

These kids were my age – maybe ten years old. There's no way they could keep someone from stealing our car, or anything inside it. This was just another form of employment, like Kéta's job was at our house. We would pick out one of the boys from the mob to stand by our car, and my mom would pay him some centimes when we got back from our errands. It was something my mother was always happy to do – the kids were clearly quite poor, some with their bellies distended from malnourishment, and others with shirts that they'd borne on their backs years beyond their proper fit. It was obviously all they had, and a few coins for their labor was the least Mom could do – although she wished she could do more.

I watched Kéta crouching close to the ground with his hamstrings smashed down against his calves, as comfortable as could be. He was tending to his fire and I could smell burning flesh in the air. He must be cooking his dinner, I thought, as Josh and I wandered out of the gate – a grey metal portal through the thick concrete wall that surrounded our house and yard; it squeaked on rough hinges each time it was pushed open.

The wall was topped with thousands of pieces of broken glass that had been set into the wet concrete when the wall was first built. These were meant to act as deterrents to a potential *voleur* with unscrupulous intentions of sneaking into our yard and stealing something. The sharp points of broken bottles were meant to slash fingers and hands if anyone tried to grab onto the top of the wall to pull themselves up, aiming to scale the wall.

Josh and I would still crawl over the top of the wall as a shortcut to school, gingerly avoiding the sharp edges and corners of the multi-colored glass fragments. We had our reasons for wanting to take this path despite the glass on the wall; we were too fearful of what awaited us at the other end of the alley, and we avoided that route if at all possible.

We sauntered up to Kéta, curious about his dinner. He was nursing the fire with little pieces of wood, feeding it with one hand and poking at it with the other. He was chewing on a stick the size of a cigar, a short twig completely frayed at one end, knobbed with slivers of woody white fibers. I had asked him before why he chewed on a stick all the time. He explained that it was his *miswak*, the African version of a toothbrush.

Apparently, this method of brushing your teeth from a twig of a *Salvadora persica* tree had more benefits than just clean teeth. Kéta said it kept him from getting malaria and kept his tooth enamel strong. The bark contains an antibiotic that suppresses bacteria growth and contains natural nutrients like Fluorine and Vitamin C. It made me wonder why we didn't use these twigs, but instead brushed our teeth with plastic bristles. Just one of the many things it seemed we *Toubabs* did the hard way.

Toubab was what all the African kids called me and Josh – it means "white man." They would actually chant it to us in a little sing-songy way as they followed us home from school.

"Tou-ba-bu! Tou-ba-bu! Tou! Tou! Toubabu!"

I asked Sungalou one day how to say "black man" in Bambara, their native language. But when I started chanting that word back to the kids the next day as we walked home from school, they got offended and started throwing rocks at us. I had even tried to sing it to them the same way they did to us, mimicking their song as best I could, but using the new word Sungalou taught me. It really didn't go over well.

We ran home as fast as we could. I guess it wasn't offensive to call us whites, but it was really distasteful to call them blacks. I didn't understand it, but I refrained from countering chants after that.

When we got close to Kéta's fire, we realized he had some sort of small animal on a spit, turning it slowly from time to time in order to roast it on all sides. He had skinned it, and its flesh was shiny from basting in its own fat, however little it possessed.

"C'est quoi ça?" I asked Kéta what it was, since Josh and I were scratching our heads at what this varmint could be. It looked nothing like a chicken – we'd seen plenty of those on our farm. This creature had four small legs and a long tail – more like a small cat.

"C'est un rat," he answered. *"Je l'ai attrapé chez les voisins."*

I looked at Josh. Did I hear that right? He caught a rat at the neighbor's house? If that was a rat, it must be an enormous mutated variety, because it looked more like the size of a jackrabbit!

"Mom! Dad!" we called as we ran back into the house. "You've got to come see this!"

"What is it?" Mom answered.

"Kéta is cooking a rat over his fire. He caught it, and now he's eating it for his dinner!" Josh explained.

Our parents happily followed us back to the alley-way, camera in hand. We had never heard of someone eating a rat before, and we'd never seen a rat this big!

There are some things that must be documented on 35mm film – things that are otherwise too fanciful to be believed.

Kéta was quite a character. He did more sleeping by the fire at night than guarding the house. But he provided a lot of entertainment, as well.

"Sir, I want to show you this pistol," he said to Dad.

"That looks like an old black powder muzzle-loader." My dad was admiring the gun.

"My Uncle gave it to me," Kéta said to Dad as he loaded the weapon. He pulled back the hammer, held his arm straight out in front of him, and aimed it toward the mouth of the alleyway. Then he rotated his head so that his face was looking in the complete opposite direction of his aim.

"Qu'est-ce que tu fais?" Dad stopped him, and asked him what he was doing,

"Ah," Kéta continued in French, "well, you see, I learned my lesson the first time I shot this pistol; the kick was much more powerful than I had anticipated." Dad was listening to his story, unable to imagine a scenario where you wouldn't look in the same direction as your aim.

Kéta went on. "I wasn't holding my grip tightly enough, and the gun kicked back with such force that the hammer buried itself into my forehead, just between my eyes." He brought the gun back toward his face slowly, touching the hammer to his forehead to demonstrate.

"See?" He showed us the scar as proof. "Now I know better; now I look the other way!"

10

When our airplane first landed in Bamako a year before, the door was opened to allow all the passengers onto the portable stairway that had been pushed up against the plane. Hot, humid sub-Saharan atmosphere gushed into the fuselage, flowing with it a smell that is uniquely Africa. To this day the thought of that smell conjures so many memories for me, more intensely than a photograph ever could. If you're ever present when a traveler returns from Africa, and they open their suitcase for the first time since returning home, you'll relate. The scent is emitted from each piece of clothing, filling your olfactory senses with vivid memories of past travels.

The airplane ride itself was an adventure. I'd been on airplanes before, but never one where farm animals traveled with the passengers. There was an African woman dressed in robes of the most colorful and exotic fabrics. Each vibrant cloth was printed with striking yellow patterns on a brilliant blue background. It draped around her torso, and she wore a matching cloth wrapped around her head, enticing my wondrous gaze. She was sitting two rows back from us, and in her lap was a wire cage that held a live chicken, softly clucking its nervous objection to the journey.

"Dad, look!" I tugged on his sleeve and pointed at the chicken.

Dad smiled at me, and said, "Yep, that's sure different, isn't it?"

"Maybe we should have brought our chickens with us," I suggested.

"I don't think that poor chicken likes flying very well," Dad said. "I think our chickens are a lot happier at Jude's house. Besides, now he and his dad can have fresh eggs every day. Right?"

"Yeah," I replied. "I hope he knows what he's doing with my chickens. They'd better still be alive when we get home."

I took another look at the hen in the woman's lap. I suddenly wondered if my hen would be hatching a new brood sometime soon. Jude was going to have his hands full.

As I emerged from the plane and out into the sun, the humidity hit me, and I was instantly drenched in sweat. That was our introduction to the climate in Mali – immediate misery and discomfort, profuse sweating, and temperatures as hot as the underworld.

We spent the first couple of weeks at the Hotel L'Amitié, and Josh and I spent almost every moment in the swimming pool – the only place we could keep cool. Our skin was swiftly burned; our initiation to the harsh sun and tropical heat had commenced.

Staying at the hotel was a benevolent and gentle entrance into the Third World for us; it could have been baptism by fire with instant integration into the African way of life. Since my dad wasn't a "Direct Hire" by the US Government, we didn't get the comforts of home from the Embassy Commissary. We hardly got medical care from the Embassy doctor, unless it was a dire emergency. Our home – when we found one – would be among the locals. It was a small modest house made of cinder blocks with a polished concrete floor. So the hotel was a little softer landing for us, coming from the comforts of the States – a place where we could eat ice cream and spaghetti before being tossed to the wolves in the *Grand Marché* of Bamako for our daily shopping.

Josh and I swam across the pool at the hotel and popped our heads out of the water at its edge, resting our arms on the hot concrete as we gazed across the grounds. There was a white man with a thick brown beard sitting under a big tree, and a monkey was lingering at his feet, waiting for him to throw it some scraps of food.

"Look, Josh, there's a monkey!" I pointed so he could see.

"Oh, wow!" He was just as impressed as I was. "Come on, let's go see if we can pet it." He lifted himself out of the pool and I followed, water dripping from our suits, the sun working quickly to evaporate the droplets from our skin. We walked slowly toward the man and sat quietly at a safe distance; we didn't want to scare the primate away.

"Have you ever seen a monkey?" the man asked us. We shook our heads, and he said, "Watch this." He put some crumbs of bread next to his shoe; the monkey came closer, took the bread and ate it.

The monkey's face and hands were black, but its fur was light with tinges of brown. Its hands were tiny, black, and creased. They looked like they might be the size of a doll's hands. My mom had brought my old Mrs. Beasley doll with us, even though I protested loudly that I was too old for that kind of thing. The monkey's hands were about the same size as Mrs. Beasley's, though. I imagined the two of them shaking hands with each other, introducing themselves as new acquaintances, and Mrs. Beasley complaining to the monkey that it was far too hot here in Mali for her long dress and frilly cap.

The monkey held the bread in both hands and gnawed on it with quick tiny bites, its eyes darting all around, filled with paranoia and suspicion.

"Cool!" we cooed. The man put a crumb of bread in his shirt pocket and the monkey climbed right up on his belly, fishing the bread out of his pocket with one hand.

"I want a monkey!" Josh said.

"Me, too!" I echoed. We were completely amazed.

The monkey sat there eating the scrap of bread, and when it was finished, it touched the man's beard, starting to scratch at it. Soon it was working with both hands, picking little morsels of goodness from the man's beard, and putting them straight into its mouth. We laughed and giggled with delight.

The monkey groomed the man for five minutes, or so, and he smiled as the monkey combed through his hair and beard. We just sat there in awe.

Josh and I ran back to the hotel and begged our mom for a monkey.

11

We found a place to live in the Zone Industrielle area, just south of the Koulikoro Highway, and east of the city center. The small K-8 American School was an easy fifteen-minute walk from our house, so Josh and I made the trip on our own most days. The school was just a house, too, surrounded by a wall, and safeguarded by a gate and a *guardien* all of its own.

We lived at the end of an alley. As Josh and I walked down the alleyway to the road, we passed a tree just to the left on the corner, growing out of the dirt next to the wall. It grew the most peculiar fruit called *Zaban*. We would pick the fruit and break them open, finding tightly packed seeds inside. Each of the seeds was a little bigger than an almond but covered with orange fibrous flesh. We sucked on each little pebble of the tart, sour fruit. "Mmmm, it's like sour candy," Josh said.

We stood there eating our *Zaban* fruit, gazing up and down the dirt street.

"Look, Josh, is that a school?" I pointed just across the street to a blue gate that was closed off from the street. There was a big gap under the gate, though, and we could see the feet of what looked like lots of African kids standing near the entrance.

"Hmmm, I don't know. Kind of looks like it, huh?" Josh said.

Just then, the gate was unlocked, and the double doors flew open, coming to rest against the wall. A wave of kids poured out of the schoolyard, flooding the street with scuffling feet, and filling the air with clouds of dust and their chattering voices.

"Whoa, I didn't know we'd have a school so close to our house!" I said, already inventing visions in my head of how much fun we were about to have with this endless supply of playmates.

"Me neither," Josh admitted.

The kids started kicking a deflated soccer ball around, working it between their bare feet with fancy footwork. A little boy wearing only a pair of ragged shorts pushed the tireless rim of a bicycle in front of him with a stick, running after it and steering it with the stick which fit into the groove where the tube would usually go.

I noticed the girls jumping rope and singing a song that was so rhythmic and metrical; their jumping was more of a dance that kept time with their tune.

"They're on recess, Josh!" I said, as we both just stood under the *Zaban* tree, observing these kids as if we couldn't be seen. But we had been.

"I think they just saw us," he elbowed me. He was right. A lot of the kids had stopped what they were doing; they were bunching up together, very curious about these *Toubabs* that had suddenly appeared at the end of the alley.

"Bonjour!" I said, waving my hand at them. I saw some girls smile and wave back at me, then shyly hide behind their older friends.

We sauntered back to our house, hearts lifted by new friendly possibilities, and tongues tingled by tart seeds of the *Zaban* fruit.

A few days later, though, my heart sank with disappointment when my innocent imaginings of playing soccer with our newfound friends were crushed. We weren't so beloved by our new neighbors after all. In fact, instead of gaining friends, we had unwittingly acquired a schoolyard full of enemies.

This was so atypical for our experiences in Africa. Usually we were met with open arms everywhere we went. Whether in the city, or in villages miles away, we found people interested in us because we were so foreign to them; they wanted to show us how welcoming their countrymen could be, and how helpful they were. We were usually met with smiles, friendly faces, helpful hands, and warm embraces.

So, this school at the end of our alleyway was really an enigma. We could never figure out why we were so despised by these kids – but we were certainly determined to defend ourselves!

It all started when Josh and I drove our family's moped down the alleyway to run an errand for our mother. It was a small, light blue moped with pedals that were used to start the engine. When it was parked, we put the moped up on the kickstand and then pushed the pedals around like a bicycle. The pedals turned the crankshaft until the motor started. Then we just took it off the kickstand, and it was like a little motorcycle. Our moped had a 50cc engine and could only go about thirty miles per hour at best. Our mom wanted us to go buy some baguettes at the nearby bakery, so we set out on our task.

Josh was driving, and I was riding on the seat behind him. We were in shorts and tank tops, and of course wearing shoes. Unlike back home, we had to wear our shoes here all the time so that we didn't incidentally pick up a worm through the soles of our feet by stepping in some stagnant water. Schistosomiasis is a disease from a vile worm that can enter your body through your skin, just by playing in contaminated water.

The grossest worm we could ever think of, though, was the Guinea worm – the one you could get by drinking contaminated water. That's why we boiled, filtered, and treated our water with iodine before we could drink it. A Guinea worm was worse for me to imagine than a tapeworm would be – at least you could just poop out a tapeworm, but a Guinea worm would bore itself out of your leg or foot, right through your skin.

Kéta was plagued by the Guinea worm once. I saw him nursing his foot one day, so I came up behind him to see what he was doing.

"What's wrong?" I asked.

"I got a worm, and it's coming out of my foot," he explained.

I came closer and stood next to him. He pulled back the cloth bandage that he'd wrapped around his foot, and I saw a puss-filled wound that was swollen and red, with a round bulbous thing poking out. The worm was captured in the "V" of a small stick that kept it from pulling itself back inside his foot.

Bile came up the back of my throat, threatening to erupt. "Ew! That's disgusting!" I offered, as if this would be something of which he wasn't yet aware. "What's that stick?" I asked.

"I'm helping this worm get out of my foot," Kéta patiently explained. "I twist the stick every day, and little by little the worm decides to get out."

"Can't you just pull it all the way out now?" I was curious enough to keep staring at the ugly wound, but sickened and gagging at its sight so much that I pleaded silently to God that I'd never get one of these worms myself.

"No!" Kéta exclaimed. "No, no, you cannot just pull the worm. He will break. And then you have a terrible infection. No, you must be patient, helping the worm to come out when he feels like it, but making sure he never goes back inside."

"Oh," I said, feeling so sorry for Kéta. I wondered how many more days until his parasite would finally crawl out of his foot. "Does it hurt?"

"Yes, it hurts. My foot is on fire. But, I'll be ok," he reassured me, not wanting to worry me.

"I can bring you some water, so you can soak your foot. Would that help?" I offered.

He agreed that might help, so I ran inside to get a little basin of water. I carried it carefully outside to the alley where Kéta was waiting with his foot still exposed. He gently immersed his foot in the tiny bath.

"Ahhh," he breathed a sigh of relief, leaning his head back, and closing his eyes. "Yes, that feels better."

"Good," I smiled, happy that I could help.

As he soaked his foot, the worm was expelling thousands of its larvae – contaminating the water. Kéta threw it out onto the dirt when he was done soaking his foot, leaving the contagion to soak into the dirt and die.

It was a poignant lesson. I dutifully wore my shoes, and I faithfully drank only boiled water.

Josh turned the pedals and the moped started up. "Get on!" he instructed. I climbed aboard, and we were on our way down the alley. We turned left past the tree with the *Zaban* fruit and were suddenly faced with the crowds of school children playing on the road. When they saw us, they stopped and stared, and started to gather together.

Josh stopped the moped because they were directly in our path. Instead of the friendly waving girls, suddenly there were older boys standing in our path; admittedly intimidating. There was a boy I'd never seen before who seemed to be the oldest, and the rest were looking to him for direction. I tried waving again, showing him that I wanted to be friendly. But he wasn't having any of it. He made a rude gesture back to us, and the chorus of kids crooned their laughter.

"Let's go back home, Josh," I said into his ear, my grip around his waist tightening with anxiety.

"Okay," he answered, and turned the wheel to make a U-turn.

The dirt caught the front tire, though, and made his turn too tight. The moped fell over, and the engine died. We jumped off as it fell and stood next to it as Josh grabbed the handlebars to pick it up again. I looked at the crowd and saw that they were walking closer, pointing and laughing at our little accident.

Suddenly, I realized that they were starting to gather up rocks from the dusty red dirt road; once the tall boy started throwing them in our direction, several more of them followed his example. One rock scampered across the dirt and hit the moped with a loud clang against the metal frame.

"Hurry!" I was getting scared now. "They're coming, Josh!" My heart came to life, pounding harder with fear.

"Help me pick it back up!" he ordered. I grabbed the seat and helped him heft the moped to an upright position. He hopped on, ready to pedal the engine to life.

"Get on!" he barked.

Right then, a rock struck him in the arm, and he reflexively covered the spot with his other hand. It hurt, but all he cared about was getting the two of us back inside our heavy grey gates.

I climbed on back and we sped away, but not quickly enough. A rock hit me on my back, just under my shoulder blade. It stung, and I said, "ow!" loudly, voicing my objection to their rude behavior. What had we done to them? The rock hurt alright, but not enough to make me cry, or anything. I looked over my shoulder and saw them flinging rocks at us still, but we had made our escape. We pulled the moped back into our yard, telling our mother that we'd wait until their school was out before we went for bread.

We couldn't believe it. Completely unprovoked! That tall kid was looking for a fight, and for no good reason.

"I can't believe I waved at that kid," I told Josh. "What a waste of trying to be friendly," I added with some resentment.

"Don't ever be sorry for trying to make friends," Josh imparted. "Maybe he just needs to get used to us. He probably thinks we're just a couple of *Toubabs* invading his territory."

"Doesn't mean he has to throw rocks at us!" I defended.

"No, you're right. All I'm saying is...one of these days maybe he'll wave back."

I furrowed my brows together, pulled my chin down with the corners of my mouth pursed together, displaying my doubt in his optimism.

Everywhere I turned in this new city – whether it was downtown, or in the suburbs, or even on the outskirts – all I could see was litter. Trash literally lined the streets, blowing along in the breeze, and gathering in the gutters or along mud brick walls. Paper, plastic, cardboard, banana peels, discarded food, old shoes, pieces of furniture, cans, bottles, and all manner of refuse. It was everywhere.

I know I became accustomed to it, because when I got back to the States and threw a can out my friend's car window after I polished off a soda, she slammed on her brakes and made me get out and pick it up off the street.

I looked at her in surprise. "What did I do wrong?"

"We don't litter in America," she looked me up and down like I was some sort of heathen.

That was the first time I longed for my African home, and her beloved dark-skinned people. I longed for their rhythmic songs and matchless cadences of their mystic dancing. I missed their slow and easy pace, their vivid fabrics and deeply soulful eyes, the sound of their voices, and the inflections of their speech. I missed my friend Modibo.

12

Our yard was full of tropical foliage and was surrounded by the wall with broken glass. We even had our
very own swimming pool. Josh and I couldn't believe our
eyes when we first saw it. We spent countless hours in
that pool, playing games, competing in elaborate contests, and most of all, keeping cool.

There was a giant mango tree next to the pool, and
on the other side of it, my dad set up the trampoline that
was sent over in our sea freight. As part of the benefits
of his job, my parents were allotted a wooden container
in which they could send any household items. The
trampoline was part of that shipment, and it provided us
countless hours of entertainment. Dad had to cut the
legs of the trampoline in half so that they would fit into
the shipping box. He welded them back together when it
arrived, and it was like new.

"This isn't my Joshua Tree, but it sure is a lot easier
to climb," Josh said, as he made his way up the mango
tree, with me in short pursuit.

We made our way out onto the limb that hung over the pool, and he asked me, "Are you ready?" We crouched down on the branch, holding on to other smaller branches for support and balance.

"Yep," I answered. Water was dripping from our hair, soaked from having repeated this routine five times already.

Our toes were curled around the branch as far as they would go, but never as adept at holding on like the monkey at the hotel. Josh squatted there, ready to jump, and I was right next to him, waiting for his count. "One, two, three, jump!"

We both pushed off with our feet, sailed through the air from the tree down to the pool, our faces glowing with glee. We landed in perfectly synchronized orchestration, composing two of the most picturesque cannonball splashes ever performed.

Our heads surfaced, and we shook the hair out of our faces, bellowing our approval.

The pool wasn't just used for our childhood enjoyment, though. The first few months at our house were miserable as far as the heat and humidity were concerned. Bamako, despite being the capital city, had just one main hydroelectric plant in a small dam of sorts that was made in the Niger River to the east of the city. But when the rainy season ended, and the dry season emerged, the waters receded significantly, and that power plant didn't produce electricity.

The smaller backup power plant had a generator that was not powered by water, but rather by diesel fuel. The power during the dry season was unreliable at best because sometimes the delivery of the diesel was delayed – sometimes re-routed to corrupt officials and sold on the black market. We went three weeks straight without electricity during the hottest time of the year. It was not unusual for temperatures to be in the 115-degree range.

During those three weeks, my parents took our three mattresses out onto our porch, along with the requisite mosquito nets. Malaria was common in Africa, so we slept under the nets at night, and we also took a quinine pill once a week. These little white pills had antimalarial properties, but they were the most bitter things known to man. Josh and I just pushed those pills as far back in our throats as we could, and then gagged them down with a full glass of water, trying desperately to wash away the bitter taste. There were some wimpy kids at our school, though, who couldn't swallow the bitter pill like we did. Their moms spoiled them by putting little chunks of the pill into peanut butter or jam that they got from the Embassy commissary. Their parents had to coax them into taking those quinine pills, and we thought they were fragile, little, overindulged kids who needed to toughen up.

Our mattresses were on the porch at night during that time, so that we could benefit from any breeze that might come our way.

"Ok, time for bed. You can dip in the pool if you want," Dad said.

We jumped into the pool and then lay down on our mattresses, soaking with water.

"Maybe we'll get a little breeze tonight, and you'll get some natural air conditioning on your damp skin," Dad offered.

"I wish we had our fan," I said.

When there was electricity for a day, or a few hours, we had an oscillating fan that would rotate back and forth, moving the air with its miniature propeller blades.

When the air blew on me it was heaven, and then pure hell when it turned its head away from me. Heaven....and now hell. Heaven....and now hell.

"Just be sure to keep your legs and arms away from the mosquito net," Josh reminded me. "You don't want a giant welt again."

We learned to keep our limbs away from the mosquito nets that were tucked under our mattresses. Once I fell asleep with my knee up against the net. By morning, I had one giant mosquito bite all over my knee cap. The mosquitos had bitten me through every tiny square opening of that net where my knee had touched it.

Dad came down with malaria - maybe from camping out in the "bush" on his work trips all the time. He had to stay in bed because he was so sick. He got the sweats, and then the chills, over and over again. It went away after a while, but he had one relapse of malaria a few years later.

"Dad, when will the *current* come back?" We tried to be patient, but oh, how we missed our precious *current*. Our dialect was infiltrated with French words the longer we lived there. We called the melding of the languages "Franglais" - a mix of French and English. If it was hard for us to go without power, I knew it was even more of a hardship for our mother. After six months of living in Mali, we got our diesel generator, and along with it, the luxury of air conditioning. And I think it came just in time; otherwise, mom would have been on the next boat home.

"We need to be ready for those kids at the end of the alley," Josh told me as we swam in the pool one night a few weeks later. The power was back on, and there were a couple of short lamp posts in the yard that provided enough light for me to see Josh's face hovering just above the surface as we tread water.

"How do we do that?" I asked. "There are way more of them than there are of us."

"Well, I was thinking...really there's just that one taller kid. All the other kids follow him around, so I guess that means he's in charge. Right?" Josh was pedaling his feet under the water, waving his arms back and forth on the surface. He spoke a little haltingly, breathing between phrases.

"Yeah, I guess so," I agreed.

"We should call him *Kuntigi*," Josh suggested. "It means 'boss' or 'chief' or something like that in Bambara. At least that's what Sungalou told me."

I thought that was an appropriate nickname, since he seemed to be the boss of his gang of school kids. He stood almost a foot taller than most of them, although he had a few lieutenants that were closer to his size. He was the one we saw when we wrecked the moped, and all the other kids looked to him for direction.

"Kuntigi? Sounds good to me," I said. I spotted a bat swooping down from the mango tree to take a drink from the pool and then fly away again, leaving concentric rings of ripples where it quenched its thirst.

The light from the lamp posts glistened on the surface of the water, the undercurrents from our movement making small waves that bent the light in every direction, shining fleeting liquefied spotlights on the wall around the yard. Our heads bobbed above the silvery skim and our churning arms formulated ripples just under the plane where the water met the warm nighttime air.

The comforting halo of light around the pool faded into immediate blackness beyond its boundaries; the heavy atmosphere dampening the usual nocturnal commotions. Only the sounds of our breathing and our diminutive splashes filled our ears, until Josh continued his original thought.

"Ok, so we need to be ready for Kuntigi and his gang," he said. "They're always trying to throw rocks at us, and we need to defend ourselves. It's like we can't even leave our own house by ourselves unless we climb over our wall and get out to the street the back way."

"They really aren't that great of rock throwers, Josh," I said. "Especially the girls. You can tell they play soccer here, and not baseball."

"Still...until I can figure out a way to make peace with them, we'll have to take the short-cut, and start gathering rocks for our protection," Josh planned.

"Peace?!" I asked incredulously, the volume of my voice abruptly interrupting the serene surrounding. "Why would we want to make peace? They started it!"

"I don't want to have enemies, do you? I mean, we have to be smart and keep our guard up – don't get me wrong. But one of these days I would like to not have to worry about the end of the alley. Wouldn't you?" he asked.

"Well, yeah," I submitted, still pedaling my legs through the heavy water, the liquid flowing swiftly between my toes and through my fingers as I skimmed the surface with my arms.

"Besides," he said with his voice a little lowered, almost reluctant to admit what he said next. "It bothers me when someone doesn't like me for no good reason."

I stopped treading and tipped my head backward, floating effortlessly now on top of the surface. I breathed deeply, enjoying the break from keeping upright in the water. I stared up at the darkness. Poor Josh – he was such a peace-loving soul. He was right; he didn't like confrontation or bad feelings. His world was upside down when someone held a grudge against him or didn't like him.

LEAH MARTIN

13

Despite the hardships of the Third World, mom was such a trooper. She melded herself into the African way of life quite seamlessly. She'd go to the *Grand Marché* in the center of town with the two of us in tow to do her shopping. The smell of the fish market was almost unbearable, the fish having lain in the sun for hours, drawing thousands of flies to feast on their scaly slimy bodies. The odor of the fish was mixed with the open sewage that ran along the streets. I don't think I'd ever seen so many people in one place at the same time. The scene was almost more than I could take in; all my senses were dynamically working, trying to absorb and consume every morsel of sound, smell, and sight.

There was a contrast of colors – some people dressed in vibrant clothing, while others were barely clad in the drab rags that were clearly all they had to wear. There were burlap bags of spices set out for sale, so piquantly pungent to my nose that I could almost taste the chilies, peppery grains of paradise, curries, and the cardamom and coriander seeds on the back of my tongue. People rushed by on mopeds, the wake of their breeze fluttering my hair and shirtsleeves and wafting the smells of the market all around me.

The streets were the antithesis of order. It was a mass of chaos: cars and motorcycles, women with babies slung to their backs carrying huge bowls of fruits and vegetables on their heads, and even cows and goats wandering through the throngs. My ears were encumbered with the honking, the motors, people talking or yelling, dogs barking, and other daily sounds of a major city in the Third World.

"Mom, what are we going to buy today?" I asked, as I held tight to her hand so that I wouldn't get sucked into the black hole of the massive market mob.

"I thought we'd get some meat for dinner, and then maybe some rice," she answered. Rice was a major staple in our meals, just like it was for the Malians. We even fed rice to our dog, Rahtchy. He was a little white dog that we inherited from our neighbors when they moved away; such a good dog. There wasn't any dog food here, though – not like we know in the States. So, we fed him rice and table scraps.

Most people in Mali were Muslims, so they saw dogs as filthy animals and wouldn't have them as pets like we had Rahtchy. My dad's driver, Pierre, was a Christian from a village south of Bamako, though, and his family actually ate dogs for dinner.

"Dogs are delicious," Pierre would tell us. We'd scrunch up our noses and act like we were going to vomit.

Josh told Dad in English, "Don't let Pierre get too close to Rahtchy."

While we were walking toward the area of the market where they sold the beef, we saw some older people sitting under a covered portion of the sidewalk, holding out their hands begging for money. One old and frail woman was blind, her eyes clouded over, with her hands reaching out to us, and her mouth making sounds that I didn't recognize. My heart tightened, and I felt sad. Another man was asking us for money, but his hand was missing all its fingers.

"What happened to his hand, Momma?" I asked. I couldn't help but stare at him, sitting there on a piece of cardboard, bony legs crossed underneath him. The flies were everywhere. If we were back home, these flies would be considered a plague. We make up songs about how annoying flies are: "Shoo, fly, don't bother me!" But here, people didn't seem to care if flies were scurrying all over their faces, on their lips, and eyelids, and noses. I go crazy anytime a fly brushes my lips; I have to rub them raw to get the tickly feeling to go away. But they just didn't seem to be bothered; flies were at home on the eyelashes of children, and on their runny noses. They were so much a normal part of their lives that they didn't even realize they were bothering them. I wanted to yell "shoo, fly!" for them, and wave them away from the babies. But it was a lost cause. The flies were there to stay.

"His fingers had to be cut off because he had leprosy, sweetie," she said. There was still a Leper Colony somewhere nearby where amputations happened frequently.

"What's Leprosy?" I responded.

"It's a disease that affects a person's skin and limbs. Sometimes they have to get their fingers or toes cut off so that it doesn't get worse," she explained.

"Oh," I replied.

"That's gross," Josh added. "I hope we don't get it."

"You won't get it, Josh. Now go give these centimes to the man." Mom gave Josh some coins and pointed to a younger man who had just scooted himself across the road on a piece of cardboard. His legs were so skinny that they didn't even look like legs; they were withered and small like a little bird's legs, and they didn't move. He sat on the piece of cardboard and pushed himself along with the sheer strength of his arms and upper body. When he got across the street, Josh added the coins to the little can that was hanging around the young man's neck. He smiled at Josh.

"Did he have Leprosy, too?" Josh asked mom.

"No – his legs are that way from Polio. That's another disease. I had a friend in high school who had Polio, and one of his legs is smaller and doesn't work very well, either," Mom said.

We continued on our way and came to the beef vendors. The cut of meat that you got on any given day just depended on how many other people had already purchased some ahead of you. The side of beef was just hanging from a hook out in the open market, flies crawling all over it. The butcher just hacked off the next piece from the bottom. If we were lucky, we'd get a good piece of the cow.

"*C'est combien?*" Mom asked the man with the machete in his hand, ready to chop off the next piece of meat. My mom was getting really good at bargaining just like the locals, so she started out asking how much.

When he told her a price, she said, "*Oh, non...c'est trop chèr.*" He looked at her and smiled; she'd earned some of his respect already, having told him it was too expensive. They bantered back and forth for a while and finally settled on a price. He whacked off a piece of meat, put it in a small plastic bag that had probably seen some previous use, and handed it to her. She placed the coins in his hand, and off we went.

"Can we have some ice cream today?" I asked Mom anxiously, and Josh eagerly joined in the pleading. We couldn't have ice cream from the local shop very often at all, because the milk they used wasn't pasteurized. This wasn't your typical ice cream shop, either. It wasn't like the one where Mrs. Aspromonte took me for the prize of an ice cream sundae in the third grade. There was no bar with stools affixed, or soda machines and freezer cases full of various flavors. It was a small retail space just off the street, with the door propped open for customers to walk inside. It was a tiny shop with a dirty tile floor and a small fan straining to make a breeze in the heavy heat. The place was empty except for the solitary soft serve ice cream machine that stood against a wall. That was our ice cream parlor in Bamako.

Mom's answer today to our pleadings was the usual, "Not today, kids." However, she followed quickly with some promising plans, "But dad's going to take us on a picnic next week, and we'll make some homemade ice cream then, ok?" We cheered our approval.

I held my mom's hand as we walked back to the car, and Josh carried the meat and the produce and rice we had picked up at the *marché*. My hand felt secure in hers, and my confidence flourished when I was with her; she always knew how to make me feel like I could do anything in the world if I just tried. Wonder Woman had nothing on me, according to my mother. She filled my reservoir of self-conviction with her steady flow of encouragement and faith in me. She nourished the tiny sprouts of my fledgling talents and abilities with her careful assurances and dutiful pruning. I felt safe in her hands.

On my tenth birthday, my mother gave me a gift that I still treasure even to this day. We didn't have much available in Africa that we could buy for birthdays; we couldn't go to the water park or go bowling. And she couldn't drive down to the department store to buy me some new clothes or take me out to McDonald's. So, she did something from her heart – something that meant far more to me than any of those other things ever would. She handed me an envelope – one she fashioned herself from a sheet of paper. She had typed my name on the out-side, and added, "From Her Mother."

I lifted the flap of the envelope and pulled out a small card on which she had typed a poem for me. She had written this poem specifically for my birthday. It was a poem about my smile, my laugh, and my essence. It told me just how much she saw in me and loved me. I put the gift in my journal for safekeeping.

14

From the time I can remember, I've known that Josh was special. I felt it, and I knew my parents felt it, too.

When my dad married my mom in 1965, they couldn't have kids for a long time. They were stricken with a sense of sorrow from being the only ones among their friends without children. My mother felt like she was broken; she was convinced that she had somehow disappointed God, and that He was keeping His favors from her, consigning to them a void of posterity.

She prayed to return to His good graces; of course, that wasn't it at all. She was a good and righteous woman, and God wasn't punishing her; but she couldn't find an answer in any other theory or supposition, so she blamed herself. Her friends would all be pregnant with their second or third child and would blather on about how fun it was to be pregnant, without a thought of how it injured my mother's already wounded heart.

But then my dad had a dream one night – a vivid and powerful dream that he can still recount with perfect clarity. In the dream, he was working in a wheat field, but the swaying swells of grain were a vivid white instead of amber. He stopped working to take a drink of water when he heard a distant voice calling him.

"Daddy!" He heard the voice, and somehow knew that it was beckoning him. He turned toward the voice and took a few tentative steps.

"Daddy, where are you?" He heard it again, but this time a little louder. He took stronger strides toward the voice, plowing his legs through the shafts of grain.

Suddenly into his view appeared a young boy, maybe four years old. They ran toward each other and my dad, in his retelling of the dream, said his heart felt like it would erupt with pure joy. He said it was a feeling he imagined only belonged in heaven and wasn't known on Earth.

When they met, my dad took the boy in his arms, swung him around once, and then hugged him tight.

The boy said, "Daddy, you're here!"

And my dad answered, "Yes, Joshua, I'm here."

And then he woke up from his dream.

This was like a vision to my father – a sign. He woke my mother and told her right away what he had dreamed.

"We're going to have a boy, sweetheart, and his name is Joshua." She looked at him a little skeptically, unsure if she should allow her heart to hope. In the end, she believed in his dream, too, and within six months, she was pregnant. They named their first child Joshua.

And that's how I knew my brother was special.

But it was more than knowing; I felt it about him, too. In my gut, in my heart, and in my soul. He was re-markable.

One day when I was alone with my mother on our farm, I asked her, "Momma, do you dream about me?"

She looked at me and asked what I meant.

"Well, Daddy dreamed about Joshua before he was born, and I just wondered if you dream about me," I explained, wanting to feel special like Josh was.

"You know what, my dearest girl?" She had stopped what we were doing and crouched to my level so that she could peer deep into my blue eyes. I could see my reflection in her pupils, and I remember how tiny I looked in them.

She made sure she had my attention, and then went on. "I may not have had a dream about you before you were born, but I dream about you every day of my life."

"Really?" I suddenly felt my heart leap a little with a sense of importance. "Every day?"

"Yes, every day," she confirmed. "You can't even believe how many dreams I have about you. I dream that you will become a very important person."

"Me?" I asked her in surprise.

"Yes, sweetheart, *you!*" She didn't even hesitate, certain and convinced of her own words. "You will be so important to other people because you will make a difference in their lives."

I thought about that for a second, not really sure how I could do that.

She went on, "I dream that you will show so many people the special kindness that is inside of you, and you will help them see how extraordinary they are."

I stared at her in wonder, engrossed in each of her words as she held my shoulders in her hands, our faces mirroring one another – mine just a younger, smaller version of hers.

She continued, "I dream that you will be smart and competent, and that you will figure out complicated problems." I imagined the grown-up me, wearing glasses that made me look smarter. I saw myself going to work and doing something important.

When I was in school before we moved to Africa, Mrs. Gonzales, the grade school secretary, told me that she just *knew* I would be the first woman to be President of the United States. I almost believed her, because the birthmark on my leg just above my knee was the shape of the United States, and besides, why *couldn't* I be the President?

My mom fervently imparted her words to me that day on the farm, taking both of my smaller hands in hers as she did. "I have a dream about you that you will be a Mommy someday, and you'll love your kids just like I love you."

I was fascinated to learn that she dreamed about me even more than Dad had dreamed about Josh. Maybe I was just as special as he was, after all.

"I dream of you each day, because you are my girl, and because I love you," she finished.

"I love you, too, Momma." She hugged me tight, and then I ran off to play, my heart bolstered by her precious words that had been forever and indelibly written on my heart.

15

As we drove home from the *marché*, my mom turned the car into the alleyway, just in time for us to see our archenemy, Kuntigi, standing near the gates of his school. I saw him eye us warily as we passed him by, lowering his lids to show his contempt for us, and even demonstrating a few choice hand motions that punctuated the insult in case there was any doubt.

We parked the car inside the walls of our little oasis and unloaded our groceries. Josh and I had some coins that we wanted to add to our savings, so we ran out to the secret hiding place in our yard: one pace north, and two paces east of the banana plant that my dad had planted when we first arrived. He had also planted some papaya seeds, and those trees were thriving, as well as the bananas. We were in a fruit paradise, always eating papaya smothered in lime juice, mangos and bananas to our hearts' desire. Even unripe mangos came in handy when my mom would use them to make us an "apple" pie. They were perfect for that.

"Ok, let's find our buried treasure. Start at the banana plant," Josh instructed.

I stood at the banana plant and took a giant step,
then two more giant steps to the right of that spot. "Do
you see the X?" I asked.

Josh looked down around my feet, found the spot we
had marked, and started digging.

"Here's mine, and here's yours," he handed me my
film canister, just the right size to fit coins inside if you
stack them one on top of another.

I added my centimes to my canister, and Josh did the
same with his before we covered them again with the
rich African soil, hoping subconsciously that the coins
would multiply and grow like our corn back on the farm.

My mother's job at our home was much harder than
any of the rest of ours were. Josh and I had to go to
school. This was hardly a chore – we played four-square
and kick-the-can, learned French and other core sub-
jects, but that was easy duty compared to hers. Dad
seemed to travel into the exotic "bush" and see wild animals and collect plants into his press for safe-keeping.
He met so many people, and always came home with
something new that he'd bought: a boomerang from a
cattle herder, or a sword from a Touareg. Our shipping
container that we brought to Mali would be just as full
going home, but with souvenirs and keepsakes from
Dad's work trips.

Mom had the most demanding work in her kitchen.
The food preparation alone was a daunting, time-con-
suming task. Water must be boiled and filtered, with
iodine added before consumption – we didn't want to be
plagued with any unwanted parasites. Lettuce and other
vegetables and fruits must be washed, and then soaked
in a solution of treated water and a bit of bleach. Flour

had to be sifted to eliminate the ever-present weevils, and then kept in bags in the freezer. Meat had to be cooked thoroughly well-done, and milk came in a carton that sat on the shelf until opened – or it came in the powdered form, to which we would add water that had been boiled, filtered and treated.

She would make yogurt for us by adding existing yogurt as a starter to milk and letting it sit out on the counter in a covered bowl to incubate in the warm air; there was no need for heating the mixture in this tropical weather. We would eat the new yogurt for breakfast with some sugar and sliced bananas – I can still taste the tangy sweet mixture just thinking about it. I liked that morning meal better than rice and milk, which my dad and Joshua loved and would eat every day if Mom let them.

I was lying in the hammock on the porch that afternoon, watching a lizard doing pushups on our wall. There were lots of reptiles that ran around in our yard and even in our house. The house lizards were smaller and scaled the walls in our home, scurrying here and there, eating the mosquitos and flies. The ones on top of the walls of our compound were a little bigger, with yellow heads and sage green bodies. Josh caught one by the tail; it just fell off, allowing the lizard to run away and escape Josh's grasping hands. These yellow-headed lizards did pushups as some sort of way to communicate with their reptile comrades, but I always thought it was funny to watch them "exercise" each time they paused in their journey across our wall.

I heard Josh call my name, so I scrambled out of my lazy hammock and listened for him again. He was calling me from up on the roof, so I climbed the stairs attached to the side of our house to join him on the rooftop. The homes were all flat-topped in the African towns and villages of Mali, having no pitch to them at all. Our roof was like many others, insulated from the heat with a layer of straw and sticks. It was the same straw that I saw girls use for brooms to sweep their dirt floors.

There was a framework of large sticks on our rooftop, and the bundles of straw were fastened to it, creating a space under the insulation that was sheltered from the sun. The breeze could blow through that shaded space and keep our roof much cooler than it would be without the insulating straw.

From our vantage point on the roof, we could see our entire yard on one side – our pool was a clear bright blue, and I could see something glimmering from the bottom, resting on the tiles. It must be a coin that we left there from our games in the water – we'd have our mom throw the coin while Josh and I stood on the edge of the pool, our eyes closed. When she saw that it had sunk to the bottom and rested on the floor of the pool, she'd say "go!" and we'd try to be the first to dive down and retrieve the treasure.

On the back side of the house over our wall we could see the large gardens where strawberries and a variety of vegetables grew. The lush and fertile soil was a stark contrast to the bright green lettuce heads growing there. Workers were bent over; they toiled in the soil with short crude hoes in hand, some with babies on their backs, weeding their crop. Some would draw water by hand from a deep well at the side of the fields, carrying one bucket at a time to the thirsty plants, quenching their parched roots.

Further than the garden was the highway; pedestrians, cars, bicycles, and *bashés* crammed full of people wove in and out of the congestion. *Bashés* were small pick-up trucks with wooden benches and metal frames built into their beds for people to hold on to as they were taxied to their destinations; bursting at the seams with passengers, they were small buses of a sort.

On one side of the house was an empty lot that Josh and I cut through on our way to school. The lot took us to a small feeder road that led to the highway where our school was located. And of course, on the other side of the house was our neighbor's home, separated from ours only by the alleyway. We could walk from our rooftop to the metal roof of our duplex garage, which led over to the roof of their house. But we always stayed on our side.

Our garage wasn't used for parking our car; it housed our diesel generator, and also our large wooden storage crate that had previously contained our sea freight shipment. Each step we took echoed loudly underneath our feet, forbidding any stealthy progress on the metal roof.

"What's up?" I asked Josh when stepped onto the roof.

"Kuntigi is in the alley right now, so let's go onto the garage to see what he's doing." He led the way over to the roof of the garage, and we stood at the front edge, staring down the alley.

Trees lined the way, large boughs stretching their tired arms, yawning and reaching for the other side of the alley. There he was. Kuntigi. He and his deputies were slowly making their way closer to our house, testing the waters and braving the enemy that now stood guard on top of their garage.

"Toubab!" he yelled. Then he hollered some other words that we didn't understand, but we took them to be slurs because he also launched a big rock toward our fortress on the garage; it hit the door below us.

We had a cache of rocks up on the rooftop for just such an occasion, and we launched our own stones at our adversaries, scattering them in all directions. It was a game we played with them, and they with us. It worked – for now.

"You can't get us, Kuntigi!" we taunted, and launched a few more rocks their way. They lobbed more at us, and we ducked to avoid the missiles.

I wasn't sure how we would ever make a truce to this war – a war made up of small battles, each comprised of rocks being thrown by one side against the other. This feud between us and Kuntigi's little band of kids was perplexing to me; of all places throughout this country, our fiercest rivals – our *only* rivals – were right next to our home at the end of our alley.

Because they had thrown rocks at us, we retaliated, and it just continued on from there. It wasn't right, and we didn't really like it. But at this point we were scared of Kuntigi, and I didn't see how that was ever going to change, despite Josh's plan to somehow make peace.

Suddenly, they went their way out of the alley, and we went ours; it was as if their mother called them for dinner at the same time as ours called for us. The game was over today, and it was time to go home.

16

Josh got a letter from Jude.

I was a little jealous that I didn't get my own letter, but he did write a small line about me at the end of his letter to Josh, so that made me feel a little better.

Dear Josh,

School is a drag. Mostly because you aren't here. I got in a fight and got a black eye. That's ok, though, it kind of makes me look cool. Johnny Porter is the one who hit me, but I have to admit I hit him first. He was calling my dad a drunk. Nobody but me can call him a drunk.

I wish he wasn't like this, but I don't think he will ever change. I love my dad because he's my dad. But I don't like him that much. I don't think anyone likes him. Not my teachers, or my Coach, or my neighbors. This may sound dumb, but I don't think he likes himself.

I think sometimes I feel the same as he does. Like I'm no good. Like I'm just like him. Before school sometimes I sneak some of his booze and drink it. If it makes him feel better and helps him forget stuff, maybe it will do the same thing for me. Don't tell your mom or dad. I know they wouldn't like me doing that. It does kind of make me forget about worrying, though.

I got your letters. Thanks. Sounds like such a wild place over there. I wish I was there.

I wish every day that I was there with you guys. Not here.

I can't wait for high school so I can play football. The coach is new here, so you don't know him. But he thinks I'll be good at it, and I think maybe he's right. I hope so, anyway. You'll be back by then and we can be on the team together.

Tell your mom and dad hi. Tell them I miss them. Tell your little sister that nobody here can play football like she can, and nobody can even come close to how far she can jump off the swings. She still holds the record. You don't have to tell her this part, but I miss her, too. I miss how sweet she is to me.

Got to go. Dad's calling.

Your blood brother, Jude

The letter had been written two months before, so Jude probably hadn't mailed it for a few weeks after he had scribed it. The letter made Josh's day because he heard from his best friend – but it made him sad to know that Jude was getting into trouble and even trying to drink once in a while. Josh was already a worrier when it came to Jude. And now he was worrying even more.

"Can I read your letter again, Josh?" I begged.

"Come on, you've already read it at least ten times!" Josh exaggerated.

"Please? I just want to read it one more time," I whined.

"You just like the part where he says you're sweet," Josh teased.

Actually, I just wanted to read the part again where he said he missed me.

17

Josh and I made the trip to the bakery for baguettes pretty regularly. I use the term "bakery" loosely. It was more like a little hole-in-the-wall shop, with a brick oven inside to bake the fresh baguettes each day.

We would bring the long warm sticks of bread back home on the moped, break a piece off and eat it as we rode, our bellies loving the warm soft inside of the bread and its crunchy exterior. That bread was a little bit of heaven, and we never tired of this errand. I hung on to Josh's middle as we headed home from the bakery, the bag of baguettes slung over my shoulder.

Shopping was a daily thing – it meant a trip to the *marché,* to the bakery for bread, or just buying directly from women who would come to our gate carrying over-sized bowls of fruits and vegetables on their heads.

As we rode along, I thought about those women who came to our gate almost every other day. They'd announce their presence, and then Mom would bargain with them for their produce after she looked it over.

They were always dressed so colorfully, and sometimes their babies were slung to their backs, secured with a cloth to hold the little bundle close to its mother's body, the fabric wrapped around her middle and tied in front.

I had seen a mother tie her baby to her back before. She would lean over at her waist until her back was flat, and then she'd sling the baby onto her back so it would lay there, its head between her shoulder blades. Then she would wrap the long swath of cloth around the baby and pull it in front of her. She'd tie it tight, and then straighten her back upright again, securing the tie in front.

One woman who came to our gate was feeding her baby with one long breast tucked under her armpit, her baby eating right there from its cozy hammock on her back. The women's necks were solid and strong, balancing and carrying heavy bowls full of their goods, babies on their backs, hands laden with other burdens in plastic sacks.

"It must be an old wives' tale that babies' heads need to be propped up safe and secure," Mom told me one day after the women left our gates. She had made her purchases and was watching the babies on the backs of their mothers. I marveled at the beauty of these black women. Their ebony skin was simply gorgeous, and I tried to imagine mine just as dark and stunning.

"What do you mean?" I asked, not sure what a wives' tale really was.

"Well, in America, everyone is always so worried about holding a baby's head up in the crook of your arm," she said, and she showed me with her arms how to cradle a baby, keeping its head safe. "I guess the African women were never let in on that little tidbit of information. They let their newborn babies' heads flop around, flinging to-

and-fro everywhere they go, tied onto their mothers' backs."

I looked after the women as they sauntered down the alleyway.

"Do you think we're right, or do you think they're right?" I asked, wondering how everyone can do things so differently.

"I kind of think these African women are right," Mom offered. "We're just overly paranoid. Don't you think so?" I smiled when she asked my advice, feeling so grown up that she thought I might have a valid opinion.

"Yeah, I think so, too," I agreed.

I was amazed by the strength of those women who came to our gate, and captivated by the way they gracefully walked away, babies' heads bobbing behind them, their giant bowl of goods on their heads, their willowy gait disappearing down our alley.

My attention returned to our moped ride home when Josh called to me over the noise of the engine. I couldn't hear what he said, though; his voice got caught in the hot breeze and was carried over my head and out of my earshot.

"What?" I said into his ear, so he could hear me over all the traffic sounds.

"Let's stop and get a pop," he said, as he quickly turned his chin over his shoulder so I could hear him better.

"Good idea!" I agreed.

I spied the little roadside stand that we always passed on the way home, just ahead of us on the right side of the road. The same young man always had a cooler, selling soda pop. His name was Goussou, and he was proud of his little business. His entrepreneurial spirit impressed me, too. I loved stopping here.

I held on to the bag of two baguettes with my right arm, my other arm around Josh's middle, and we pulled over to the side of the road next to our friend, the drink vendor.

Goussou smiled wide as he saw us coming, his bright teeth prominent against his face, his skin glistening in the sun. He opened his cooler for us to inspect the flavors he had today.

"*Bonjour, mon ami, Joshua*," Goussou said, shaking Josh's hand and smiling at me.

"*Salut, Goussou*," Josh echoed his greeting.

Inside his cooler I could see the bottles bathing in their icy tub, waiting to be chosen. I pulled out an orange Fanta, and Josh did the same. We gave him our coins as payment, and he used his bottle opener to liberate the built-up bubbly inside.

I tipped my head back to guzzle a few gulps, and then let out a satisfied "aaaahhhh," my thirst having been thoroughly quenched. Josh was just as satiated, so we loaded ourselves back onto our moped for the rest of the ride home.

That's when I noticed a man squatting on the ground just a few paces away, his elbow resting on his knee, his forehead resting in the palm of his hand. He was probably our dad's age, with a close-shaved beard covering his handsome black face. His short hair was receding a little, and his eyes seemed kind.

When he saw me looking at him he smiled at me, the edges of his eyes wrinkling into their familiar happy place, revealing his habitual expression. I smiled back as we drove our moped away and gave a small wave of my hand. I looked back over my shoulder, watching him get smaller and smaller as we put distance between the soda pop stand and ourselves.

I turned back around to face forward – my face in Josh's back – and I saw the man's smile lingering in my mind, a notable gap between his two front teeth.

We covered the ground quickly between Goussou and home; as we navigated the dirt roads I saw little girls bent over at the waist sweeping the packed dirt court-yards with whiskbrooms made from sorghum plants. Stray dogs roamed around scrounging through garbage for scraps. I saw a dried-up water collection area – right now it was full of trash that had collected there, blown in with the breeze. But when the monsoons came, this ba-sin would be full of water, kids playing and bathing in its liquid reservoir. The kids would even throw a fishing line in to catch the little fish that would come out of hi-bernation in the dried-up mud, freed from their sleep by the quenching rains.

The rainy season brought with it a deluge of water with nowhere to go. It flooded the streets, and people would wade through it up to their knees at times. But just as fast as the waters had come, they were gone again, leaving the dirt packed solid and dry. The only remnant of evidence of the soaking rain was small stagnant ba-sins scattered here and there around the city.

Josh and I turned onto our street, relieved right away that Kuntigi wasn't there with his friends in front of their school. I could feel Josh's stomach move my arm with his deep intake of breath, then again as he let out a sigh of relief.

As we turned the corner by the *Zaban* tree and started into the alley, Josh slammed on the brakes and caught me off guard, our moped coming to a skidding halt in the dirt. Kuntigi and about five of his friends were standing right there in the alleyway not fifty feet away from us. Now what were we going to do? They were standing between us and our home. We sat there on the moped, its engine idling, baguettes under my arm, trying to figure out our next move.

Kuntigi and his pals turned toward us. They must have been a little disconcerted, too; despite their show of bravado and confidence, I sensed some nervous energy about them. Maybe they were more like us than we thought. Maybe they were scared, too, just like I was.

Kuntigi and his friends started picking up stones from the ground to arm themselves for what they thought was sure to be an ensuing rock fight. My eyes widened with alarm, and I was about to jump off the moped and scurry for some earthen ammunition myself. I hadn't considered that Josh could easily save us by speeding off on the moped and carrying us away from the impending brawl.

Just then, Kéta came out of the neighbor's gate into the alley. I couldn't believe his providential timing. It took him just seconds to see what was happening. He said something to the kids in Bambara, and they slowly started walking toward the mouth of the alleyway, hugging the wall as they went, trying to skirt our position. He yelled louder at them, I think telling them to go faster, because they picked up their pace a bit. He bent over, picked up a small rock, and flung it toward them, and they scurried past us sitting there on our moped, and bolted from the alley into the street. Just like that, the standoff was over.

We drove up the alley to our gate, and Kéta asked us, *"Ça va?"*

We told him yes, we were ok, and he smiled, saying he would protect us. I was glad for Kéta that day; he turned out to be a good *gardien* for us after all.

18

"Do you want to ride into the city with me to buy some paint?" Dad asked me.

"Yes!" I readily agreed, excited for the adventure.

He took me on the moped, and we rode toward the store where he could buy some paint for his project. He was going to paint our gates – both the one that we walked through, and also the big double door gate that we drove our car through to park inside the wall.

Dad drove the moped along a wide swath of packed dirt running parallel to the main road. This was essentially a dirt avenue where pedestrians walked, away from the maddening traffic. The highway was especially dangerous, full of *bachés* and other cars and trucks – not a route my dad wanted to take with me on the back of the moped. As we rode along this frontage pathway, we encountered bicycles, other mopeds, and lots of people walking to their various destinations.

We passed a man with a massive goiter protruding from the front of his neck. I had seen many Malians with goiters, but none as large as the one he had, and I felt sad for him. These goiters were enlarged thyroid glands, caused by a lack of iodine in their diet. I had asked my dad about them the first time I saw one, because it looked to me like there was a big grapefruit stuck in the person's throat.

"What's wrong with that lady's neck, Daddy?" I asked, thinking that the woman must not have to try very hard to hold her head up; it seemed like she could just rest her chin on the big sphere that ballooned from her neck.

"She has a goiter – her neck has a swollen gland in-side of it because she doesn't get enough iodine," he explained.

"What's iodine?" I asked.

"It's a chemical element that we need so that we can be healthy. Back home, our salt has enough iodine added to it so that people don't really develop those goiters. But here in Africa, people don't always get enough iodine," he taught me.

I just didn't understand why it was so hard in Africa for people to stay healthy. There seemed to be so much more disease here than at home. In Bamako, we had to go into the clinic every few months to keep up on immuniza-tion shots so that we wouldn't get diseases that I'd never heard of before.

There were some things we just couldn't prevent, though. For example, everyone in our school got lice. My mom worked hard to get them out of our hair; it took a lot of effort for her to kill the lice and comb all the nits from every strand on our heads. I also got a tick behind my ear, and my mom had to get that out, too. Somehow, she knew that you had to twist that tick counter-clockwise to unscrew it from my skin, and smash it with the flat part of her fingernail so that it popped, squirting my blood out in its moment of death.

My dad slowed down as a man in a dirty uniform stepped in front of our moped with his hand raised. Dad came to a quick stop and I just listened as the man questioned my dad, asking him where we were going, and what we were doing. He looked like he might be a policeman.

It became clear fairly quickly to my dad that the policeman wasn't going to let us proceed on our errand. He kept talking to us in his accented French, stalling and keeping us from driving away.

"I think you may need to come with me, sir," he stated this with as much authority as he could muster.

"No, I don't think so, sir. As you can see, I have my daughter with me, and we need to get back to her mother," my dad tried.

"Come with me to the station, sir, and we will talk about things there," the man continued, not giving up.

"Talk about what, *Monsieur*?" My dad was starting to get impatient. "I've done nothing wrong. Why exactly did you stop me?"

"You cannot drive over here. You must drive on the main road. Come with me, sir. Get off the moped and come with me." His words were louder, and my dad knew he had to do something.

"Ok, ok, I think we can come to an understanding," Dad said, confident that he knew why we had been stopped. We were *Toubabs*, and this was simply a money-making opportunity for this policeman. My dad took his wallet from his pocket and pulled out some bills. The exchange took place as Dad shook the policeman's hand, slipping him the money, and then they broke their hands apart. After looking discretely at the cash, the policeman contemplated for a moment before deciding that it was adequate, then simply turned and walked away.

On the way home, Dad didn't show any fear, or un-ease. He was steady as ever, and this put me at ease, as well. He talked loudly over the sound of the engine so that I could hear him from behind.

"I'm going to Pierre's village tomorrow – do you and Josh want to go?" he asked.

"Yes!" I yelled in reply, excited to explore a new place.

We got home, and Dad took Mom by the hand and led her into the kitchen. While they talked in hushed whispers, I told Josh what had happened, and then in-formed him that we would get to go with Dad the next day to visit Pierre's village – they were Christians from the Bobo tribe, and we were hoping to find a pig to bring home to Mom. Pigs were hard to come by in a Muslim country – they didn't eat pigs because of their religious health code. We thought perhaps in Pierre's village we might find one that we could buy.

The next morning, we loaded up in the Land Rover. Dad sat in the passenger seat and Pierre drove, with Josh and me in the back seat. Dad would be collecting some plants from the area and would add them to his plant press to preserve them for later classification.

When we got to Pierre's village Josh poked me in the arm, and said, "Look!" pointing out his window. I stuck my head next to his and looked at where he was directing my gaze.

Two teenage boys were walking with a sturdy stick on their shoulders, one in front, and one behind, sharing the weight of their cargo that hung between them from the stick.

I looked closer, and then blurted out, "Dad! Those guys are carrying dead dogs on that stick!"

Dad looked over, and then said, "Yep – you know the Bobo tribe is mostly Christian, and they eat both pigs and dogs."

Pierre said, *"Les chiens – ils sont délicieux!"* The grin on his face let us know that he loved eating dogs.

The poor little dogs hung upside-down from the stick, flopping back and forth as the boys walked along the road. They were scrawny dogs, not nearly as big as I was used to seeing. I felt so bad for them, and I imagined Rahtchy hanging from that stick; I had to look away, closing my eyes to try to rid my mind of the thought.

After my dad did some work with his plants, he asked Pierre if he could help him find a pig to buy. Of course, he was more than willing to help out, and he found a distant relative in his village who would sell us one. This pig was nowhere near the size of Jack or Nelly-Jack from our farm back home; it was a skinny little thing – more like the size of our family dog than anything else. But we were happy to have it.

The man killed the pig for us and singed the hair from its hide. He gutted the pig and covered it in a burlap sack. Dad and Pierre tied the sack to the roof of the Land Rover and poured water on it to keep the burlap damp. As we drove home, the air would flow through the burlap and create evaporative cooling to keep the pork from go-ing bad in the heat. Each time we stopped, Dad would douse it with more water to keep the burlap wet.

Once we got the pig back home, Dad went to work to process the meat. First, he cut some pork loins that Mom would roast, and we would eat with vegetables. What a luxury. Then he made both ham and bacon from the other cuts. He would first soak them with a brine of salt and saltpeter. Then, he would smoke them in the garage. His smoker was an elaborate setup that he fabricated using the shipping crate that he had set aside from our sea freight.

To smoke our pork, Dad tipped the sea freight crate upside-down, and made hooks that would hang the meat from the now top of the crate, on the inside. He hung the various pieces of meat from the hooks and built a small fire under the crate on the floor of the garage, propping the wooden crate up a tiny crack so that it would allow oxygen in to feed the little fire. He kept the fire low enough to create enough smoke, but hot enough that the curing process wouldn't take days; otherwise, the meat might go bad. Instead the smoke and heat inside the crate cooked the meat in just a day, and in the end, we had bacon and ham for months. Pork never tasted so delec-table. We felt like pampered royalty.

One side of our garage was filled with the diesel generator. Josh and I were now experts at starting it up whenever the *current* went out. As soon as the lights shut off, one of us would go out to the garage, grab the crank handle from its peg on the wall, and fit it into the crankshaft. We'd turn it on, and then give the handle three or four cranks, until the engine roared to life. It was loud. But it gave us light in the darkness, and cool air during the hot season.

It also gave a sense of security to some friends of my parents who were about to have their first baby. They were a Canadian couple who lived and worked in Mali - assigned here by their church. They were of the Baha'i faith, and they were asked to live in Mali to spread the word of their teachings through the example of their daily living. They found work after they arrived in Mali, and now they were going to have a child.

My parents offered our home to them for the birth of their baby because we had a generator to fall back on in case of a power outage. They were relieved at the offer, and that's how a tiny baby girl was born in my room one night. I had moved out for this occasion, and Josh and I were nowhere in sight when the baby came into the world. But we heard the tiny cries from out where we sat, perched in the mango tree. We looked at one another and smiled.

19

Mom picked us up from school and drove us around on a few errands. The last chore was a stop at the bakery for some daily baguettes, and we pleaded with her to let us stop by Goussou's for an orange Fanta. We cheered as she pulled over where Goussou stood with his cooler and ran over to fish out a bottle from the icy water.

As I took a swig from my Fanta, I saw the man with the gap between his front teeth again. He noticed me, too, and he smiled and waved. I waved back, and decided I'd walk over the few steps to where he was standing while Josh and Mom finished paying for our drinks and got their bottle caps removed.

"*Bonjour*," I offered.

"*Bonjour, mademoiselle*," he replied, politely. He continued in his African accented French, and I conversed in my American accented French. Mine was rudimentary, not really knowing how to converse in the future tense, and barely knowing how to conjugate many of the verbs. His French, though, was very refined and articulate. I thought he belonged in a bank or in the government, or something like that – not sitting here on the street next to the soda pop guy.

We continued our conversation in French.

"Where do you come from, miss?" he asked.

"I come from America. That's my mother and my brother over there," I answered.

His voice was smooth and silky, caressing my senses as music would, enticing my young mind to hear more. His smile was infectious, and I asked him what his name was.

"My name is Modibo," he offered. "And yours?"

I told him my name, and I asked him why he was here by Goussou all the time.

"I live not far from here, and sometimes I come out here to listen to the sounds and see the people."

I nodded my head, feigning understanding, and then Josh walked over to get me.

"Let's go," Josh said to me in English.

"Josh, this is Modibo. Modibo, this is my brother, Josh."

Modibo tried his English on us, "Nice to meet you, Josh."

I could see in Modibo's discernible eyes that he was proud of his linguistic effort. I smiled at this and decided he should be our friend.

"We have to go," Josh said, and he pulled my hand toward the car.

"Bye, Modibo," I said as I took a few steps toward our mother who was starting the car now. "I hope we see you again soon!"

Modibo bore the gap between his teeth, a wide smile having sprung to his face. *"À la prochaine, les enfants!"* He called to us – see you next time, kids!

20

Our family was planning a trip together over the Christmas break from school. We decided to venture north to see the ancient trade city of Timbuktu. The city is hundreds of years old and situated on the ancient trade route for gold, salt, ivory, and even slaves. Salt was a very precious commodity, and at one time would trade evenly for gold, ounce for ounce. We wanted to explore the ageless city and experience her architecture, people, and culture.

The trip was still a few months away, but we were anxiously awaiting the adventure; dad said we would be traveling there by boat. Josh and I could hardly contain ourselves, and eagerly counted the days until we would leave.

School kept us busy while we tried to restrain our anticipation. Schoolwork itself was a blur - homework simply a means to an end, a duty before we could run outdoors and play. We were quite skilled at four-square, a game I'd never played before coming to Mali. It involved standing in one quadrant of a large square with your opponents each occupying one of the three other small quadrants. The goal was to try to get your opponents out by bouncing the rubber ball into their square without them returning it. You get one touch on the ball; if you couldn't return it after a single bounce in your square, then you were out, and the next kid in line would take your place. We loved this game and would play it at every recess.

We would play Kick the Can with the other kids at school, hiding behind trees, and trying to set all the captives free. One night we played Kick the Can with all the American kids that had come with their families to the Marine House to watch movies on the exterior wall of their big garage.

The Marines who were stationed at the Embassy all lived in the Marine House. Every now and then, we'd pass them in our car along the roads in Bamako as they jogged for their morning exercise routine. They would show movies each week, and Americans like us would sit outside and watch them for a small entrance fee.

One of those nights, we kids were all playing the game in the dark, stealthily hiding from the person who was "it" until an opportunity arose to run into the open and kick the can away from its place before getting caught and tagged. I was hiding behind some bushes when a boy from the class above me at school came over and hid next to me. He took my hand and held it; I didn't know what to do, so I just stood there gauchely with my hand in his.

"You know I have a crush on you, right?" he said.

"No, Justin, I didn't know that," I answered awkwardly. There weren't that many kids in the entire American school. Maybe seventeen of us between the

4th and the 8th grades. Justin was a cute boy, and I had to admit his blond hair and hazel eyes had caught my attention more than once.

"Well, I do. I mean, I have a crush on a lot of girls, but you're one of them," Justin said.

I let go of his hand, and ran out from my hiding place, bolting for the can in the clearing. Even young girls know how to play hard-to-get. It's just born inside of us, I guess.

I kicked the can across the yard freeing all the captives from the "jail" they were in. These were the kids that had already been caught by the person guarding the can. Kids scrambled everywhere in search of new hiding places, screams of delight filling the hot night air. I hid behind the same bushes, hoping Justin would find me there again.

Suddenly, a pair of hands grabbed my waist from behind me, and I jumped. I turned around to find Justin there again, with one finger against his lips indicating for me to shush.

He leaned into my ear, cupping his hands against any listening eavesdroppers, and whispered into my ear, "I want to kiss you."

He stepped back a little and looked at me, trying to discern my reaction. Like any eleven-year-old girl, I was awkward and shy when it came to this side of boys. Roughhousing with them was easy. Tackling them in football was a cinch. But kissing them? My face turned red, and I was so grateful for the darkness around us, hoping he wouldn't see my embarrassment.

"Ok," I said shyly.

He leaned in toward me and I didn't move, allowing him complete control of this situation that was so foreign to me. His lips touched mine; I stood there, and involuntarily closed my eyes. My neck started to tingle, and I noticed how warm his lips were against mine. And then, too soon, it was over. He ran away into the night, and I stood there in the dark cover of my hiding place, savoring the memory of just moments before.

I must say, it was magical.

Nothing ever came of it beyond that one kiss; my first kiss. Justin and I were just friends at school like anyone else, and we were both fine with it that way. Sometimes I wonder if Justin ever looks back years later, though, and remembers that brief moment in time that we shared – a sweet and innocent kiss under the African night sky. I remember.

21

I wanted to spend our money on some gum like we used to back home. Only in Bamako, there was no grape flavored Bubble Yum; there was a pink colored gum that came in the shape of a small Tootsie Roll, each one cost just one *centime.* It would do.

I informed Josh I was going to buy some gum down at the *petit magasin* – a little shack on the side of the road that sold sundries.

We jumped off our porch and walked over to the banana plant. One pace north – I took a giant step. Two paces east – two more giant steps. We dug up our film canisters, and clambered over the wall, carefully avoiding scratches from the broken glass. The path led through the empty lot, and to the dirt road. We took a left, walked over the railroad tracks, and there was the little shack on the other side of the road.

The roadside store was nothing more than a stand with a small square of tin propped on a few poles to shed any sun or rain. We could buy a can of powdered milk here, and small bags of sugar if needed. But we had come for something better than that; we had come for the gum.

"One hundred pieces of chewing gum, please." Josh placed our order, and then made the purchase with our coins. We felt like pirates with our plunder – a big bag of gum for mere pennies as our loot.

As we headed back toward our house, I heard a rumbling noise, and looked to our left.

"Josh, is that a train coming? We're going to have to wait for it if we don't hurry!" I worried.

Sure enough, it was a train coming down the tracks. No signals or warnings or whistles here – just the rumble of the train as she came toward us laden with her masses of cars full of mysterious cargo.

The train started passing in front of us, so we slowed our pace, realizing we'd have to wait for it to pass after all. There was one boy already waiting for it to go by, standing there in front of us. We walked up toward him, and stopped beside him, waiting patiently as the train passed by, one car at a time. People were riding all over the cars, holding on to the sides of open boxcar doors and sitting on top of the cars, too.

I glanced over at the boy who was now standing next to me.

My heart stopped. My eyes grew big, and I froze for a moment unable to move a muscle, statuary as Lot's wife. My heart remembered to start beating again after stuttering from its sudden fear. Now it was racing, pounding wildly as if insisting to come out of my chest!

I had always heard of "fight or flight response" – a phenomenon where animals in the wild, when faced with danger, would either fight their enemy, or flee from them. They would manifest physical reactions to the danger, like increased heart rate, increased adrenaline, dilated pupils, and a surge of energy. Humans have similar responses when faced with danger or fear. I thought to myself in that brief second that I didn't have *either* response; instead, I just froze in paralysis. I wouldn't do well in the wild, I thought. I would be eaten by my predator because, when faced with fear, I couldn't move a muscle.

Finally, after what seemed like a long time to me, but was probably just a couple of seconds, I forced myself to reach out toward Josh, and I touched his hand next to me. He looked over and saw my fear. I pointed with my eyes and leaned my head in the boy's direction, whispering intensely to Josh, "Kuntigi!"

Hearing my fierce whisper, Kuntigi looked over at us, and his own eyes widened in shock. He didn't move, either. There we stood, the two of us staring at him, and he back at us as the train slid slowly by. He wasn't as menacing as I had made him out to be in my own mind. He didn't look like the threat to our very lives that we had built up in our imaginings. He actually looked...normal. He wasn't as tall as he seemed from a distance, either. He wore a faded and worn shirt that had jersey numbers on it. His shorts were a dusty dark blue and stopped above his roughened knobby knees. No shoes.

We looked at each other, nowhere to go. The three of us were detained from escape to the safety of our homes by the train that was blocking our paths.

And then Josh changed everything.

He slowly raised his arm up toward Kuntigi, holding out the bag of gum, still clenched in his hand. It was hanging there in front of him as an offering of peace between rivals. Kuntigi just stood there and looked at the bag, and then at Josh. He wasn't sure what he should do.

"*C'est pour toi. Tu peux partager avec tes copains.*" Josh offered the gum to him, so he could share it with his pals. "This is for you."

"*Pour moi?*" he asked, making sure he had heard Josh right. He looked at the bag and could see there was some sort of candy inside. Josh held it a couple of inches closer, reassuring Kuntigi that he really meant it.

Kuntigi slowly reached up, accepted the gift, and opened the bag to peek inside. When he saw the gum, his eyes widened again, and then he looked up at us, almost in disbelief of this encounter he was having with the *Toubabs*. The fear that had been in his wide eyes at first now turned to surprise and elation.

The train had already passed us by, the heavy humid air all around us was now void of its commotion. But we didn't really notice. Our powwow had the three of us enthralled, and our peace treaty was almost sealed.

"*Nous sommes des amis?*" I asked him if we could be friends now, and I offered my hand up to shake his. He looked at my hand, and then his eyes slowly came up to meet mine. His face broke out into a wide smile, his teeth the brightest white I think I'd ever seen. His dark eyes lit up and he put his hand in mine, shaking Josh's hand next.

And then Kuntigi was gone, running across the tracks toward his friends, leaving us standing in the dust.

Josh and I looked at each other, and all we could do was grin.

"Around the world?" Josh asked me.

We gave each other a high-five and swung around for another down low. We smiled all the way home, and we didn't even care that we were empty handed. Our hearts were full.

22

Josh and I saw Modibo again a week later and spent some time talking with him. He enjoyed practicing his English with us, and we were willing teachers. We found out that, like many Malians, he was out of work. His extended family consisted of seventeen people, and he was responsible for supporting them all. They lived in a small walled-in compound with a courtyard of compacted dirt that the women frequently swept clean. There was a well in the center of the courtyard and sleeping quarters on each side near the walls. It was very modest, and all Modibo could afford as a secondary school teacher.

He was an educated man, but down on his luck. He had lost favor with one of the government officials in the Ministry of Education because of his opposing political views. Modibo was vocal and led the teachers in dissent, so the government official made sure he lost his job.

"Modibo," Josh said, "we told our parents all about you, and they want to meet you. Next time we come by, we'll bring them and introduce you."

"Joshua, that would give me great pleasure. I would love to meet them," Modibo answered.

Shortly after that, my parents came with us and met Modibo. They got to know him a bit, and decided to invite him over to our house for dinner. Our family got to know him over the course of the next several weeks. We met his wife and his oldest sons, and my parents hired him for a couple of hours each week to tutor us in French. I taught Modibo English words and phrases, and he started calling me, "*mon professeur*," which made me swell with pride.

Modibo and I sat on the edge of our swimming pool one afternoon in the shade of the mango tree. I watched his lips make the shapes of the foreign words, his tongue forming the tiniest of lisps. His dark skin was beautiful, and the linens of his African garb were hypnotic. I asked him questions about his people, and he in turn asked about America.

"Modibo, can I ask you something?" my voice intonation rising at the end, just as I lifted my head to meet his eyes.

"Of course, *mon professeur*," he listened intently, genuinely interested.

"Well, I hear the girls singing songs while they play at the end of our alley. And I hear women singing, too," I started. He nodded, patiently waiting for my question. "Do you think you could teach me a song in Bambara? I want to sing like your people do."

He showed me the gap in his front teeth again, as his lips parted into a wide grin. He was delighted that I would have such an interest in his culture and his people. He tilted his head down to meet my gaze, and said, "But of course, it would be an honor to teach you one of our songs."

He taught me an African folk song in Bambara about a boa constrictor and a crocodile fighting underneath a fig tree.

> *Ban toro*
> *Bi nabi le*
> *Mininyan ye bama*
> *Bi nabi le*
> *Mininyan ye bama bi le*
> *Ko tu ro toro koro*
> *Bama bila mininyan ba*

I studied the sounds of the words and mimicked the melody as Modibo sang it to me, over and over again. He sang it with me as I learned the words, but try as I might, I could never quite capture the modulation of Modibo's deep and resonant voice, or the inflections that made this song Africa itself. I couldn't help that I was a *Toubab*, and as much as I wanted to sway to the drumbeat the way I'd seen African women dance, I just wasn't born with their West African rhythms.

Modibo wanted us to teach him a song that we knew from America, so Mom suggested that we teach him "Buffalo Gals!" We held our splitting sides as the air peeled with our laughter, Modibo smiling broadly as he sang out in his accented English, "*an a-dahnce by da light ah da moon.*"

Josh and Modibo occasionally spent time talking about religion. They exchanged questions and offered attempts at answers. Modibo was fascinated by our Christianity. Josh and Dad would expound the basic doctrines to Modibo as they sat outside on our porch. They would sit in chairs talking away while peeling green, hard mangoes, slicing them up like apples for Mom to bake into another pie.

We loved Modibo. My parents found him to be a man of good character, trustworthy and noble. They invited him to come along with us to Timbuktu as our guide, and he accepted willingly.

To me, Modibo was a man who captivated my attention; he was intriguing and exuberant, a teacher and friend. He was handsome, his skin an exquisite black, his broad nose and clear eyes elegantly framing his face. But it was his smile that was the most striking – the gap in his front teeth always the trait that I will remember most from the first time I saw him, when Josh and I stopped to buy our bottles of orange Fanta.

23

"Let's load up for our picnic!" Dad called out to us. As promised, we were heading out of Bamako, driving into the unknown just to see what we could see. We had driven east before, toward Mopti, and we had explored the roads to the north, as well.

"Where are we going today, Dad?" Josh asked.

"I think we'll head south, toward Ouelessebougou. We might not make it that far, though; we might see something we like and stop there first. We'll just see," he answered.

Mom had prepared some food for our picnic. Some of the ham Dad had smoked, along with some baguettes to make ham sandwiches. Boiled eggs, and some home-made yogurt. As a special treat, though, we were going to make some ice cream. My parents had packed an ice cream maker in our sea freight – it was one of those wooden buckets with a crank handle on the top.

Mom brought the ice cream mixture – made from eggs, sugar, powdered milk, and treated water – all ready to go. We could hardly contain ourselves with our excitement!

We drove south out of the city, past the airport and on toward an unknown destination. We saw several herds of animals walking along the road, each being shepherded by a young boy with a stick.

Dad had told us about a trip he took once in the Sudan, where he bought a boomerang from a cow herder. He was flying in a small propeller airplane, piloted by a Swiss man, landing in various latitudes of a very large ranch owned by a Saudi Sheik. The Sheik hired my father's consulting company to conduct various studies on his million-acre ranch to determine the viability of developing it into an operational enterprise, eventually to ship beef into Saudi Arabia.

In the southern part of the ranch, Dad and the Swiss pilot, along with a Sudanese animal scientist who was with them, searched for an adequate place to land the plane. They spotted some grassland and decided to land the plane there, conduct some land classifications, talk to the locals about grazing and herd sizes, and then take off again to the next location. When they landed the plane, the grass turned out to be six feet tall. They mowed down a huge swath of the grass with their propellers and were immediately concerned with how they would take off again. Their Sudanese counterpart coaxed the nearby villagers to scythe the grass down by hand, so it would be short enough for the airplane to take off again.

At the next place they touched down, the Sudanese animal scientist interviewed some local cattle herders, while my dad chatted with one of them who was holding a wooden boomerang. This wasn't the kind of boomerang that would return to the thrower; it was pointed on one end, and was meant to be used as a weapon, hurled through the air to penetrate a predator threatening the herd. Dad offered to buy it from the herder, and he readily agreed.

Dad would come home from his trips into the "bush" often bearing souvenirs such as these – authentic tools, trinkets, and even weapons that he purchased out of the hands of their previous owners.

On a different outing we had seen the Bandiagara Cliffs where the Dogon people still live – cliff dwellings that were eerily similar to the Anasazi Cliff dwellings that we were so familiar with at home in the States. Josh and I had found Anasazi artifacts buried on our farm, and we thought it would be fascinating if we could dig up some old potshards near the Bandiagara Cliffs, too.

Today, though, we drove until we saw a little village, and decided we'd pull over near some large outcroppings of rocks. "I'll race you to the top of that giant boulder!" Josh yelled to me as he took off running. We spent the next half hour playing around the rocks, and soon we started to see several little Malian kids approaching us from the village; some even scurried up the rocks to join us.

The four of us sat down together to eat our picnic; the ham sandwiches tasted divine. "Start cranking on this handle, kids. You can take turns," Dad said.

I started to crank away at the ice cream maker's handle as Dad poured rock salt onto the chunks of ice he had broken from a block and crammed along the sides of the bucket. He taught us that the freezing point of salty water is lower than it is for pure water, so the rock salt melts the ice in the bucket and the water becomes super cold. And that's how the ice cream gets cold enough to freeze.

Before long we had quite a large audience. Kids of all ages, and even adults stood around us watching with curiosity, wondering what in the world these *Toubabs* could possibly be up to now. There were smiles, and stares, and words in dialects we couldn't understand.

"*Qu'est ce que vous faites?*" a teenage boy asked us, brave enough to find out what we were doing. He wasn't much older than I was, but he wore his few years pronouncedly on his face, his unforgiving existence eroding the childhood from his life as each year slipped away.

"*Nous faisons de la glâce.* Ice cream," Mom answered.

After Josh cranked the handle for a while, Dad took over and finished the job. We took the container from its icy cold saltwater bath and took off the lid to reveal the creamy goodness inside. Mom scooped some into bowls for each of us, and we enjoyed the cold milky treat.

She turned to our audience and asked, "*Vous en voulez?*" Do you want some?

Smiles broke out all around us, with choruses of "*Oui! Oui!*" singing in our ears.

We didn't have any more bowls, but that didn't even matter. Each of them cupped their hands, reaching them toward her for their serving, chattering away and vying for position in front of the crowd nearest my mom. I thought of my little chicks back on the farm. They would always surround me whenever I went out to feed them, scurrying at my feet and calling to me with their high-pitched cheeping. I saw my mother sharing our ice cream with this precious brood, and I imagined her gathering them under her wings, sheltering them from their dismal subsistence just for this moment in time.

Mom looked at Dad with an eyebrow raised, knowing hands weren't going to work very well as bowls for the melting ice cream. But without anything else, she shrugged her shoulders and forged ahead. She dipped the spoon into the ice cream and plopped it into the hands of our nearest new friend. The girl ate from her hands, trying something brand new to her palate, cold and smooth and sweet. Her eyes opened wide in surprise, and then a smile crept over her face. She licked at the ice cream as it quickly melted in her hands, dripping through her fingers.

As Mom continued to serve the ice cream into the cupped hands all around, sounds of pleasure and delight erupted as their taste buds tingled with the delectable sugary sweetness they were all tasting for the first time in their lives. They licked their hands clean.

We set the container back into the ice bath to keep the ice cream cold. When our friends asked for more, I went to get the container out of the bucket, and some of the salty water accidentally seeped into the container of sweet ice cream.

"Oh no!" I cried in dismay. "I just ruined the rest of the ice cream, Mom! I accidentally let some salt water in there." I felt so bad that I had just spoiled the last of it.

The kids cupped their hands and held them out again, and I tried to explain to them that it would taste bad. I kept trying to convince them that the salt would ruin the flavor. They kept holding out their bowl-shaped hands, though, so Dad said, "Go ahead and give it to them – if they don't like it, they won't eat it."

So, I spooned out the rest of the now salty ice cream, and the kids ate it up just as fast as the last time, not batting an eye at the salty taste. I suddenly felt like an overindulged prissy girl, too finicky and fussy for salt-spoiled ice cream.

Days like these made me wonder why I hadn't been born in Africa. Why had I been born a *Toubab* in America, born to comparative privilege and opportunity? I could just as easily have been born to a family in this very village, and spent my days toiling away preparing food for my family, and then bearing several children, carrying each one on my back until they could walk. Some would maybe even die, given all the disease in Mali. I'd spend my time sweeping dirt floors and steaming couscous, washing clothes by hand and carrying pitchers of water on my head.

Days like this I looked at the kids gathered around me cupping ice cream in their hands and I asked, "Why not me?"

And then I got back in the car with my family and drove back to our house in Bamako – the house with the swimming pool and the polished concrete floor.

"Mom, look at Josh," I said as we stood next to each other just outside our garage.

She turned her head to look down the alleyway and saw him, his white skin standing out stark against the group of his disciples. He was surrounded by a flock of Kuntigi's friends from the school across the street. They followed Josh everywhere now – he had certainly made friends with them, just like he always wanted. Ever since that day when the train went by and Josh gave Kuntigi all of our gum, it was as if our feud had never happened.

"He looks like the Pied Piper," Mom said. "It's like Josh is covered in honey and they're a swarm of bees."

"He's got candy that he shares with them, Mom," I said. "So, he kind of is covered in honey. Pretty close, anyway."

"Well, good for Josh. I'm glad he finally made friends with them."

"You know Kuntigi isn't his real name, right? The taller kid?" I offered.

"No, I didn't know that," Mom answered.

"Yeah, Josh and I just called him that because we didn't know what his name was. It means chief, and since he seemed to be the chief of their little tribe, it seemed to fit," I explained.

Mom laughed and shook her head. "You guys..."

"His real name is Amadou. But it's hard to stop calling him Kuntigi," I said.

Josh kept some candy in his pockets when he went to the end of the alley to play with our new friends. He'd hand a piece to each kid who came to play, and they'd smile and crowd around him, chattering in Bambara words that we didn't understand.

Once when I was with Josh, a girl took my hand and pulled me over to their jump rope game. I clapped along and tried to learn their fun jumping tricks. I sang along the best I could. We'd bring our soccer ball, full of air, and engage in friendly competitions with them, seeing who could keep the ball in the air the longest by bouncing it off our knees, our feet, or even our head. Josh and I wanted to teach them a game, too, so we taught them how to play freeze tag. They thought it was the best game they'd ever played.

Today, though, Josh was at the end of the alley with-out me, and Mom and I were watching from outside our gate.

"It seems like forever ago that we thought Kuntigi hated us," I told my mom.

"Maybe he thought we were invading his territory," she offered her theory.

"Yeah, probably," I agreed. "But now, you can hardly pry the crowd of kids away from Josh!"

Josh really was like the Pied Piper. Or maybe more like a shepherd of his flock since he wasn't leading the kids out of their village with a magical flute. Rather, he knew them by name and led them around the neighbor-hood, retrieving a piece of candy from his pocket and placing it in the hand of a chubby-cheeked little girl, tod-dling after her older sister along the dusty road.

"He said he'd make a friend out of Kuntigi one of these days. And look, he was right," I said, my eyes smil-ing into a happy squint.

Several days later, Kuntigi pounded on our gate, banging loudly and yelling frantically. Nobody an-swered, so he opened the unlocked gate and ran up to our door, scared of Rahtchy, who growled at him, but deter-mined to get someone's attention.

"Patron! Patron!" He was calling for my dad, pounding now on the door of the house.

"Oui? Qu'est-ce qu'il y a?" Dad came to the door, opened it and asked Kuntigi what was wrong.

"Joshua! Joshua!" Kuntigi kept repeating, grabbing my dad's hand, and leading him out of our yard, and into the alleyway.

Kuntigi led my Dad to where Josh was sitting against the outside of our wall, holding his left hand tight in his other one, blood dripping through his fingers and streaking down his arm, his face ghostly white.

Dad ran over to him and picked him up, cradled him in his arms, and brought him inside the gate. He told me to run and grab a kitchen towel, which he wrapped around Josh's bleeding hand. He applied more pressure to the wound and lifted it into the air above Josh's heart to try to slow the bleeding. Once Dad knew the oozing blood had slowed its course a bit, then he'd have a look at it to see how bad it was.

"What happened?" he asked Josh.

Through tears, he explained, "I was just trying to feed the horse some grass, because he looked really hungry. You could see its ribs, Dad."

"Ok, so you tried to feed it? What horse?" he probed for more information.

"The horse that pulls the cart with diesel drums on it," Josh said. "After he delivered our diesel, Kuntigi and I followed it down the alley. I thought he needed some grass, so I tried to give it to him. He lunged for it and got my finger. I'm sorry, Dad." His dirty face was streaked with tears that he had shed from the pain. He used the inside of his elbow to try to wipe them away, but it just smeared the dirt and made his face even messier.

"Don't be sorry, Josh. It's ok. You're going to be ok," Dad said.

"Dad, Kuntigi really helped me." Josh was looking around now, wondering where Kuntigi went. "He got me back home. I don't think I could've made it back here by myself. I was so dizzy."

"Good, I'm really glad he was there," Dad said.

"Where is he?" Josh asked.

"I think he's still outside the gate," Dad answered, more concerned about Josh's finger right now. He got a look at it and saw that the tip of his finger was gone, but the bone was intact. It was serious, though, and Josh would need a doctor.

"Kuntigi!" Josh yelled. Amadou answered to the nickname we had given to him; I think he was happy to be considered the chief of the school kids. "Kuntigi! Come in here!"

Kuntigi poked his head into the gate, and Josh waved him in. He looked uncomfortable, like he didn't think he belonged inside the walls. Josh kept waving him over, until Kuntigi stood next to where he was sitting. He pulled Kuntigi's hand down, so he would sit next to him.

Josh put his arm around Kuntigi, and said, "*Merci, mon ami.*" Thank you so much, my friend. Kuntigi smiled, and Dad patted him on the shoulder, adding his thanks.

After a visit to the Embassy doctor, and the local Leprosy clinic that offered amputation of the finger, Mom and Dad decided to send Josh to Paris for surgery. Dad flew with him, while Mom and I stayed home. It was strange being on our own, and we both worried for Josh. But everything went well, and within a couple of weeks they were back with us, life back to normal.

24

The day finally came for our trip to Timbuktu. Josh and I woke up feeling like it was Christmas morning. That same feeling of excitement and anticipation was flowing through our veins, and we couldn't wait to get going on our newest expedition.

Mom packed a few things for the trip, including a water filter – even though Dad had brought three days' worth of water for the trip there. Once we got there, we could boil and filter more. I looked through the bags that Mom had packed, and to my horror, I saw my old Mrs. Beasley doll.

"Mom! Why are we taking Mrs. Beasley? You know I outgrew her years ago!" I complained.

"Should we just throw her out, then?" Mom asked, knowing I still had some sentimental attachment to her, having had her practically my entire life. But I'd left dolls behind years ago, and I was horrified that she would think I needed Mrs. Beasley to come along with us on our trip.

She was one of those dollies that had a pull-string and would say things to you when you pulled the ring that was fastened to her back. She would say things like, "Speak a little louder dear, so Mrs. Beasley can hear you," or "Do you want to hear a secret? I know one!" I did love playing with her when I was a lot younger, but I was too old for dolls now.

"We can just throw her away, I suppose," she said again, waiting for my reaction.

"No, I didn't say that," I quickly replied. "I just think we can pack her away and keep her in the chest. I can give her to my little girl someday," I said, not wanting to be rid of her completely.

"Oh, ok..." Mom smiled. "Well, the reason I packed her is because I'm sure there will be some girls we meet along the way who have never seen a doll like Mrs. Beasley. I thought we could make some friends with her."

"Oh. Well, yeah, that could be a good idea," I reluctantly agreed. So, Mrs. Beasley came with us to Timbuktu.

We loaded up the car, and then drove by to pick up Modibo. He was thrilled to be our guide, and to show us areas of his country that we hadn't yet seen. It seemed he had distant relatives everywhere, and he spoke several of the local dialects. We were so happy to have him along with us on our trip to these heretofore-unknown regions of the country.

We drove to Mopti, a town a few hours away that lay along the banks of the Niger River. We would be taking a boat ride up to Timbuktu, and it was supposed to be a three-day journey.

The boat docks were filled with people. The banks of the river were turned into a marketplace, covered with bright fabric of all colors, fruits arranged in piles, and solid slabs of salt for sale. The boats waiting for their cargo lined the shore, and my eyes were trying to survey every detail.

Our boat was a *pinasse,* which is another word for "giant canoe." The body of the boat was about twelve feet wide, roughly seventy feet long and eight feet deep, but only about a foot of the boat was still above water, being so laden with cargo. Several massive curved ribs fabricated the structure of the roof, with smaller curved lengths of thin wood strips filling between the larger ribs. The roof was covered with a large sturdy canvas that went the entire length of the *pinasse*. The sides of the canvas were rolled up during the day, providing open air. At night they would be rolled down to keep the bugs out and make it a little cozier for sleeping.

The boat was filled with cargo of all sorts – drums of vegetable oil and diesel, burlap sacks full of peanuts, and then bags of oranges and onions loaded on top of those. Various consignments filled the boat to the brim; the last cargo, sitting on top of it all, were the people. Modibo found us passage on one of these canoes, and the *Toubab* family was sent to the back of the boat, near the two outboard motors that slowly powered the vessel through the meandering river.

There were close to one hundred people aboard our *pinasse*. There was a galley of sorts where a few women cooked for the passengers. It was just an area void of cargo where a fire could be built in a large clay fire pit on the bottom of the canoe that the women filled with hot coals. Several people could stand and maneuver around the makeshift kitchen. My dad made pancakes in the galley one morning, and the women and other passengers nearby were flabbergasted. First, that a man would be in the kitchen cooking, and second how fast his meal was finished and ready to serve. Their meals took all day to cook, but we had brought some pancake mix that Mom had made from scratch, and Dad just added water from the gallon jugs that we had brought along. Flip, flop, and presto – the pancakes were done.

Josh and I watched Dad as he cooked, and Mom visited with the passengers in the back of the boat, waiting for breakfast to be served. Josh jumped up on the edge of the boat in the galley area and folded his middle over the wooden side. I did the same thing, and we rode like that, hands playing in the water as we moved through the river, our butts hanging into the galley, the legs of our jeans wet and our feet bare, having just run up and down the sandy banks while the boat was stopped for a short break along our route. Now we were back in the boat, leaning over the edge and running our hands through the river's flow. Dad snapped a photo.

The captain of our boat was a very social guy – he had friends everywhere along the way, and he liked to stop and visit every single one of them. We didn't mind the stops. Usually it meant another chance for us to explore and discover something new; we'd get off the boat to buy some flatbread in one town, or shop for trinkets at the local market of another. At one place along the river, we disembarked at a small hut where some teenage girls were outside drying fish and smoking them over a fire. They were bare-breasted, and had beautiful African fabric tied around their waists. Their necks and wrists were adorned with bracelets and necklaces, and their feet were bare. Their hair was tightly braided in intricate patterns. We bought some of the fish they were selling and ate it later for dinner.

Each time we were ready to leave shore and get back on the journey, the "deck hands" of the *pinasse* would stand on the edge of the hull and use a long pole to push off from the river bank. Our canoe would glide out into deeper waters where they could start the outboard motors. One guy positioned his pole in the marshy waters against the bank of the river, and I thought he was going to lean so far away from the boat onto his pole that he might tip over and fall into the water. But he never did – he pushed himself back from the bank against his pole every time, and never fell into the river.

It was a lazy life on the river – we slept, and sat on top of the canvas roof, gazing out into the marshes of the delta as we made our way closer to our destination. Modibo and Josh sat on top of the roof toward the front of the boat, pointing at birds, or ripples in the water that revealed something wild lurking beneath its surface.

"Modibo, do you think you'll stay in Mali forever?" Josh asked him.

He pondered for a couple of seconds, "Hmmm, I don't know Joshua. I think maybe one day I will travel – maybe I will come visit you and your family in America. But I'm not sure."

They sat in silence for a few moments, and then Josh asked again, "Why do you think you were born here, and I was born in America?"

"I think only God knows that, Joshua," Modibo answered. "I am a son of Africa, and you are a son of America. We are simply born this way, and we cannot change this."

Josh thought about that, and then said, "Maybe it was God that brought us here, and maybe it was His plan that we met you."

"Yes, I think you are maybe right," Modibo contemplated, and then agreed. The chance that he would make friends - more like family - with someone from America here in his own country...seemed more than just mere co-incidence. It was Providence.

"I think so," Josh was considering the idea. "Modibo, do you ever get the feeling that you're supposed to do something significant with your life?"

"Joshua, are you sure you are twelve years old? This is an ageless question that old men usually ask themselves," Modibo said.

Joshua looked down at his hands, and then back out into the river.

Modibo quickly added, "I know what you mean, though. Yes, I feel God has plans for each of us."

Joshua looked over at him, glad to hear that he wasn't the only one to feel this way. "I just want to do something that will help people and make a difference to them. I'm not sure what it is yet, but I have a feeling inside me that I'm meant to do that."

Modibo said, "I think you will change people, Joshua. Even though you are still young, you can influence people for good. Look at you and your sister. You are young, and yet you have made a change in me for good."

"Really?" Josh asked.

"Yes, really," Modibo confirmed. "Just think of it - you have made perhaps a small difference here in Africa - so far away from your homeland - and when you are gone, the ripples from you having been here will continue to grow out from you, and touch many more people."

Josh thought about that for a minute, and then with sudden perception he said, "Yeah, and you have changed us, too. So, when we go back home, you will keep living on inside of us, and maybe in that way you will shape and influence something or someone – even far away from your homeland, too."

Modibo smiled. The two of them sat on the top of the covered canoe, contemplating their words for a few moments in silence, as the prow of the canoe plowed through the river's calm waters.

"I'll never forget you, Modibo," Josh said. "None of us will."

"I'll never forget you, either, Joshua."

❧

Our trip was taking a lot longer than three days; we were running out of treated water, with no way to boil and filter more. We tried to conserve what we had and wondered how much longer until we arrived at our journey's end. We knew clean water was going to soon become a real problem.

Sitting in the back of the boat on top of the oranges, we chatted with our neighboring passengers and Mom asked me if I wanted to show their little girl Mrs. Beasley.

"Yes!" I answered with enthusiasm. She was up in our luggage on the top of the boat, so I climbed onto the edge, standing with my toes on the wooden hull, leaning into the canvas, curving my body along its shape. I'd slide one foot, and follow with the next, holding on to the canvas. I got to our bags and fished out Mrs. Beasley, shuffling back to where mom was still sitting.

We showed the little girl – she must have been four years old – how I could pull the string on Mrs. Beasley's back, and to listen as she talked. The girl's eyes lit up with interest. Her mother had a small baby in her arms and was watching as we played with her older daughter.

I asked Modibo to translate for me, which he did.

"Will you let me hold your baby? Your daughter can hold Mrs. Beasley," I offered.

Modibo conveyed my proposal, and the mother didn't hesitate, handing me her swaddling bundle. Mom handed Mrs. Beasley to the young girl, and her eyes beamed with delight. There we were, in the middle of the Niger River, in the middle of the sub-Sahara; I was holding a tiny black baby who couldn't be more adorable – a tiny bracelet around her wrist, and big round eyes looking back at me – and the little girl was holding Mrs. Beasley, admiring the wired glasses that framed her face, and stroking her blonde hair.

After a while, I handed the baby back to her mother, and smiles lingered all around. My mother talked to me quietly so only I could hear. "You know, that little girl will probably never see a real doll like that ever again in her life."

"Yeah, you're probably right," I agreed.

"I know you wanted to keep Mrs. Beasley in your treasure chest for your own little girl one day. But what do you think about maybe giving her to this little girl instead? She will probably love her and treasure her just as much as you did when you were her age," Mom submitted.

I thought about it, and saw that Mom was right. This little African girl clearly loved Mrs. Beasley already, and it would probably make her very happy to keep her.

"Ok, yeah – I'm ok with that," I answered.

My mom put her arm around me and pulled me into her, whispering, "I'm so proud of you."

My heart filled with joy – because the little girl was so happy that she could keep my doll, and because my mother was proud. I wonder if that girl – a grown woman now – still has Mrs. Beasley. Is she covered in dirt, clothes torn and glasses long lost, kicked along the streets with the other trash and no longer important to anyone? I like to think she's strapped to the back of a little Malian girl as she plays outside and carries a basket on her small head, my old dolly having been handed down to her by her mother, the little girl I met on the Niger River.

After five days on that oversized canoe that became our floating home, we finally arrived at the port near Timbuktu. Once upon a time the city was built right next to the river, but over hundreds of years of wind-blown erosion, the sand moved, and thus the river shifted and curled away from the city.

We had run out of our drinking water, and we ended up using our portable filter to attempt to cleanse the river water. At least the larger particles would be filtered out, including the dreaded Guinea worm. We also treated the water with iodine tablets to kill some of the unseen germs and bacteria. Anything and everything was dumped into that river, though, and we knew we were bound to contract something unpleasant. It was just a matter of time now.

We took a local taxi, drove the short distance into Timbuktu and set up camp in the compound of Modibo's distant cousin. They were a Touareg family, and many of them wore clothes made from stark indigo blue fabric. Their skin was fairer in color and their hair smooth – they were more like the Arabs of Northern Africa than the black Africans we knew in Bamako. They welcomed us into their home – we were friends of Modibo and that made us "family," too. We quickly set up our tents in their courtyard. This was amazing to our hosts. They had never seen tents such as ours and were astounded at the ease of their assembly, and how quickly they were ready to use.

"Come look at this," Josh grabbed my arm and pulled me out to the courtyard. Our green two-man tents were pitched on one side of the yard, and the communal outdoor latrine was located on the other. The dirt was packed tightly, having been swept clean with whisk-brooms just like I'd seen in Bamako. Chickens were running around the enclosed yard, and a goat was tied up in the corner.

"Look, that kid is going to kill a chicken," Josh said. I saw the chicken hanging upside down from the boy's hand, its legs firm in his grasp.

The boy was about Josh's age, and he wore the bright blue clothes, too. His skin was an olive color, and his features were long and willowy, his nose thin, and his eyes bright. He looked exotic to me, and his eyes caught my gaze each time I saw them.

He held a hatchet in one hand, and with the other he started swinging the chicken around in the air like a windmill, a lot like Josh used to do with the milk bucket after we milked our cow, Lucky. Around and around went the poor chicken, and I started to feel sorry for it.

"What in the world is he doing, Josh?" I implored.

"He's making it better for the chicken – don't worry. He's getting it dizzy so that it holds still to chop its head off," he explained.

After several turns of his arm, the boy laid the chicken on the block, and smoothed out its neck to make it as long as possible. Sure enough, the hen was so dizzy and disoriented that she just lay there, and her life was over in an instant, without suffering.

The women of the family prepared the meal, and when it was ready I was ushered into a room where the women ate, which was in a separate room from the men. I didn't understand why we had to be isolated, but they told me that's how Muslims do it, so we followed their customs.

Mom and I sat in a circle on the floor with the other girls and women. I could smell the wonderful aromas of the couscous and sauce that were in front of us in a big bowl, waiting for us to partake. The sauce had been stewed with the chicken that I had seen at the end of its life just a couple of hours before.

Each of us had our own assigned section of the bowl in front of us, as if the round vessel were divided into wedges like a pie. They didn't use forks or spoons for their meals – we were instructed to eat only with our right hand. We each took small amounts of couscous and sauce in our fingers, tried to mold it into a little ball with our thumb, and did our best to get the food into our mouths. Mom and I weren't very good at using our hands to eat, and the other women laughed demurely at our struggle.

I reached for a piece of flat bread, and Mom warned me, "Be careful not to chew too hard on the bread. You might bite down on some sand."

Sure enough, the bread had a gritty texture to it, so I ate with caution. The wheat came straight from the fields without being washed or cleaned, so the sand from the desert would often find its way into the bread in Timbuktu.

Women also weren't permitted into the most ancient mosque in Timbuktu; only the men could go inside. We felt a little vindicated when my mother and I were ushered across the alleyway from the mosque into the home of an Arab family, while Dad and Josh got to go inside. The gracious Arab women hosted the two of us in their home, during which time they made a point not to allow any men to come inside, and that made me grin.

We had to take several steps down from the street level into their home. The sand had piled up over the years throughout this ancient part of the city, burying the homes inches at a time. The sand had accumulated a couple of feet around all the buildings in the area, and that's why we had to step down to get into the home of the kind Arab women. Their house was cool, clean and simple. They didn't speak a word of English and we didn't speak any Arabic. But lots of smiles and offers of food passed the time while Dad and Josh toured the ancient mosque.

We rode camels in Timbuktu, and I wished for a moment that Jude could have been there with us. He would have loved riding these camels. We made some wonderful memories with our family and with Modibo, and then it was time to head home.

On the trip home we rode in the mail courier Land Rover through the edges of the Sahara to a large river port where we planned to gain passage back to Mopti on a river boat – one with a paddle wheel like I'd read about in Huckleberry Finn. When we got there, we could only get tickets for third class, which meant the bottom of three decks, with the animals, and only standing room. This wasn't acceptable to Modibo.

"Follow me," he instructed us. We obeyed and followed him as he started to scale the boat. He climbed on the railing of the lower deck, and then climbed up to the second level, each of us in pursuit. Mom climbed up the side with some attentive assistance from Dad, and we all landed on the top deck of the boat, out in the open air.

"I'll go talk to the captain," Modibo told us, and then he disappeared for a while. We were hoping for some successful negotiations, because the last thing we wanted to do was ride on that lower deck with the animals, and crude overflowing toilets.

After a while, Modibo returned.

"What happened?" Dad asked.

"I told the captain that I was showing my friends from America what Mali is like, and that I didn't want to be embarrassed by having them ride on the bottom deck. After much discussion and gentle persuasion, the captain agreed that we could ride on the top deck. The cabins are full, but we can remain outside on the deck and sleep here at night," Modibo reported.

We were all relieved, and we enjoyed the quick overnight trip to Mopti. Along the way, my dad met a young schoolteacher who had been visiting his family and was returning to work. Dad teased me by negotiating back and forth with the man on how much he would take in trade for my hand in marriage. How many camels and cows would it take, he asked my father, who played along. I knew he was kidding, but still felt a tiny panic of, "what if he weren't?"

I didn't like to think what girls my age had to endure having been born here. They couldn't fall in love and choose their own husband all the time – their dads would choose for them. I thought about Jude and wondered if it was still possible for me to end up with him. I knew that was a silly notion from an innocent childhood dream. But maybe he thought of me sometimes like I did of him. Maybe.

By the time we got home from our amazing family vacation, all of us – except Modibo – had amoebic dysentery. The water had gotten to us, and we became intimately familiar with our commodes. It was still worth the experience of our enchanting and exceptional trip to Timbuktu.

Just a few days after our trip, my father baptized Modibo in our swimming pool. His conversations with Josh and my father over the last several months had led him to a conversion to Christianity. He had studied and read the scriptures, had prayed for himself, and had made this decision. Josh was so moved by this development, his heart so touched, that his feelings overflowed from his eyes in a few tears as he stood by the pool to watch.

Modibo was dressed in white clothing, and as he came up out of the water, the liquid trickled from his eyelashes and ran in small beads from his beard, falling back into the pool. He gave my dad a hug, and then looked at the rest of us – my mom, Josh and me – standing at the edge of the pool to witness the occasion. We smiled at him, and his face broke into a rejoining smile; the gap in his front teeth etched itself into the archives of my memory.

LEAH MARTIN

25

As we explored the African landscape, we would often stop in isolated villages where rural life was in motion as people eked out their daily subsistence. These were the places where children would swarm around us, gathering from the crannies of their huts and courtyards. Some younger ones had never seen a *Toubab* in all their lifetime.

"Bon-bon!" The kids called out for candy, following us as we walked around the village. Some would reach out and touch my hair, having never before seen the straight long hair of a white person.

Women in these Malian villages worked so hard, all day long. The hardships they endured in their daily routines aged them harshly and swiftly, their worn and ragged shells much older than their true inner age. The men in those rural areas were responsible for cultivating the grains; plowing and planting. Once that was done, the women took over and did all the weeding, the harvesting, and then the preparation. The men, cultivation complete, would retire themselves to the shadows of the big village fig tree, philosophically solving the world's problems as they lounged the days away.

Most of the women's time and energy was spent preparing food for their families. They would collect wood to build their small fires, over which they would boil water to prepare their meals. Hours upon hours they would pound sorghum, millet, salt or other foods in their varying sizes of mortar and pestle. I witnessed women in villages, on roadsides, in courtyards, in front of their fires – all pounding away at their chore with long, thick wooden sticks, beating their meal into submission, grinding it little by little into smaller and finer morsels that would cook down and be more readily edible.

Pounding, pounding, pounding – such a dreary task. But I saw these remarkable resilient women turn this dreary duty into a metrical musical cadence, transforming the hours-long burden into something bearable, and even enjoyable – at least for me, a young spellbound girl fascinated by their phenomenal talent.

I saw a pair of such women, hammering away with these sticks, their grains in the wooden vessel that sat on the ground. They stood, holding the pestle in two hands, high up in the air above their heads, then smashing it down into the grains, pulverizing the sorghum, or whatever their meal would be that day. In the northern regions of Mali, they would have more millet, and even irrigated wheat near Timbuktu. In the southern areas, it would be sorghum, and the women made what they called *gateau*, the French word for cake. It was a sorghum porridge that was allowed time to set up, then cut into squares and fried, forming a base over which they could pour their sauces.

The women were singing a song to keep the pummel of the pestle in a steady tempo, thumping their mortars to the beat of their chanting tune. The song was entrancing to me, and I stood there, oblivious to anything else around me, watching as they sang and worked in perfect synchronization. Their velvety voices harmonized in a hypnotic refrain that I found myself longing to learn. They sang to the drumbeat of their own strikes, a percussive metronome that persuaded their toil onward through the long day under the African sun.

Some women took turns with one mortar, alternating their sticks in the same bowl. Others would throw their stick with one hand, catching it with the other as it moved down to smash the meal. All to the tempo of their songs.

It seemed like a game to me. A diversion from the toil. An amusement to distract from the drudgery.

I drank those rhythms in; the African songs were living waters that gave sustenance to my young soul. They became part of me, seeping into every crevice of my being.

These tribal hymns, Modibo's smile and kind gleaming eyes, Kuntigi's handshake, the babies' bobbling heads on their mothers' backs, the kids eating our homemade ice cream from their hands – my youthful being was immersed into the font of these experiences. My childhood was buried in their flowing stream; I arose from these waters a new and altered young woman marked with the imprint of this people. They are still a measure of me; they are a portion of what makes me who I am and can never be rubbed out or washed away.

LEAH MARTIN

26

We entrusted Rahtchy to Modibo as we said good-bye to our Malian home. We made sure he promised not to let Pierre get his hands on our family dog. He pledged his watchful care over Rahtchy, and we said our tearful goodbyes. I wasn't sure I'd ever see Modibo again, our worlds so far apart, separated by the vast ocean and thousands of miles thwarting our connection and threatening the nearness of our friendship.

I hugged him tight, my arms encircling his neck. "I love you, Modibo."

"I love you, my child. Goodbye. May God bless you," he said into my ear.

Joshua shook Modibo's hand, trying to be mature. Modibo pulled him into his embrace, and a tear rolled down Josh's cheek.

My parents gave Modibo all the food that was in our house. He was overwhelmed with gratitude, happy to be able to feed his large extended family for quite some time.

The last day in our house, Josh came into my room and said, "Let's give all of our clothes to Kuntigi and his gang."

"You mean to your fan club," I corrected, and smiled at him impishly.

"No, I mean to our friends," Josh said, sternly. "I don't have a fan club."

"Ok, Josh," I said sarcastically. "But we'd better ask Mom first."

Mom told us to save back four days' worth of clothes, and that she was fine with us giving away the rest. We didn't have a big wardrobe as it was, but we had more than Kuntigi and the other school kids had at the end of our alley.

We had Kuntigi bring all the kids up to our gate, and we handed out shirts, and shorts, jeans, and socks. And several pairs of shoes. I had a white ball cap from my dad's work that I wore sometimes, and there was a young boy already wearing it, bright against his black hair, his eyes peering from beneath the brim, a wide smile across his face. We gave Kuntigi our soccer ball, and I handed out each of my leftover centimes, placing one in each little black hand that reached toward me. I remembered when we first moved here, seeing their legs through the gap at the bottom of the gate at their school at the end of our alley. They were a mystery to me then, but now I knew each one of these friends, and was sad to leave them behind.

"*Au revoir, Kuntigi,*" Joshua said. We stood facing him, now clad in Josh's old blue tennis shoes, but without socks. He also had on a shirt that Josh had given to him, bright green with a wide white stripe across the chest. His face beamed with pride.

Kuntigi held out his hand first to me, and then to Joshua. They shook hands, and Kuntigi covered their clasped hands with his other hand, emphasizing what their friendship had meant to him. They couldn't really communicate very well; neither of their French was wonderful – more rudimentary than anything. But lots of words weren't really needed right now. They looked into each other's eyes, and they smiled.

"*Tu es mon ami, Joshua,*" Kuntigi said.

"You are my friend, too, Amadou," Josh said.

They hugged briefly and said goodbye. We turned back to our house, and they turned down the alleyway. Before Josh went into our gate, he looked back, and caught a glimpse of Kuntigi glancing back at him, too. They waved for the last time.

As we flew out of Bamako, I watched as we climbed further and further away from the city below. I realized in that moment that everything we had just lived and experienced was no longer our present existence but had, in an instant, turned to memories. Memories that became more and more distant as the hours and days progressed. I was sad that it was over. Excited to venture homeward, but forlorn that Mali and her indelible influence were now in my past.

27

We hadn't been back home for a full day before Jude came by to see us. He hugged Josh and slapped his back, their smiles as big as they could be. Jude even picked me up and twirled me around once, placing me back on my feet and stepping back to look at me.

"I can't believe how much you both have changed!" He was genuinely amazed. He had changed, too – he was so much taller, and broader in the shoulders. We were all in our early teens now, and his voice had changed, deeper than before and more mature.

"You're different, too. I can't believe how tall you are!" I responded. I couldn't pull my eyes away from him. His skin was tanned from working outside, but his eyes were still that stunning chocolate brown that I remembered. His dark eyelashes were long, and I think he knew how charming his smile could be, because he flashed it at me as if he knew its spellbinding power. I blushed and turned away.

He and Josh went out the back door and headed for Joshua's Tree to hang out and catch up on everything that had happened during their absence from one another. I stayed with Mom to help organize the kitchen. My parents had let Josh and I know that in two months, we'd be moving on to my dad's next job. We'd be living in Africa again, but this time all the way to the southern limits of the continent in a town called Maseru. Dad would be doing land cover classification again, mapping the entire country of Lesotho with his findings.

We were all excited for another adventure, but the one thought that kept nagging at the margins of my mind was how Jude would handle the news again. The first time we left, he seemed to take it especially hard, and being alone with his dad had only driven Jude to rebellion. He was still drinking before school from time to time, looking for ways to punish himself for nothing other than his own sense of self-worth. Or lack of it. He got in fights and spent hours in detention. I was worried about him, and so were my parents.

I looked out the window and could see Josh and Jude sitting up in the platform of the tree in the distance. I knew if we could stay here, we could help Jude and maybe provide some sense of family and stability for him. But we couldn't stay here. So, my heart was troubled.

"Mom, I wish we could take Jude with us," I sighed, thinking this was the only other plausible solution to helping our friend – our blood-brother.

"I know, honey. I was talking to your dad about the same thing. Maybe we can work something out for him to come visit us in Maseru." My eyes lit up at this suggestion, and instantly my heart was lifted from its worrying, hope now in its place.

"Really?" I asked eagerly.

"Well, it would have to be ok with his dad, you know. We'll have to talk to him and see what he says. So don't get your hopes too high. You know how he can be sometimes," she warned.

"I know," I said, and put the dishes in the cupboard, suddenly full of optimism and hope. "Can I go tell the boys?" I asked.

"Not yet – let's all sit down as a family and ask Jude if that's something he even wants to do, ok? That's a long way to travel, and it's far from his home. Let's make sure we take one step at a time. We'll talk in a couple of hours when your dad gets home, ok?" she suggested.

"Ok, Mom," I agreed. I walked over to where she was standing and put my arms around her, hugging her tight. "Thank you," I said, sincerely full of gratitude that she would be willing to do this.

A few hours later after we had all eaten dinner, we sat around the living room, and Dad started the discussion.

"Jude, we want to ask you something, and I don't need you to answer right away. You should probably think about it," Dad said.

"Ok...," Jude looked around with some apprehension, wondering if he was in trouble, or if he had done something wrong already. His internal defenses had been well-trained to anticipate fault and blame lying squarely with him, no matter the circumstance. Living with his dad had instilled that reflexive response in his psyche.

"We're going to be moving again in a couple of months," Dad started. I saw Jude's expression change immediately, his face dropping, and his shoulders slumping beside his body. "But this time, I think you're old enough to maybe come visit us while we're there," Dad finished his thought, and Jude's eyes opened a little with cautious anticipation.

"What do you mean?" Jude asked cautiously. I think he'd experienced enough disappointment in his short life already that he wasn't eager to trust good news on its face.

"Well, you have the summer coming up, and we thought if it was ok with your dad, you could come spend it with us in Africa before you have to come back here for school," Dad said.

"Oh, my gosh...really?" The corner of Jude's mouth started to twitch up in a tiny smile, but then realization hit him, and he answered, "Oh, but it costs a lot of money to fly that far, and you know how my dad is. We don't have a lot of money. And then there's talking my dad into it in the first place. You guys know better than anyone that he's not your most friendly person." Jude was starting to doubt the possibilities and lose hope. His smile had quickly faded.

Mom broke in, "Jude, you just let us worry about the money – and if you think about this for a while and decide you want to come visit us for the summer, then we'll take care of asking your dad about it. Ok?"

Jude looked at Josh, and then looked at me. He rubbed the palm of his hand with his thumb, smoothing out the little scar he had from cutting his palm with Josh when they made their oath of brotherhood to each other.

I figured it must help him to think better because he kept rubbing it until he had something to say.

"I don't need to think about it. You don't even know how much I want to go! If you can talk my dad into it, I wouldn't want to be anywhere else." Jude's eyebrows were lifted in the middle of his brow, the sincerity of his voice tugged at my heart, and I could see how much he was still aching from being left behind the first time. I couldn't imagine how he must have felt before this conversation, expecting that we would be leaving him behind yet again.

"I'm just worried my dad will say no again," Jude stressed, his eyes glistening a little with impending tears.

"Just leave that to me," Dad said resolutely.

Our family was in awe of City Market. It had transformed in our eyes from our local grocery store to a produce paradise, full of amazing foods and fancies that we hadn't been accustomed to now for a few years. Mom was filling her cart with gallons of milk out of the cooler, the wonderment of it all showing on her face as her eyes lit up and sparkled. She added a bag of Oreos to the cart, planning a treat later that night for our family. One we hadn't had in what seemed like ages.

Josh and I scanned each area of the store, our jaws dropping at the cereal aisle. We couldn't believe our eyes when we saw every inch of every shelf filled with copious flavors and brands of cold cereal. We begged Mom to let us have Captain Crunch and Cheerios. She felt overwhelmed by the choices, and almost wanted to run out to the car instead of facing the colossal task of choosing one brand over the other fifty. But she readily agreed to buy us the cereal we wanted.

Now that we were home we relished the little things that we took for granted in the past. Drinking from the tap, running around without shoes, and no more need for the weekly bitter quinine pills. I missed Bamako. I missed Modibo. But the comforts of home helped temper the longing and pacify the fears of change.

A few days later, Dad knocked on Jude's door. The trailer house was in shambles, siding falling off the exterior, boards missing from the porch leaving gaps that had to be avoided on the way to the front door. The door handle itself was missing, a round hole where it should have been made a large peephole through which someone could look inside the house if they wanted. Trash was left all over the small yard; metal springs, shelving, old tires, and all sorts of junk was discarded there for all to see. Dad rapped on the door again, and this time he heard some movement from inside.

The door finally opened, and Jude's dad stood there, peering at his unexpected visitor. His clothes were in desperate need of laundering and the stubbles from his week-old beard hid the deep creases of his seasoned face.   He squinted, looking my dad over, wondering where he'd seen him before.

"Yeah?" he asked abruptly.

"Hi, I'm Josh's dad," Dad opened the conversation, waiting for Jude's father to recognize him. "Jude's friend, Josh, who used to live here a while back."   The stench from the house was dense and foul.

"I know who you are. I remember. Tried to take my kid with you when you moved. How can I forget?" He was a bitter man, and looked a lot older than my dad did, the alcohol addiction having aged him significantly.

"Yeah, that's me.   Listen, we'll be moving again, and I just wanted to ask you if you'd consider a proposition I have for you." My dad took out his wallet, and just stood there, waiting for Jude's dad to react.

"A proposition?   I'm listening," he answered, eyeing the wallet.

"I'm going to need some help this summer where we're moving to, and I was hoping I could hire Jude to come work for me," my dad said.

Jude's dad narrowed his eyes.   "Well, sorry, but I need him here."

"I was thinking that I could make it worth your trouble.   If he spends the summer with us, I'd make sure you would be compensated for not having him around," Dad said.

My dad still had his wallet out and held it in his hand. He lifted it now and started pulling hundred-dollar bills halfway out of the billfold so that Jude's dad could plainly see where he was going with this. He pulled out three, four, and finally five bills. Dad stopped, standing there with five hundred dollars half-way out of his wallet, just waiting for Jude's dad to make a move.

Booze reeked from the pores of the man's skin, and he looked like he hadn't showered in a few days. He licked his cracked lips, his eyes never leaving the money, and he said, "He's yours." He snatched the five bills from my dad's hand and brusquely shut the door, leaving my dad standing on the porch, staring at the door.

Dad walked down the rickety steps of the porch, and even though he felt a little sullied after the deal he had just brokered, he knew it was for the greater good. At least for Jude's greater good. Now he could watch over Jude for the summer and get him away from the influence of this broken man for a season.

28

I couldn't believe the difference between our first African home and the newest place we had settled into.

Maseru was the capital city of Lesotho, a very small country that was completely surrounded by the country of South Africa. It was 1984, and the South African economy helped lift Lesotho's simply by being geographically surrounded and therefore influenced by the larger, more developed nation.

The climate was much more temperate than in the southern Sahara. Here, it would even snow in the mountains; they call this country the Mountain Kingdom of Africa because a large majority of it lies higher than six thousand feet above sea level. It can get cold here in the winter, which is during the summer months of our home in the States; Lesotho is far into the Southern Hemisphere, so the seasons are opposite of what we were used to.

When it gets cold, the people wear their thick wool blankets, fastened with large brass safety pins. The blankets came in various colors, each with unique patterns specific to Lesotho and her culture.

The people of Lesotho are called Basotho, and their language is Sesotho. My favorite Basotho in the entire world was Bernice, the eighteen-year-old house maid that my parents hired to work for us. My mother taught her how to cook and bake the food that our family enjoyed. Bernice would bake a chocolate cake every day of her life if my mom let her. That, and toasted tuna and cheese sandwiches. Bernice in turn taught my mom how to make steam bread, common to Basotho fare.

Josh and I attended an International School in Maseru, which was based on the British school system. It was called Machabeng High School, and enrolled students from all walks of life. There were Basotho students, of course, but also many from Scandinavia, the British Isles, the United States, Australia, Ethiopia, India, Sri Lanka, East Asia, and many more. Our school was a true melting pot of the world and her various cultures, and I loved making friends from so many different nations.

The King of Lesotho was King Moshoeshoe II, and he sent his son and daughter to our school. They were the same as the rest of us, all dressed in school uniforms, ties and blazers, skirts for the girls and slacks for the boys. We had teachers from Scotland, India, Ireland, Sri Lanka, America, and more.

Josh and I were involved in after school activities and spent a lot of time with our new friends. Often, Dad and Mom would take us across the Maseru Bridge and into South Africa to do some shopping at the nearby town of Bloemfontein. They even had an orthodontist there, and a restaurant that served burgers and fries.

This was not the Africa we were used to, but we adjusted quickly, and learned to love our new home.

"Ok, kids - your turn to drive." Dad pulled our Volkswagen camper van, known as the "Combi," over to the side of the road. Josh got behind the wheel to drive and spent his fifteen minutes in the driver's seat. We were on some back roads with very little traffic, and this was how Dad was going to teach us how to drive. We had driven tractors and even hay trucks at a particularly young age, but that was always in a farm field, far away from any other traffic.

My turn came up, and I slid behind the wheel. I worked the clutch and the gas pedal in tandem, with Dad instructing me when to shift gears.

We were younger than the driving age would be back home, but Dad was excited to teach us how to operate a vehicle on the open road. It was a rite of passage for my dad and for us, and the road between Maseru and Bloemfontein was a perfect place for our initiation.

29

The day finally came when Jude was due to arrive. We'd been waiting for a few months already, and now our anticipation would finally be over. My parents had arranged for him to get a passport before we left and instructed him carefully on keeping it safe. They purchased airfare for him to fly from a nearby airport, through Washington D.C., and on to Johannesburg. There was a refueling stop in Africa just as the plane got across the Atlantic, but Jude didn't have to get off the plane there. People were friendly and helpful to him, showing him where to go for his connecting flights. I thought he was so brave for traveling by himself.

We all drove to Johannesburg to pick him up at the airport. My parents had packed the Combi for a month-long family vacation; the first stop on the trip was retrieving Jude from the airport.

"Jude! Over here!" Mom yelled above the crowds as she spotted Jude coming out of the Customs area at the airport. Hearing his name, he turned his head and waved back, a huge grin covering his face. He looked better than ever.

The four of us surrounded him and smothered him with hugs.

"I can't believe I'm finally here with you guys," Jude said through an enormous smile. "I'm in Africa!"

He really couldn't have been happier, and we shuffled him off to gather his luggage.

Our family trip took us through the Karoo Desert, the three of us teenagers in the back of the Combi, with Mom and Dad in front. We stopped at an ostrich farm and bought some ostrich jerky and a raw ostrich egg. Dad drilled a hole into the top of the egg with the tools on his pocket knife, and Mom cooked a huge omelet after she shook the egg out of its shell into the sizzling pan in the small kitchenette of the Combi. It fed all of us, with some left over.

Josh and Jude rode on the backs of the ostriches, racing around a little track the farmers had set up. I was content just to sit on one of the giant birds, but I wasn't about to take a ride. I envisioned Road Runner speeding off with me on his back, and then stopping abruptly so that my momentum would throw me forward into the dirt. No thank you.

We stopped in Cape Town and rode the cable car up to the top of Table Mountain. Facing the oceans south of us, we could see the wide Atlantic on our right and the Indian Ocean on our left. Our route would take us to the Indian Ocean side of the continent following along the Garden Route, a coastal highway that would take us from town to town. In each place, Josh and Jude and I would pitch our two small tents in the campgrounds along the beaches. I had my own tent, and they shared one. Mom and Dad slept in the Combi – it had a bed that folded out the back of the van.

We met a guy in his twenties who was traveling along the same route as we were. He was a Dutch man named Jan traveling alone on his motorcycle. Everything he brought with him on his trip fit in a backpack that he carried on the back of his bike. He must have been one of those lone adventurer types; he rode his motorcycle all the way down here through the entire continent of Africa all by himself. We traveled along with him for a while, camping in the same areas along the coast. He even stopped off to visit us in Lesotho a couple of weeks later after we got home.

At one beach in Port St. Johns, there were several young African boys selling lobsters on the water's edge. We had been swimming in the ocean that day, jumping in the waves and making friends with the other campers. All three of us got stung by jellyfish. The boys peed on the welts of their wounds because we were told that it would heal the stings much faster that way. I refused to participate in this restorative cure, preferring to suffer with my stinging skin.

The African boys were selling the lobster for one Rand each. At the time, one Rand was almost equivalent to one US Dollar. My parents bought each of us our own lobster, and we feasted in the Combi that night, dipping our lobster in melted butter.

This just *couldn't* be Africa, could it?

Jude was in heaven, loving every moment of his time with our family.

"I don't want this to end," he told me after we were back at our house in Maseru.

"What do you mean?" I asked.

"I can't explain to you what it's like to be part of a real family," he continued. "But my time with you guys is going to be over. And the day I have to go back home is just looming over my head. I wish I could stop thinking about it and just live in the moment."

I reached over and put my hand on his. "I feel the same way," I reassured him. "I wish you didn't have to go home, either."

He looked into my eyes with those big brown pools of his, and we just sat there in silence for a few moments. I could see a hint of emotion brimming in his eyes. Just then, Josh walked into the room, and Jude pulled his hand away from mine, instantly suppressing his tears.

"Hey, Josh," Jude said, nonchalantly.

"Hey, you guys. Mom just signed us up for Outward Bound, so we're going to an adventure camp next week!" he announced.

"That's so cool!" Jude exclaimed. We were all three excited for another quest. We wanted to make the most of Jude's summer vacation, and there were more memories to be made with him before he had to go back home.

The following week, the three of us set out with a group of kids from Machabeng who had all signed up for the adventure camp. The outfit was set up in a remote area of the mountains of Lesotho where we rode horses, went through obstacle courses, went on long hikes through the back country, and slept in round huts with thatched roofs called *rondevals*. One for the girls and one for the boys. Of course, we frequently visited each other's *rondevals* at night, sneaking across the grassy field under the noses of the camp counselors.

Our group was setting out on an overnight hike; we each carried a backpack with supplies and our sleeping bag. We walked and hiked all day until we made camp in the shelter of a massive rock face that had been eroded into a smooth shallow concave shelter by ages of wind howling against its face. We built a fire and told stories, Josh and Jude and I huddled together near the fire's licking flames. I liked having to huddle near Jude. He put his blanket around both of us as we sat next to the fire, listening to the camp counselor tell his stories.

Jude held my hand under the blanket.

I closed my eyes as we sat in front of the fire, enjoying the warmth on my cheeks and eyelids. I could perceive through my closed eyelids the fire's flickering light, dancing around in the blackness of my unseeing.

The next day we continued our trek across the African veld, following an ambling river and stopping in a large prairie full of lanky grass. Everyone needed a bathroom break. We could see a village in the distance, a few huts poking their heads up through the grassy plains.

"Ok, kids, listen up. I don't want any toilet paper left out here in the field, so when you're done going, you need to burn the paper," the counselor instructed. The breeze was pleasant, cooling my back after I took off my pack, some sweat evaporating in its draft.

Obediently, I grabbed the matches and a roll of TP, and headed out to some tall grass for a pit stop. I squatted down and dropped my pants, peering over the tall grass to make sure no one was watching. When I was done, I lit a match and set fire to the toilet paper. The fire consumed the paper quickly, and the flames died almost to nothing as the remnants of the paper charred away into thin air.

That's when I noticed that a few little frays of grass had caught on fire, too, and I stomped on the rising flames to suppress them before they got out of hand.

Another flame burst into life before my eyes, born of the last one that I didn't quite squash with my shoe. My heart felt the panic of adrenaline, starting to race faster as I stepped on the new flame, trying to choke it with deprivation of oxygen. Now the flames were growing and were starting to consume the larger clump of grass. I knew I had to get help fast. I ran back to the group of people, yelling, "Fire! Fire!" as I went.

The counselor sprang into action, pounding at the flames, but not able to ebb the escalation. The fire was already leaving a charred path of stubble in its wake, a cancer spreading across the African grassland. I was in a complete panic. I'd already found Josh and was crying on his shoulder, his comforting arm around me.

By then, several Africans had come from the nearby village, and they pounded the fire with clumps of brush, pounding it into submission and smothering the flames until they were dead. Smoke was oozing from the ground across the two acres of grass that I had burned.

I found our counselor later and apologized profusely, insisting that I was dutifully burning the toilet paper as I'd been instructed.

"Are we in trouble with the villagers?" I implored, wondering how we would ever pay them back for the damage I'd caused.

"No, it's ok. I gave them a couple of boxes of cookies that I brought along with us, and that seemed to assuage any sort of issues. We're fine."

I was so relieved, and so grateful for those villagers who came to put out my fire. I envisioned its flames going on for miles, only to be stopped at the river's edge. I said a silent prayer of gratitude that it hadn't been worse.

"We'll just call you Pyro for short," Josh teased me.

"I didn't do it on purpose!" I insisted, whining to them like a child.

We started our trek again, walking in single file away from the village. I felt horrible having entered their peaceful little valley, and now leaving it in shambles.

"Ok, whatever you say...Pyro," Jude smiled as he joined in the ribbing.

That night we were back in our *rondevals*, relishing in the week we'd had, but looking forward to getting back home to our showers, Bernice's cooking, and our beds.

I was lying in my bunk thinking about Jude and started to get a little sad that he would have to head back home to the States pretty soon. I wondered what would be back there waiting for him. His neglectful father, for one. I knew Jude couldn't stand living with his dad, but at the same time, he knew he had to go back there because he felt a duty toward him. Someone had to make sure he didn't drink himself to death.

Football would also be waiting for Jude. The coach really recruited him hard; this would be his second year in high school, and the team was really benefitting from

Jude's athleticism. He'd been talking to Josh about football non-stop since he'd come to visit us. They would talk about certain plays, and they'd spend hours in our yard playing catch and running patterns. Josh would throw the football to Jude, who planned on being a star receiver on the varsity high school team. Occasionally they needed my help to stand in their way as they ran their routes. Gone were the days where I would risk bodily harm to tackle these boys in a game of football.

With all of these things coursing through my stream of contemplations, sleep escaped me, so I slipped quietly out of my bunk and took a walk not far away from the *rondeval.* The night sky was actually bright, the stars providing more light than I expected. The tall grass looked silvery in the moonlight, glistening as the breeze pushed and pulled the tops of the shafts like the luring tides of the sea, waving in the night.

I could see the shadow of someone sneaking out of the boy's hut, and realized he was walking my way. Suddenly, there was Jude standing in front of me.

"What are you doing out here?" I asked him.

"I could ask you the same thing," he smiled with this retort.

"Well, I just couldn't sleep. Thought I'd look at the stars for a while."

"I couldn't sleep, either. Those guys are too loud, between the talking and the snoring, I just wanted to get out of there," he said.

We stood there in silence for a few seconds, and I looked up at the stars, feigning interest in their constellations and astronomical wonders. Really what fascinated me wasn't the Southern Cross, or the Scorpio constellation. It was this young man standing in front of me. I was intrigued by this rebel, this renegade figure who was so different from anyone else I'd known. He had been in my life since I could remember, and I knew most of this nonconformist persona he portrayed was simply an armor protecting his soft and vulnerable core. He trusted me with his true heart and had shown me his tender side before, so I knew it existed. His life experiences, though, had taught him to defend himself with a rough outer shell, and that was the maverick most people could see.

His face was shadowed, the colors muted by the night. But I could see his eyes on me, and my heart skipped a little beat, my stomach constricting with a kind of thrilling nervousness.

"I've had such a great time with you and Josh," he said. "I'm not looking forward to going back home again. It's gone by too fast."

"I know. I wish you could stay longer," I agreed.

"I'm lucky to have a friend like Josh. He's so good at everything. So smart, and just such a genuine guy," he told me. Of course, I knew all of this already.

"Sometimes I wish people would see me that way," he admitted.

"What do you mean? People think you're a good person," I reassured him.

"No, not like Josh. He's different. I don't think I'll ever really measure up to him. Not that anyone would expect me to."

"I love you for who you are," I offered. Then I realized I'd said the "L" word, and I was so grateful for the night hiding my embarrassment in its obscurity.

There was too much silence after that statement, and finally he said, "I'm really not good enough for you. You know that, don't you?"

"Stop," I insisted. "Don't say that. I like you just the way you are, Jude."

He stepped a little closer to me, and he reached for my face, lifting my chin with the side of his index finger. I was looking up at him; he was at least three inches taller than I was.

"I'm not good enough for you. I know that. I've done stupid things in my young life." His tone was suddenly subdued and serious. "I probably should have had more of a childhood than I did. I've had to grow up fast because of my dad." He was talking in hushed tones; he didn't really want anyone else hearing this.

"Just trust me; I'm not like Josh," he concluded.

I wasn't thinking of anyone else, though. I was lost in his dark eyes, and I felt like we were all alone, secreted away by the night's embracing shadows. He leaned toward me and kissed me softly, then looked into my eyes, maybe to consider my reaction. But I kept my eyes closed, hoping if I did, he'd kiss me again. And he did.

We were two tiny beings, insignificant specks of dust standing under the vast African night sky, endless in her galaxies, infinite in her potential. And yet, I felt as valuable and significant in that moment as any of those orbiting planets or clusters of stars. We could hear the chirping of insects, the flow of the nearby water, and muffled voices from the huts. But out there under the immense cosmos, amidst the panorama of this African landscape, we found ourselves together, continents away from our childhood home sharing this tender moment of our youth. Our moment.

30

"Let's go for a spin on the old race track!" Josh suggested to his new friend, Matt, who was visiting his parents in Maseru. Matt was seventeen and went to boarding school. They were from Washington State, and my parents knew Matt's parents.

"Yeah, let's do some doughnuts in the dirt tracks!" Jude agreed from the passenger seat. Josh was in the back, but leaned up between the two front seats, an elbow next to each headrest so that he may as well have been in the front with his two buddies.

Matt's parents had just bought him this used car across the border in South Africa, so it still had the South African license plates on it. They wanted him to have something to drive around for the time he would be in Maseru over his summer break from school. Even though Josh and Jude were a couple of years younger than Matt, he liked hanging out with them and trying to find fun things to do.

"Ok, tell me where the race track is, then," Matt said.

They sped toward the river that doubled as the border between the two countries. The racetrack was near the river and was hardly used anymore. It was a perfect place to try out the new car; a wide-open space where they could skid around in the dirt and fling gravel from under their tires as they peel out and skid to a stop.

"Ok, just a little further, Matt," Josh directed. "Right there – see that little road? Take that, and it'll take us up to the track."

Matt found the dirt drive and peeled off the main road. Their route took them up a few feet to a plateau where the old racetrack was. Matt opened up the carburetor, speeding along the flat open concourse, and the boys all whooped their approval.

"Ok, my turn!" Jude said after a few minutes. He took his turn in the driver's seat, and spun in circles, cranking the wheel to the far left as gravel spewed in a contrail behind them.

Josh took his own turn, shifting gears like a pro, and sliding sideways to a skidding halt.

Suddenly, the boys heard "pop, pop, pop!" like fireworks were going off. They looked around and saw some men running toward them.

The blood drained from their faces when they realized they were soldiers and were heading straight for them. Even though they didn't know what they had done wrong, they knew they were in serious trouble.

"They have machine guns!" Matt yelled.

"Whatever, man," Jude said with sarcastic doubt, figuring Matt was either paranoid, or trying to scare the two of them. "There's no way those are machine guns."

"Jude, I think he's right," Josh said, craning his neck to see the men running their way.

"Are you serious?" Jude asked, worried now. He looked around, too, and they all heard the firecracker sound again.

"They're shooting at us!" Matt yelled in a panic. "What do we do? Should I drive away?"

"No, let's just get out and let them know we don't want any trouble," Josh said, trying to be calm.

The three boys climbed out of the car just as the men came up to them, shouting at them to put their hands in the air. The three boys complied, both scared and confused all at the same time. The men were dressed in military uniforms, and they each had a machine gun in their hands, pointing them straight at the boys.

The three were scared to death, wondering what in the world was going on.

"What did we do?" Matt asked the men.

"Who are you, and why are you avoiding our road block?" one of the men demanded, dismissing Matt's question.

"What? What road block?" Matt asked.

"We can see you are from South Africa – your car license." The man pointed his gun at the plates of the car. "We have a road block and you are trying to go around."

Josh was starting to put two and two together. He remembered now that there was a military base further down the main road, and they would have run into its gates if they hadn't turned off onto the small road leading to the racetrack. They must have a road block set up somewhere just beyond where the boys had turned onto the unused road, and these soldiers probably figured they were trying to evade it.

"No, sir, we were just trying out his new car. We are not from South Africa. We are Americans," Josh offered, knowing that the Lesotho Military didn't always get along well with the South African government. Maybe they would let us go if they know we're Americans, though, Josh thought.

Jude stood silently, hands still in the air, not wanting to rock the boat.

Just then, another soldier pointed his gun at Jude, a sardonic smile coming to his face. Jude felt an immediate sense of terror and fear. He realized in that instant that despite how hellish he thought his life was back home with his dad, he didn't want to die! He squinted and turned his face away just a little, still watching the man from the corner of his vision.

The soldier pulled the trigger.

There was a loud "click"; Jude and Josh flinched, closing their eyes hard and cowering a little as they stood in place. The soldier was intimidating them by dry-firing his weapon at the boys. When he saw the fear on their faces, the soldier smirked and laughed out loud.

"What the hell?!" Jude yelled, fear in his eyes, and panic starting to arise in his gut.

"Jude, look at me," Josh whispered to Jude fiercely, but as quietly as he could.

Jude was starting to feel the anxiety build, though, and all he wanted to do was run. He was fidgety, and Josh could see it. His breathing started to get more shallow and quick. All he could think of is that he couldn't stand here for one more second. He wanted to run!

"Jude!" he yelled at him sharply to get his attention, and Jude snapped his head over to look at Josh, their hands still high in the air.

"Listen to me, ok?" Josh said more calmly. "Look into my eyes, Jude."

Jude's eyes fixed on Josh's, and he started breathing more calmly.

"Jude, I have a plan, ok?" he said in a low voice. The soldiers were chatting amongst themselves, probably trying to figure out what to do with next these white kids. Could they get away with taunting them longer, or would they get in trouble if they really were Americans, and had friends in higher places than they did?

It gave Josh an opportunity to try to talk some sense into Jude.

"What plan?" Jude asked.

"Yeah, what plan?" Matt joined in.

"Just trust me, ok?" Josh implored Jude. "Please – don't do anything. We're blood brothers, right?"

Jude breathed heavily a few times, scared that he might be starting to hyperventilate. He nodded in reply.

"Ok, good. Blood brothers can trust each other. Just have faith in me, ok? Please?" Josh whispered.

Jude nodded again, and then he turned back to the soldiers.

"This is my friend's car," Josh told them, pointing with his chin over at Matt. "He's from *Washington*," he emphasized the last word for their captors.

"Washington?" the soldier asked, suddenly intrigued. "Washington D.C?"

"Yes," Josh nodded. "Washington D.C. Where the White House is. Where the Ambassador is from," he added. "We know the American Ambassador here in Maseru."

Josh could see the soldiers murmuring something to each other, and he knew this tactic was working.

Matt looked at Josh and Jude, and then back at the soldier. "Yes. Washington D.C." He slowly started to pull one hand down, joining in now with Josh's idea and asked, "Can I show you my identification? My papers?"

The soldier looked nervous for the first time and told the boys to put down their hands.

"Show me," he demanded of Matt.

Matt pulled his wallet from his pocket and retrieved his driver's license from Washington State.

"See?" He pointed at the word *Washington* at the top of his driver's license as he held it in front of the soldier's face.

That was all it took for the soldier to believe him, and the men started a discussion amongst themselves in their own language. Without another glance or single word to the boys, they suddenly turned around and walked back in the direction from whence they came, and it was over.

The boys stood there for a while to let their hearts calm down and slow their rapid beating. Josh looked at Jude, whose eyes thanked Josh without words.

The ride home was slow and almost all in silence. The boys were pretty shaken, and when they told my parents what had happened, they went to the Embassy to have a discussion about the incident. It could have ended very badly instead of the way it had. I'm not sure what ever happened to the soldiers, if anything. But it felt like an international incident when I heard about it, even though the boys were able to laugh about it after a while.

In the back of their minds, Josh and Jude knew the outcome could have been much worse. The experience tacitly fortified their friendship. Surviving something together so terrifying formed even more of the bedrock of their burgeoning brotherhood – a solid and steadfast foundation whose strength and firmness would one day be tested; hopefully their bond would be strong enough to endure.

Jude would dream later of the machine gun's empty "click" and wake up with a jolt.

Jude was leaving the next day. My dad would be driving him back to Johannesburg to catch his flight. The three of us were a little somber, none of us wanting Jude to leave. After dinner, Josh and Jude went outside while I helped Mom and Bernice in the kitchen.

"Want to play some catch?" Jude asked Josh, picking the football up off the grass.

"Sure," Josh agreed.

They started throwing the ball back and forth in silence for a while. Neither of them really knew what to say.

"I wish you didn't have to go," Josh was the first to break the silence.

"I know. Me, too," Jude agreed.

"I'm so glad you came, though." Josh threw the ball in a perfect spiral. Jude caught it with one hand, a skill he had been honing for a while now.

"Yeah. I'll never forget it. It's been so amazing." Jude threw the ball back across the yard.

Josh caught the football, and tucked it under his arm and started walking, closing the distance between him and his friend. He motioned for Jude to sit with him on some landscaping rocks.

"Listen, I want you to know how much you mean to our family, Jude," Josh started.

"Aw, man. You're not going to get all sappy on me, are you?" Jude teased, not sure what to do with what seemed like was becoming a serious moment.

"No, but I want you to know this. I mean it. You're like a brother to me, Jude." Josh wasn't fazed by Jude's teasing. He pressed forward, trying to make his point. "I worry about you being home at your dad's place. I hope you know how stupid it would be to start drinking before school again, especially when you're going to be playing football, and all that."

"Yeah, I know," Jude agreed. "Coach is serious about that kind of thing. I can't afford to be kicked off the team. Don't worry about me – I won't do anything stupid," he assured his friend.

Josh paused for a few seconds, and then he pulled something out of his pocket and handed it to Jude.

"I made this for you," Josh held a small coin-shaped memento in his hand and offered it to Jude.

"For me? What is it?" Jude examined it, turning the metal piece over between his fingers to see the other side.

"It's just something for you to keep, and to remind you that we're blood brothers. My dad helped me make it," Josh explained.

It was a flat round metal disc with a hole punched out near the top so Jude could wear it on a necklace, or thread it onto a keychain if he'd like. On one side there were two letters "J" stamped into the metal, one near the top, and another crossing over the bottom hook of the first. On the back was the shape of a tree, with the words

"Blood Brothers" stamped carefully underneath it. The letters were a little crooked, having been stamped out by a fifteen-year-old.

"Those J's stand for Josh and Jude," he explained, "and on the back is my Joshua tree back home where we became blood brothers when we were just kids.

Jude examined both sides again and again, not knowing what to say. His eyes were getting a little blurry from a few tears that were starting to form, so he took a deep breath, and ebbed them back by sheer force of will.

"Thank you, Josh." Jude looked over at his friend and smiled, one corner of his mouth higher than the other. Josh could see his sincerity, and it made him feel great.

"You're welcome, brother," Josh replied. "You really are like my brother, and I hope you always remember you can count on me."

"Oh, I have no doubt about that, Josh," Jude said without hesitation. "You really don't know how good you are, do you?" he asked.

"Come on...I'm no better than you." Josh wasn't comfortable with this kind of praise or comparison.

"Josh, you come on! I know I'll never measure up to you. You always get the best grades, you never do anything wrong, you're always the shining student and son and brother and everything. You're just *good*, Josh, and that's great. But I would be kidding myself if I thought I could ever measure up to you." He kept looking at his coin, thinking about what we he wanted to say next.

"Plus, you just have a perfect life," he continued. "You live in Africa and have an amazing family with parents who are perfect and normal. And they love you. I'll never have that, Josh. It's just how my life is, I guess. And it's fine. Sometimes I just wish.... you know?" Jude looked over at Josh, and then looked at the grass.

"Yeah, I know," was all Josh could say.

"Look, it's fine. Let's just go in, ok? Thanks for this," he said, lifting up the metal disc. "I really like it – it means a lot." Jude stood up, and offered a hand to Josh, pulling him up beside him.

"I'll miss you, Jude," Josh said, and gave him a quick hug.

"I'll miss you, too, Bro," Jude answered. They slapped each other on the back, and then walked back inside the house.

❧

Jude had been packing his suitcase late that night and was having trouble sleeping. He was anxious about the flight but had resigned himself to his fate of having to return home to his dad. I was sleeping in my room, lost in the world of dreams when I felt someone gently shake my shoulder, trying to wake me up.

I opened my eyes and propped myself up on my elbow. It was Jude, kneeling next to my bed.

"What are you doing?" I asked, trying to wake up and clear my foggy mind.

"Sorry to wake you up, but I didn't want to leave without saying goodbye." He spoke quietly, not wanting to wake anyone else up in the house.

"I'm going to see you in the morning before you guys leave, aren't I?" I wondered if the plan had changed, or something.

"Yeah, but I mean I just wanted to talk to you alone, and not in front of everyone," he whispered.

"Oh," I said, "Ok." I turned around and sat up in my bed, trying to give him my full attention.

"Listen, I know I'm not going to see you for another year or more," he started. "I just wanted to say how much fun I had with you and Josh on this trip. And that I won't forget that night on Outward Bound – under the stars."

"I won't forget, either," I promised.

"Ok, good." He wasn't sure what else to say and knelt there in awkward silence for a moment.

"Well, I just wanted to say...I'll miss you." Then he lowered his voice even more, and almost inaudibly whispered, "And I love you."

He got up and sat next to me on my bed and put his arms around me. He hugged me tight and held me like that for a while. I don't think Jude really got to hug anyone – certainly not his dad, and probably not anyone else, for that matter. His arms held me tight like he was afraid to let go, and I melted into his embrace. I gently rubbed his back to comfort him in his humble offering of vulnerability.

"I love you, too, Jude," I whispered into his ear.

This seemed to give him the strength he needed to finish packing and leave what felt like home to him. He leaned back from me and looked at me in the dark. He took my face in his hands and kissed me tenderly. I never wanted it to end. My heart felt such a connection to Jude – not just now, but ever since I could remember. I cared for him like no one else I knew. My heart was aching already at the thought of him leaving, so when he kissed me again and then turned to leave me, I grabbed his hand, holding him back, silently pleading for him not to go. He looked back at me then, searching every part of my face for a moment – maybe trying to commit it to memory so he could retrieve it once the miles were between us. Then he let go of my hand and disappeared from my room.

The next morning, we waved as he and Dad drove away from the house.

31

School started again, and we immersed ourselves into our studies, kept up on our homework, and spent time at all our various after-school activities. We hung out with our friends, played intramural sports, and kept as busy as teenagers tend to be. The hands of time seemed to spin out of control, the earth rotating the days away, its revolutions bringing about the varied seasons.

Mom and Dad had made friends with an older American couple who was stationed in Lesotho for a job. Mr. Clark was an engineer who had a key role in developing the plans for a large hydroelectric dam up in the mountains of Lesotho, in a small town called Mount Moorosi. His wife came with him, but their children had grown up long ago and moved out on their own. They were grandparents, but their age certainly didn't stop them from traveling around the world. They were two of the most active grandparents that I knew. The Clarks went scuba diving in exotic waters, hiking on the rugged terrains of Nepal, they rode elephants in Thailand, and so much more. They were determined to live their lives to the fullest, no matter their age.

Now Mr. Clark was busily overseeing the construction of the dam, hundreds of workers under his supervision. There were construction workers from different countries there, including a large contingency from the Philippines.

I was captivated by Mr. Clark's stiff handlebar mustache that he carefully groomed on his upper lip, its long ends twisted into place by twirling them around his fingers. I would watch it twitch briskly above his mouth with every word he spoke, but it all fell on deaf ears because of the trance I was under from his rigid waxy coils.

Mr. Clark's workers all lived up in the mountains in the temporary community, each with a small portable trailer they called home for the duration of this job. They had a clubhouse, too, where they could spend their off-hours playing pool, card games, or mahjong and drinking beer.

"Where are you coming from this time?" Mom asked Mrs. Clark as they sat in our living room, catching up after a few weeks since the last time we'd seen them.

"I was just at Teyateyaneng where they make pottery. They call it TY for short," she explained.

Mrs. Clark traveled on her own all over Lesotho, visiting places where women wove tapestries, made pottery, and all kind of other cultural activities. I thought it was fun having a grandma around every time Mrs. Clark passed through Maseru.

"How would the two of you like to come up to Mount Moorosi for a week?" she asked me and Josh.

"Can we mom?" We looked over at her with pleading eyes. Josh and I had a break from school, and we'd love to go somewhere new.

"Sure, I think it would be great for you two to spend a week up there. As long as you're on your best behavior," she warned.

She thought it would be good for Mrs. Clark to have some company up there in the middle of nowhere, but she also thought it would be good for us to spend some time with a grandmother. We had been away from our own for a long time, and Mom figured the influence on us would be positive.

"We will!" Josh promised.

The next day, we left with Mrs. Clark for her home in Mount Moorosi. She drove us along the winding roads through the beautiful countryside, passing a few people on horseback. They plodded along, keeping warm with their Basotho blankets draped over their shoulders, their iconic Basotho hats atop their heads. The hat, called a "mokorotlo," is woven in a cone shape with a knot at the top, and is unique to Lesotho.

We were having a great time in Mount Moorosi. Mrs. Clark showed us how to use a rock tumbler to polish rough pieces of gemstones and rocks that we found as we went out exploring. We even made jewelry with the little shiny stones after they were polished. We glued tiger eye, amethysts and other varieties of quartz onto prongs that we then made into necklaces and rings. She cooked meals for us, and we helped her bake cookies. And whenever we wanted, she let us go up to the clubhouse to play a few games of pool. Our grandpa had a billiard table back home, so Josh and I already knew how to play.

It was early evening when Josh and I were playing a game of pool up at the clubhouse, passing some time before heading back to the Clarks' house.

"Yes! I'm solids," I claimed, as Josh sunk a striped ball into the corner pocket on the break. I was partial to solids, and eight was my favorite number. I would try to work through all the other solid billiard balls until I could finally sink the black one into a pocket for the win.

Josh was probably better than I was at playing pool, but I still gave him a run for his money now and then. I loved how I could use geometry to calculate the accuracy of my shots. If I could tap the white cue ball with proper aim, it would strike against one of my solids at the perfect spot so that it would roll at my precisely-planned angle into one of the six pockets on the table. I liked that the eight-ball was the dangerous ball, the one that could cost me the entire game up until the very end, at which point it transformed into the one I absolutely needed to sink in order to win.

The clubhouse was busy and noisy. There were about a dozen construction workers who were there enjoying a beer or two as they played Mahjong and kicked their feet up to relax. They were almost all from the Philippines, but there were some Basotho workers there, too. They chatted with us and seemed to enjoy having a couple of American kids around to break up the monotony of their evening.

"What's your name?" one of them asked, walking up to the pool table.

"Josh," my brother answered for both of us. "What's yours?"

"My name is Datu," he offered. He was a short man in his late twenties or maybe early thirties, just about the same height as I was; Josh was taller.

"Hi Datu," we said. He wanted to play pool with us, so we added him to our games. He bought us each a bottle of cold Pepsi, a rare treat for us, so we immediately took a liking to him.

His buddies hung around watching as we played, and Datu told us about his family back home in the Philippines. He was working here to make money to send back to them, and we admired that about our charming new friend.

Datu's buddy wanted to play a game against Josh, so Datu said he would teach me how to play Mahjong. We sat at a small table on the far side of the room, and I tried to learn the new game that I'd never seen before.

"How old are you?" he asked.

"I'm fourteen," I replied, studying my next move of the tiles on the table. I saw Datu look over at my brother, and then back at me.

"You're good at this game!" he complimented. "I hope my daughter grows up to be smart like you."

I was delighted that an adult would take such interest in me, even though his small stature made him seem more my age.

"Would you like to see some photos of my family?" Datu asked.

"Sure," I said, waiting for him to pull some photos from his wallet.

"Come with me," he said.

"Where are we going? You don't have the photos here?" I asked.

"No, they are in my photo album in my trailer," he said, standing up from the table. "Here, I will go get you another Pepsi."

I stood there watching Josh playing pool. He was smiling and laughing, having a great time. I'm sure he'd be just fine until I got back. This shouldn't take long, I thought.

Datu came back with another soda, and I followed him out of the clubhouse. He was such a little guy; he was anything but intimidating. We laughed as we walked the hundred feet or so over to his trailer.

"Please come in," he said.

Something in the back of my mind was telling me I should go back to Josh, but I didn't want to be rude to an adult by saying no.

I followed him inside. It was close quarters, with just a small living room, a tiny kitchenette, and a sleeping area. Datu reached into a cupboard above the couch and pulled out a photo album, then walked over to sit on the foot of his bed.

"Come," he said, patting the old bedspread beside him.

I sat down next to him as he opened the album, turning the pages and describing the scenes in front of me. I saw his wife and two little kids sitting in their yard, bright green foliage behind them. His home looked like a tropical place – it reminded me of Bamako. He told me the names of his kids, and said he missed them.

"When will you see them again?" I asked, feeling sorry that he was so far away from them.

"At the end of the year, I will go back home," he told me. I couldn't imagine being away from my parents for such a long time.

I turned the stiff album page over the big rings of the binder, Datu's wife and children peering back at me through the protective plastic, their eyes seemingly perplexed by my presence. I considered their probing stares coming through the flat photos of the album pages, and I began to ask myself the same question. What am I doing here?

Datu put his arm around me, and everything changed in that instant. I stiffened, not sure what to do. Feelings of fear started creeping up the back of my neck, and I wanted desperately to get out of there.

Datu reached his other hand toward me and turned my face to him. Before I could react, he kissed me right on the lips. It was the opposite of what I felt when Jude touched his lips to mine, which was a reciprocal connection. With Jude it was innocent and tender, genuine and even pure. This – this unsolicited and unwelcome advance from someone twice my age brought instant trepidation.

I pulled away from Datu, "What are you doing?" I asked in surprise.

"You know you want to kiss me," he coaxed.

"No, I don't!" My eyes widened, and my heart was beating faster. I knew I had to get out of there as soon as I could. How did I get myself into this?

I stood up from the bed and headed for the front door when he grabbed my wrist and pulled me back toward the room.

"Stop!" I yelled.

Datu pushed me onto the bed, flat on my back. He put his hand over my mouth so that I wouldn't make any more noise or draw attention to his little trailer that was nestled so close to the other ones where his friends lived.

Now I was genuinely starting to panic. My breathing was more labored, all my air having to flow in and out through the small openings of my nostrils. My anxiety demanded more oxygen, and faster! But Datu's hand was covering my mouth, making me feel like I would suffocate.

"If you don't shut up, I will have to hurt you," he hissed. "And your brother, too! You know I don't want to do that, so be good," Datu ordered.

He was significantly stronger than I ever imagined the little man could be. With one hand covering my mouth, he used his other hand to pin down one of my arms. I used my one free hand to shove against his arm, trying to break myself free so I could get some air. He was irritated with my struggling, so he let go of my mouth and pinned my other arm down. Now I was completely captive.

As soon as his hand uncovered my face, though, I sucked in an enormous breath of air, and then again and again. My lungs seemed starved for the oxygen, and it was a relief to them to breathe freely and fully again.

I wanted to scream and yell out, but I couldn't; I felt paralyzed in my fear. I suddenly remembered standing at the train next to Kuntigi, recalling the fear I felt then, and my inability to move. But this was a hundred times worse, and I didn't have Joshua standing next to me to save me like I did at that train in Bamako.

My heart was pounding, and my eyes were frantic and wide. What did he want from me? I just wanted to leave and go home to my Mom. Please, God, I prayed silently. I know I somehow got myself into this situation. But please help me get out of here!

Datu was hovering over me now, staring callously into my eyes. I looked away, not ever wanting to see those small beady eyes again. He forced his knee between my legs, and I tried with all my strength to keep them together, whimpers escaping from my throat. But he was so much stronger than I was; so much power packed into the small frame of his body. I couldn't stop him. He forced my legs apart and kept his knee there on the bed between them.

"Please," I whispered to him. "Please, let me go. Please, I beg of you."

"Shut up!" he said again, desperation plain on his face.

I was crying now, tears streaming down my face and into my ears, my hair dampening from my salty sobs.

He took one hand away from mine to work on his belt, fumbling awkwardly with the buckle. I couldn't scream. I couldn't move. I couldn't breathe. Please God, help me.

That's when I heard Joshua calling my name not far away outside.

Datu heard it, too, and he looked toward his door, frozen like a scared gazelle.

I took my chance. Mustering a deep breath, I smashed Datu as hard as I could across the front of his face with my free arm, a piercing scream erupting from my throat, wet and raw.

Thank you, Father in Heaven, I prayed. Thank you for freeing my voice.

Datu was stunned. I must have scraped his eye, because he grabbed at his face with both of his hands. I pushed him away, and he didn't fight back yet, so I scrambled off the bed, and headed toward the front door.

"Josh! Joshua!" I yelled.

Just then, Josh pounded on Datu's door. I opened the door and flung myself into my brother's arms, sobbing. He held me tight, looking into the trailer behind me with angry eyes and furrowed brow. His face was red with righteous indignation.

"Let's go, Josh. I just want to go," I begged him, suppressing my cries as best as I could.

"No, I'm going to beat the crap out of Datu. What did he do to you?" Josh demanded.

"Josh, please," I looked into his eyes and said, "Nothing happened. I promise. Please, just take me away from here." I pulled on his arm and dragged him toward the Clarks' house.

"Something happened – why else would you be crying?" Josh was angry, and if he didn't hit someone and avenge his sister, he felt like his chest would erupt.

"I was just really scared, ok? Please, don't say anything to Mrs. Clark, or to Mom and Dad, ok?" We were walking away now, and I stopped to look at him. "Please? Do you promise?"

He saw the desperation in my face and felt sorry for me.

"I don't want to get in trouble for going in his trailer, ok Josh? It was a stupid mistake – I wasn't even thinking clearly." I was babbling anything I could just to convince him to let it go. I wanted to pretend it didn't even happen.

"Please...I promise you nothing happened," I continued my pleading. I knew something bad had almost happened, but I was reigning in my fear and emotions, bridling them into my command and dominion. I was angry that I had almost given that control to someone else out of my own naiveté.

"If something did happen, I would have to at least tell Mom and Dad," he said.

I stopped in my tracks, and he stopped a step later, turning back toward me.

"Josh, stop. I promise you. Nothing happened!" I said emphatically. My tears had stopped now, and I was wiping my face, trying to remove any trace of what I'd just been through. "Look, he wanted me to see some photos of his family, but I was too stupid to realize that's not what he actually wanted. He almost..." I paused. "But he didn't. You came just in time, Josh."

As soon as I said those words, I let out another gush of tears and hugged him tight. "Thank you so much for saving me."

He heard it in my voice, and he believed me. I felt so foolish for ever getting myself into that situation, and I was humiliated. It would be so much worse if any adults knew about it. I just wanted to forget about it. Please, just let me forget.

He saw that I was ok, that I was just scared. Despite his desire to punch someone to defend me and my honor, he reluctantly agreed to keep my secret.

"Thank you," I said.

He walked with his arm around me, and I let him. I was so glad he was there with me, and my heart finally calmed to a normal pace.

"I'm sorry, Josh," I said, as we walked toward the Clarks. I breathed deeply a few times and straightened my hair so that Mrs. Clark wouldn't notice anything awry.

"I'm sorry I wasn't paying attention," he said, blaming himself. "I didn't even see you leave with him."

"It's my fault," I said. "Thanks for not saying anything. I just feel like a fool."

We took the long way to Mrs. Clark's so that I didn't look at all distressed when we finally got there. I put on my best face, tried to calm my trembling hands, and followed Josh inside.

"Just in time for cookies!" she announced. "Did you guys have fun at the clubhouse? I was wondering if you were ever coming back. I was about to come find you."

Josh answered for both of us, "Yeah, we played pool and drank sodas. Thanks for the cookies!"

We dipped the warm chocolate chip cookies in milk, and then watched some videos that she had on tape before going to bed. I couldn't wait to go home. Not just home to my Mom and Dad. But *home* home.

I was sad to have to say goodbye to all my friends at Machabeng. We had started high school together and had gone to our first school dances together. We were in plays, debate clubs, did homework together, and even dated the same guys on and off. My favorite boyfriend at Machabeng was from Ireland, and I was sad to say goodbye to him, too.

I wondered if I'd ever see these remarkable people again. They had become a permanent part of my formative teenage years, teaching me poignant social lessons without even being aware. They were there when I got my braces on across the border in South Africa, and they were there to cheer me when they finally came off. They showered me with compliments about my new smile, bolstering the struggling esteem of a teenage girl.

We said our goodbyes, promising to write letters. And before I knew it, I was back home, solidly ensconced in an American teenage life. Childhood was in my distant past, and my future was waiting for me in the distance ahead.

32

1986

"Ok, scoot over, Josh!" Jude yelled into the driver's window of my dad's pickup truck. He was standing in the bed of the pickup, leaning over into the open window so that Josh could hear his voice over the loud rushing wind. We were driving down the highway at full-speed, and Jude was getting ready to climb in the driver's side window.

I was on the passenger side, and Josh was driving. Each of us would rotate positions as the truck sped down the road. I climbed out the passenger window, the gray pavement below me flowing by in a blur, the painted dashes on the highway melding into one solid line under my feet as I clambered into the bed of the truck.

Just as I made it into my new position standing behind the cab, I saw Jude slide into the driver's seat on the opposite side. Josh had scooted over on the bench seat, pressing the gas pedal down with his left foot, and guiding the steering wheel with his left hand – essentially driving from the middle of the pickup cab. Jude slid into place and took over, allowing Josh to take my prior spot, where the seat was still warm from my presence just seconds before.

The wind was flowing through my hair, and I lifted both my hands above my head, feeling the freedom of the open road. I closed my eyes and tipped my head back, the sun basking on my face. I felt alive! The truck zoomed down the road, meeting very few cars. I could smell the evergreens as we whisked past them, the wake of our breeze coercing their needles to follow us; branches resting back into place once we were out of sight.

"This is crazy!" Josh bellowed.

"Yeah, crazy-fun!" Jude agreed.

"True," Josh looked over at his best friend, and they both smiled. "We'd better hurry, or we'll be late for football practice. Coach will make us do wind sprints."

"Ok, one more rotation, and we'll head back to the school," Jude said.

I saw Jude's hand motion to me outside his window that it was my turn behind the wheel, so I put one foot through the open window, straddling the back of the cab with my other foot still in the bed. I held onto the handle just inside the driver's side door, and pulled myself the rest of the way in.

Plopping down onto the seat, I took over from Jude and saw Josh already standing in the bed of the pickup in my rear-view mirror, having quickly rotated out of the passenger window.

"Woohoo!" I cried out with unbridled energy, and Jude echoed my elation.

We sped toward the school, and I dropped the boys off for their practice, full of adrenaline and ready to go.

They had a big game coming up the next night, and they were both excited to play. Jude was the star receiver, and when Josh joined the team after we moved home from Maseru, he won the starting spot as quarterback. This was their senior year, and they would be playing our rivals from a town just thirty minutes away from ours. The community was pumped up, school colors displayed in business windows, the excitement of the game building.

When we came back from Africa, I quickly learned that Jude had a girlfriend. He hadn't mentioned her to us at all, so when I saw him holding her hand in the hallway at school on our first day back, my heart sank, and my cheeks flushed red with a strange feeling of dejection and hurt all at the same time. I'd never felt so small and unimportant; I just wanted to disappear into a crowd or down a dark hallway. Anywhere but right there. As I passed them on my way to class, he caught my eye, but then quickly looked away from me.

So, this was what it felt like to have a broken heart. I buried the feeling away, quashing and quelling it into submission until I was in total control of my reactions whenever I saw them together. It wasn't easy, but I didn't want to show how much he had hurt me. I thought he felt the same about me as I did for him, after all we had shared when he visited us in Africa. Doesn't he remember that he kissed me? I had really believed him when he told me he loved me, but now I felt duped. I felt a breach of trust. I didn't want him to know the effect he was having on me, so on the outside, I was as cool as ever around Jude. On the inside, I was crushed.

"Who's that girl with Jude?" my mom asked me after we ran into them at the convenience store one day.

"Oh, that's his girlfriend," I tried to sound nonchalant.

"Girlfriend?" she paused, and then added, "How are you doing with that? Are you ok?"

"Oh, yeah," I waved it off like it was nothing to me. "You know, she's a cheerleader, and she's all cute and perfect. I'm not surprised they're together. He's a football jock, after all."

"You're cuter than she is," Mom tried to bolster my tender heart. She knew I was playing it down.

"Mom, no I'm not. She's a perfect size two. She's like Barbie," I contested. "It's fine, really. I'll never be all flirty like she is. If that's what Jude wants, then sorry, because I'm not like that."

"What's her name?" she asked me.

"Chrissie," I said in a high-pitched nasally voice, mimicking her the best I could.

"Well, you have plenty of boys who like you already, so just go have fun," she advised.

"I'm having fun – don't worry, Mom."

In reality, I felt a daily dose of disappointment. Worse than that. It's not like I could just forget about him and move on. I saw him every day of my life. Josh and I picked him up for school in the morning, and the two of them were hardly ever apart. Jude was always at our house. I couldn't get away from him if I'd tried.

It was strange, because I held on to the memories I had with Jude like they were jewels or coins that should be secreted away – buried next to a banana plant, perhaps, only to be uncovered with a treasure map; one pace north, and two paces east. X marks the spot.

I did treasure those cherished memories with him out on the grassy fields of Africa under the dark southern skies. It seemed like yesterday to me. I thought we had shared moments that would last through time, worlds away from here and therefore somehow more real and enduring. How could he have forgotten so easily?

The game was a close one. I was sitting in the stands next to my parents, and we were cheering on our team. Jude's girlfriend, Chrissie, was in front of the bleachers, jumping around in her short skirt and waving her pompoms around. I watched her out of the corner of my eye and wondered what made her so great that Jude would want to be with her rather than with me.

I looked away from her and tried to focus on the game. It was the last quarter with very little time left, and we were behind by a field goal. The crowds were rowdy because there were a lot of fans that had come from the rival team. My mom was a huge football fan, and she was cheering louder than anyone.

"Come on, Josh! You can do it!" She projected her voice as far as she could, cupping her hands around her mouth to form a miniature megaphone. I'm sure Josh could hear her from the huddle.

"Throw one to Jude!" Dad yelled, but he was no match for Mom's rooting.

Josh broke the huddle, and our team lined up for the first play of the drive. Josh handed the ball off to the running back, who got tackled right at the line of scrimmage for no gain at all.

On second down, Josh threw the ball to another player on our team who I didn't recognize. He was over near our side of the bleachers, and he caught the ball, but only made about two yards of progress.

"Come on!" Mom was starting to get irritated with our team's lack of progress. "You can do better than that!"

"Good thing your mother isn't the President of the Booster Club," Dad leaned over and said into my ear, but well aware that Mom could hear him. He looked at her and smiled at the glare she was giving him.

Third down, and the clock was running out of time. We're going to lose, I thought. Great – I'll have to deal with two depressed teenage boys after the game. You'd think everything in the world hinged on their football games, the way they either rejoiced in revelry after a win or sank into the depths of melancholy after a loss. And they thought girls could be emotional.

The center snapped the ball to Josh, and almost immediately, a defensive lineman plowed straight through an empty hole in our offensive line and pounded straight into Josh, laying him out flat on his back. Luckily, he still had the football in his hand. Unfortunately, it was fourth down.

"Oh, man. We're going to lose on a sack?" I commented more to myself than to my parents. "This is going to be worse than I thought. Maybe I'll go visit some friends after the game, so I don't have to be around those two moping around our house."

"Is he ok?" Mom asked, not seeing Josh get right back up.

"I think he was hit pretty hard," Dad agreed.

The coach ran onto the field with the team manager, and they knelt down next to Josh for a while. Dad started to get up, thinking he might have to go see for himself if Josh was ok. But just then, Josh got up, and everyone in the bleachers started clapping.

He talked to the coach briefly, and then called for the huddle again.

"It's fourth down. They're going for it?" I asked my mom incredulously.

"Well, there are only a few seconds left in the game, so they have no other choice." She was looking at the clock on the scoreboard.

This couldn't be good. Fourth down, last play of the game, really. This play would either win it or lose it. They were too far away for a field goal, which would tie them up and put them into overtime. They had to have a touchdown, or the game would be lost.

Josh called for the hike, and he got the ball in shotgun formation. He looked around for a receiver, and the last seconds ticked down off the clock to nothing. This was it - as soon as this play was over, that was the game. My mom was jumping up and down next to me screaming, and I was holding my breath. I saw Chrissie with her pompoms up to her face, anxiously watching Josh. Wait...Josh? Why was she watching Josh?

I looked for Jude on the field - he was trying to elude his defender way down the field, nowhere near where Chrissie was looking. That's strange, I thought.

Just then, Josh launched the ball in a high arc over the heads of all of the players. I followed the trajectory and saw that his throw was intended for Jude, who was running as fast as he could toward the end zone, trying to reach the ball before it hit the ground.

There was a collective gasp, and then silence as we all watched the ball hanging in the air. Jude was ahead of his defender, and just as the ball came over his head, he reached his hand out as far as it would stretch, catching the ball with just one hand before rolling to the ground and into the end zone. I remembered him playing catch with Josh in Maseru and practicing this one-handed catch a hundred times. I smiled at the memory and joined the rest of the bleachers in celebration. Josh and Jude had just won the game!

After the game, everyone was on the field, congratulations being offered, and plays being retold and relived. I was watching from the bleachers still, but it was fun to see Josh and Jude getting so much attention for their great game. They each had a little swarm of fans around them, one on the field, and one over near the sidelines. Their helmets were off, sweaty hair matted to their heads and uniforms stained by the grass of the field.

I saw Jude glance over at Josh, looking to get his attention and share a smile over their win. As soon as he found him, though, his smile faded, and his brow knit with confusion. Chrissie was over by Josh, laughing and flirting with the quarterback. Jude looked away, and then broke away from the people surrounding him, heading back for the locker room.

Ironically, I felt my heart twinge a little for Jude because I knew what he was thinking. I knew him so well. He had always been hung up on how great Josh was, and how he would never be as good as he was. And now he found a reason to reinforce that feeling, watching his girlfriend flirt with Josh right there in front of him. I knew there was no way Josh would be interested in Chrissie, but I still felt bad for Jude. Even though he didn't want me. I still felt for him.

I rode in the backseat of the car on the way home. Josh was driving, and Jude was staring out the passenger window, trying hard not to talk to Josh.

"That was an amazing catch, Jude," Josh offered.

Silence.

"I mean, I wouldn't be surprised if some college recruiters start looking at you. You could maybe get a scholarship, man. Seriously," he tried again.

Jude looked down, then straight ahead out the windshield. "Thanks," he said quietly. "But I'm going into the Army as soon as we get out of High School."

"You are? Really?" I interjected. "Since when?"

"I'm not the college type. You guys know that. I'm joining the Army – I think it will suit me a lot better," Jude explained.

"Are you sure?" Josh asked. "You are such a good receiver, Jude. I'm serious. Colleges will want you."

"You mean like Chrissie wants you?" Jude gave Josh an accusatory glance.

There it was. I just sat back and waited for some sort of verbal rumble to ensue. I raised my eyebrows with anticipation, the lines on my forehead creased deeper than usual with interest of what would happen next. That didn't take long to come to the surface, I thought.

Josh thought for a few seconds, while I sat quietly and uncomfortably in the back.

"I'm not interested in her, you know that," Josh said.

"She seems pretty interested in you, Josh. As usual, you win." Jude's voice was tinged with bitterness and sarcasm.

"I'm not trying to win anything, Jude. Look, she came over to me – I didn't ask her to, and I'm not interested. She's your girlfriend, and she's not my type.

That's not how I am, man. Come on..." Josh was trying to talk some sense into his friend.

"Right...I forgot. The girls who are good enough for me aren't good enough for you," Jude said.

None of us said anything else for the rest of the drive home. I wanted to yell to Jude, "Don't you see how hypocritical you are? Don't you see how I'm not good enough for you, and you're just tossing me aside? Don't you see you're not the only one who never wins?" But I didn't say anything. I just kept to myself, and quietly wiped away a tear that escaped my eye and rolled down my cheek.

33

I opened my eyes when I heard my alarm clock go off. I leaned over and hit the top of it to stop the maddening sound it was making and closed my eyes again. It was too late, though. My eyelids cracked open again on their own, and I knew I wouldn't be able to go back to sleep again. So, I rolled out of bed and started the shower.

It was summertime again, and I had to get ready for work. The boys had just graduated, and they were taking the summer off before they had to report for duty at Fort Jackson in South Carolina for Basic Training. I couldn't believe they were both leaving me at the same time, and my heart pulled tight at the thought. I tried to put it out of my mind.

I got underneath the hot steaming flow of water, and just stood there for several minutes, letting the streamlets from the showerhead flow through my hair, and cover my face. I closed my eyes and wondered how we all grew up so fast. Why were we already having to face the realities of life, instead of playing with our

Matchbox cars underneath our trailer, swinging from Joshua's Tree, or running along the dirt pathway toward the river? I could see our little selves in slow motion, running without our shoes in the summer sun. My hair was flying through the breeze, and Josh's cheeks were covered with childhood freckles.

Things were just less complicated then. I longed for that time.

I washed up and reluctantly turned off the hot water, putting my work clothes on.

My job was at Mr. McKenzie's sheep ranch this summer. He was paying me $45 per day, however long that day lasted. It was hard work, and not really the kind of summer job you might imagine for a girl. But I could do it, and I was glad to be outdoors. The sun was somehow nourishing for my soul. I had been carrying a burden for a while now; a heavy need for time alone with my thoughts. So, this job outside, mostly by myself, seemed just right for that.

I'd spend hours moving irrigation pipe and driving the tractor to rake and bale the hay. Hours of solitude and quiet, away from roads and cars, away from people and stress. Just me among a few sheep, the pungent smells of the green pasture and its wild flowers, the breeze rustling the leaves of the old trees around the ranch.

I could hear the sounds of the rivulet where I drew water through a pump for the irrigation pipes. Sometimes I'd have to wade into the stream and pull the weeds away from the foot of the pump, unclogging it and allowing the free flow of the water into the network of irrigation pipes, like veins crawling through the pasture carrying its life blood.

I could hear the birds chatting as they soared above me in their vast expansive playground. But mostly I heard the thoughts of my own soul; churning, considering, meditating as I worked. The time I had to my own thoughts was just the therapy I needed to accept everything that was happening around me; none of it within my control.

It was time to sheer the sheep, and my job today was to stomp the wool. I hung long cylindrical burlap sacks from a large hoop ring. The bags were about ten feet tall when they were hung from the ring, the top of the bag at the same level as the platform that I stood on with the sheep shearers. When they sheared the wool from the sheep, I would gather it all together off the barnyard floor and throw it into the burlap sacks.

When it was full, I'd jump through the hoop ring into the giant sack full of wool, and stomp on it to pack it down. The sack was just the right diameter to fit a person inside. I'd climb out of it only when I compacted enough wool to stand on, to where my head would reach the same height as the ring. Then I'd fill it up again with wool, stomping it over and over until the sack was packed tight and full. Then I'd unhook it from the hoop ring and sew the top of the sack closed with a giant needle and some twine. I tipped the ten-foot tall sack over on its side and attached the next giant burlap bag to the ring.

This job went on for several days because Mr. McKenzie had a lot of sheep. Some of them weren't very happy to be herded into the barn and shuffled through the network of wooden fences to where the shearers were performing their wooly coiffures. As I pushed the sheep through the maze of chutes inside the barn, one of the ewes made up her mind that she wasn't going anywhere. She backed up into the corner of the little pen she was in, lowered her head like she was gearing up for something, and launched herself forward. She galloped as fast as she could across the ten feet to where I was standing and jumped into the air, ramming me square in the chest with her head. I fell flat on my back into the layer of sheep excrement that lined the barnyard floor.

I was a little stunned to be staring at the rafters of the barn. I got back onto my feet, unsure how to react. I looked at the ewe trying to hide her wooly body by the fence, her bulging eyes staring nervously back at me. I shook my head, a smile creeping over my face. I laughed a little at myself because I was sure I was a sight to behold, covered in sheep dung. I couldn't really blame her for trying to defend herself.

"It's ok, girl," I tried to soothe her nerves. "It's just a haircut. It won't hurt. You'll be back in the pasture before you know it."

She still just looked at me, standing firm. I corralled her into the chute, grabbing big handfuls of wool on her back, using my grip to push her on her way. She finally started following the other sheep.

Standing with my back up against one of the posts in the barn, I scraped as much muck off as I could before I walked over to start stomping wool for the rest of the day. The shearers had been working for a while now, and had a big pile of wool ready for me.

I was inside one of those tall burlap sacks, stomping the wool under my feet, compacting it as it naturally provided me some height, so I could climb back out. Everything was sticking to my skin, the oil from the wool covering my arms and attracting little bits of dirt and hay from the barn. My thoughts were elsewhere, though, caught up in the events of the last couple of months.

"Josh, don't you think you should be going to college?" My parents were genuinely concerned about this decision and were trying to talk some sense into their son, while still respecting his aspirations.

"I could go to college, but I really think it's the best decision for me to join the Army with Jude," he replied.

My parents looked at each other, and then back at their wringing hands.

"Are you sure?" my mother's pleading eyes were searching for some sense of understanding. "Josh, I don't want you to just follow your friend. You need to think of your own future."

"I know, Mom. And I know you and Dad are both concerned. I don't know how to explain it to you," he said. This was hard for him, too. He couldn't defend what he was feeling. There were admittedly many emotions that went into his decision, but also a logical line of thinking that he felt made perfect sense to him. Even if it did seem crazy to everyone else.

"We'll support you in whatever decision you make, son," Dad said. "We just want to be sure that this is the right decision. That's all."

"I know," Josh said.

My brother had told me about his determination to join the Army a week before and tried his best to enlighten me with his motives. I think I understood, but it was still hard to listen to his conversation with our parents from the other room.

"Mom, Dad...the only thing I can say is that Jude is my brother. You understand that, right? I know he wasn't born to you like I was. But he is as close to a brother as anyone I'll ever know."

He looked at them, trying to assess whether or not they were really understanding him. Then he continued.

"We grew up together – for the most part. And I promised him I would always be there for him. We have a bond that is just like family. And because of that I feel a responsibility for him." Josh's voice was full of pleading, begging our parents to understand and have compassion on his childhood blood brother.

"I think we understand that. We just don't want you to throw away an opportunity for yourself. That's all," Mom said.

"I know. Just let me try this for now, and if it's not the career that's meant for me, then I can use the G.I. bill to go to college after my initial commitment," Josh said, and this seemed to relieve a lot of my parents' concerns.

Josh added one last thing, "For whatever reason, I feel really strong – almost inspired – to join up with Jude. Like I need to be there to watch out for him, or something. Not to keep tabs on him, but to have his back. To be there for him. To be his brother."

Josh and Jude signed up with the recruiter together. Josh's test scores were high enough to land him a specialized job in the Army, or even attend Officer Candidate School. But when the recruiter mentioned that to him, he waved him off.

"Let's just keep that between ourselves, ok? Don't mention that to Jude. I just want you to assign us to the same Basic Training, and to the same duty after that. If I'm joining the Army, I want to be sure that we're assigned together. Can you promise us that?" Josh asked the recruiter.

"You bet," he replied.

And now, at the end of the summer, they'd be heading for Fort Jackson. But not before a summer trip that they planned together to celebrate their graduation.

And I'd be here, working on the sheep ranch.

I had another year of school ahead of me before I graduated. I wasn't sure how I would make it through without my best friends.

Over the summer, I came to accept our inevitable procession through life and into adulthood. During those long days on the sheep ranch, I envisioned the parade of our childhood memories marching along to the beat of a tama drum, each reverie taking its place in the cavalcade of our lives, leading us to where we are now. Apart. Well, not the two of them. They were together. But I was apart from them. I was alone.

I decided to plunge into my senior year of high school full-force. If for no other reason, to protect myself from the hollow void that Josh and Jude bequeathed me with their sudden exodus from my life. I gave myself no other choice but to dive in.

I joined the track team and threw the javelin, I sang in the choir, got elected to the student government, made it into the honor society, and anything else that came my way. I was determined to fill every tick of the second hand as it circumnavigated the face of the clock, seconds producing minutes, and minutes developing into hours.

I sat out in Joshua's tree behind our house, perched up on the platform that he built so long ago. I came here when I missed them and wanted to somehow feel close to them again. Eventually, I convinced myself that the days would rotate into nights, and the earth would make its way through another revolution around the sun. Bringing me closer to what, though? I don't think even I knew the answer to why I was wishing the time away.

"Hey, wait up!" Steve called from somewhere behind me in the hallway between classes. The crowds were busily opening lockers, grabbing books, and chatting with friends. I turned around, and saw his gorgeous smile catching up to me.

"Hi, Steve," I smiled back. "What's up?"

"Nothing much. I just thought I'd walk with you to class." We had Calculus together, so when he caught up to me, I turned back in the direction I had been going, and we walked together.

"Are you going to play in the Powder Puff game?" Steve asked.

"Yeah, actually, I think I am. They need as many girls as they can to fill out the teams," I added. My school was fairly small, so if a large percentage of people didn't participate in these sorts of activities, they just didn't happen.

"Cool! I can't wait to see you play. I'll be cheering you on." He would literally be cheering me on. The football team actually dressed up as cheerleaders in this role-reversal football game and cheered for the girls as we ran plays on the field.

"Yeah, I can't wait to see you in that cheerleading uniform!" I teased.

Steve smiled. We walked without saying anything until we got to our math class, where we found two seats next to each other and sat down waiting for the bell.

He leaned over across the aisle and said in a low voice, just for me to hear, "Listen, I know we're just friends, and all. But I was just wondering..." He paused for affect.

"Yeah?" I played along, prodding him to continue.

"Well, I was just wondering if you might want to go to the prom with me?" he said, a little rosy in the cheeks.

"Really?" I was genuinely surprised. I didn't even consider that someone might want to take me to the prom. I actually felt a momentary excitement at the prospect, and I smiled at Steve so that he knew I welcomed the idea.

"Well, yeah," he said, "I think it will be fun." He looked at me with his eyebrows raised, questioning in anticipation of my response.

Steve was a nice guy, and fun to hang around. He was funny, too, which I really loved. I needed to laugh and have fun. So, this was an easy answer to give, and I didn't make him sweat the response.

"Yes, I'd love to go!" I said, and I thought I could see his shoulders relax, and his chest breathe easier.

I drove home that day with a lighter heart, and I found myself singing to the radio. I wondered to myself if this was what hope feels like. Hope in a burgeoning friendship. Hope in something to look forward to. Hope that I'm not lost after all.

The night of the Powder Puff football game was thrilling. We dressed in jerseys and put black paint under our eyes to make us look tough. The senior girls had recruited the freshman class girls to our team, and we played against the combined team of the sophomores and juniors. I was chosen as the quarterback. It was a fun game, and I laughed every time I looked over at the side lines and saw Steve dressed up like a cheerleader, doing his best to use his borrowed pompoms. He was hilarious.

We had been spending a lot of time together, and I was really starting to like him. We went to the movies, did homework together at my house, and we were looking forward to going to the prom together. It was fun to have a friend, and it was starting to develop into something more. Steve left little notes for me in my locker. He would slide them into the crack of the door, and I'd find the folded yellow paper waiting for me between classes. They always made me smile.

After one of the girls on the opposing team got a chipped tooth during one of the plays, they started some rough retaliation against our team. I came face to face a couple of times with Barbara Cotter, a very solid and muscular girl who had gotten into a few fights in our hallways at school over the last couple of years. She had a reputation, and nobody wanted to get in her way. Her sophomore year, she had broken the cheekbone of another girl in our class. She meant business, and when I saw her in front of me, ready to take me down in that game, I ran around her as fast as my feet would take me, all the way into the end zone.

Barbara had a few choice words for me. But I had to thank her, because she was the one who drove me to the touchdown.

After the game, Steve came and stood next to me. Seeing his short pleated skirt and tight-fitting top, I couldn't contain my laughter and I just let it all out, grabbing my sides to prevent them from splitting.

"You are a piece of work," I chortled the words out of my mouth, barely intelligible.

He smiled like the great sport he was, and said, "Eat it up, girl. This will be the only time you ever see this." He moved his hand up and down his tall frame, displaying himself to me like a hostess on a game show.

I laughed again, "I wish I had my camera. Wait – I'll bet my mom has her camera here with her. We should find her!" I suggested, grabbing his hand and pulling him toward the bleachers where I knew I'd find my mom.

She snapped a photo of the two of us, and I hugged her, telling her I'd be hanging out with my friends for a while before coming home.

"Before you go too far, I have a surprise for you," Mom said.

"What do you mean?" I asked, wondering why she'd get me a surprise for a measly Powder Puff game.

"Look over there by Dad," she said, pointing to the other side of the bleacher stands. I followed where she was pointing, still giggling and holding on to Steve's arm, caught up in the moment of the night.

I saw my dad standing there talking to two men with --- with short haircuts! I couldn't believe what I was seeing. It was Josh and Jude! I stood there staring, hardly recognizing them as the boys who had left a few months before. They looked like men now. They were muscular, tanned, their hair really short, and they just seemed...confident. I don't know how to explain it. They had this aura about them; they had certainly been trans-formed from who they had been when they left. I could see it even from where I was standing a distance away.

"Well?" Mom said, prodding. "Aren't you going to go say hi?"

"Oh." I woke up from my momentary trance and re-alized I had dropped my hand from Steve's arm, and almost forgotten he was even there.

I was in somewhat of a stupor, the world I had fi-nally been able to construct around me to prop me up in their absence suddenly tumbling around me like a house of cards.

I found my legs, and started running with alacrity toward them, tears looming and a sob threatening to es-cape my throat.

I had been a lone drop of dew on a blade of grass, abandoned and almost sure to evaporate into nothing-ness. But now my two heroes were here to save me, allowing me to coalesce with them into something larger and more substantial, the sun's heat no threat to our amalgamation.

I flew past everyone else mulling around the bleachers, ignoring them as I blurred by. Then Josh saw me coming, and his smile widened, his arms opened to welcome me. I flung myself into his embrace, and the tears flowed freely. Jude stood nearby waiting, and I no-ticed his dog tags hanging around his neck. There was a little coin-shaped piece of metal hanging with the two tags, and I realized it was the blood brother token that Josh had made for Jude in Maseru. I reached over and grabbed him into our little circle. All at once, everything in my world was ok again.

A little while later as we were gathering things up to drive home, I remembered Steve. Oh my gosh, I had forgotten about Steve! I felt like a horrible person. I looked around, eyes darting from one group of people to the next, but I couldn't find him. I walked back to where we were standing just a little while ago when my mom had taken our picture after the game, big smiles on our faces and my arm hooked around Steve's elbow. I saw some pompoms lying on the bleachers, but my cheer-leader was nowhere in sight.

34

"Tell us about Boot Camp!" Mom encouraged the boys, who were wolfing down the enchiladas she had made for them.

"Slow down! You're going to puke that all back up if you don't stop eating it so fast," I warned. "You'd think you guys were never fed, or something."

"Sometimes we weren't!" Josh said. "I'm glad I'll never have to go through chow time again. Right, Jude?" He looked over at his friend, who nodded in ready agreement.

"Yeah, as soon as the last person in the chow line sat down to eat, chow time was officially over, and the Drill Sergeant made us leave the chow hall," Jude explained.

"But what about the last person? He didn't get to eat?" I asked, incredulously.

"Nope – not unless he could somehow shove a few bites into his mouth without being seen," Josh said. "Boot Camp was brutal."

I was glad I didn't have to endure the long days of grueling exercise, only to be the last one in line to eat. I imagined how miserable it would have been to sit down with my metal plate of food, famished from all the physical exertion, only to have to leave it there untouched because chow time was over. That was just mean!

Josh was cleaning every last morsel from his plate, and Jude got up to put his empty plate in the sink.

"You can have more," Mom offered. "Help yourselves."

"Oh, I'm good. Thank you," Jude said, patting his full belly.

"One time, Drill Sergeant got in my face in the chow line and started yelling at me. I didn't even know what I was doing wrong!" Josh said. "I kept apologizing to him. I said, 'Sorry, Drill Sergeant! It won't happen again, Drill Sergeant! What exactly am I doing wrong, Drill Sergeant?'"

Jude started laughing at his story, and I just watched him, loving every moment of seeing him again. His smile was so familiar, and his laughter soothed my aching heart.

Josh continued his story, smiling as he retold it. "Mom, you won't believe what he said. He told me I was running my tongue over my teeth under my lips, and it was annoying him!"

We all burst into laughter, and Dad asked, "Well, what did you tell him?"

"I said, 'Yes, Drill Sergeant! It won't happen again, Drill Sergeant!'" Josh answered.

I tried to imagine how something so silly could be such a huge deal to the Drill Sergeant that he would single Josh out in line, just waiting for his food. I guess the yelling is just part of the Boot Camp experience, for whatever reason.

"Well, I almost got into huge trouble when that new chow hall lady asked me how I wanted my eggs cooked," Jude said. "She didn't know that those of us in Basic Training weren't allowed that kind of choice – that was only for the Drill Instructors," he explained.

"Are you serious? You couldn't even ask for eggs over easy?" I was shocked again, liking the idea of the Army less and less.

"Totally serious," Jude said. "We got scrambled eggs, and that was it. Whether we liked it or not. It's not like we could taste the food, anyway. We ate it so fast, because we only had a minute or two to scarf our food down. When they yelled that time was up, that was it. We were done."

"Yeah, and if you did anything other than what they told you to do, you'd end up doing push-ups," Josh added to the story.

"So anyway, when she asked me how I wanted my eggs, I looked around to see if anyone was watching," Jude recounted, moving his eyes from side to side, acting out his story for us. We smiled, loving his dramatic performance.

He continued, "I didn't see any Instructors, so I just said to her, 'Sunny Side Up, please.' And she started cooking my eggs to order. Guys kept going around me in line, getting their scrambled eggs, and I stood there like an idiot, knowing I would probably get caught."

Josh was laughing, and so were the rest of us. Oh, how I loved these boys. But they were men now. It's like they had transformed into adulthood in just a matter of those couple of months. It was stunning to see.

"So just when she gives me my eggs, the Drill Instructor comes over to me." Jude stiffened to attention as he was recounting the story to us, bringing it to life in our kitchen. "He yells at me, 'Soldier, what do you think you're eating?' he demands. I say they're eggs, and he shouts that I don't deserve those eggs, and I have to throw them out right now!" Jude's eyes are wide, and so are mine, listening for what would happen next.

"And...?" I prodded him to continue as he took a drink of water.

"Well, I said 'Yes, Drill Sergeant!' and headed to the trash in the corner, all the while shoving those eggs down my throat as fast as I could!" he said. His eyes lit up, remembering. "Those eggs were the best thing I'd ever tasted."

We all laughed with him, and they told us stories for a couple of hours sitting in our living room.

Now Josh was recounting a story to us about how they both had to endure a tear gas chamber. Their squad sat on benches with gas masks on, while their Drill Instructor set off a canister of tear gas. They all breathed easily for a while, until the Instructor ordered them each to remove their gas masks. They had to sit there and breathe in the noxious vapors for a full minute, and then they could run outside and breathe in the clean air.

"My eyes have never hurt like that before, and every ounce of mucus in my nose and lungs seemed to pour out of my body," Josh said. "It was disgusting."

Jude told us that mail call was really important to them while they were away. Everyone there was anxious to hear from home. It could be a pretty miserable experience, and a letter from home was an oasis for them in that dreary desert.

"Drill Sergeant would call out to us if we had a letter and throw it through the air toward us. We'd just have to scramble around and find our letter on the floor. He didn't care," Jude explained. "Private Jones! Private Johnson! Private Costa! He'd bark them out as fast as he could, and just toss them like Frisbees into the crowd."

Jude demonstrated for us what his Sergeant looked like and acted out his story – it was always better for us that way and made his account enthralling.

"He'd read anything that was written on the back of the envelopes, too, just so that he could mock the Private it was being sent to," Jude continued. "One time he read the back of a letter and then teased the poor guy: 'Private Stewart's mommy says she misses her boy.'" Jude's voice held the same high-pitched mocking tone that his Drill Sergeant had.

We laughed, but he wasn't done with the story.

"And then one time – remember, Josh? – Private Samson got that letter from his girlfriend, and on the back of it, she wrote, 'Love you, Poo-Poo.' Ohhh, that was the end of poor Private Samson. He never heard his real last name again from the Drill Sergeant. From then on, he only called him "Private Poo-Poo." Josh and Jude both busted up laughing at the memory.

"Drop and give me twenty, Private Poo-Poo!" Jude played the role of the Drill Sergeant.

"Yes, Drill Sergeant!" Josh dropped down obediently.

"Poor guy," Mom said.

Mom, Dad and I were all so happy to have them home. They would be sent off to their next assignment in a week, but I tried to push that thought down inside of myself and just enjoy the time they were here.

"Well, I should be getting home to see my dad," Jude said. He got up, gave us all a big hug, and walked toward the door, pulling me with him a little bit away from the others.

"Hey, can you get away tomorrow?" he asked me, opening the door on his way out, but hesitating for my answer.

"Sure," I answered, a little surprised, but excited.

"Ok, I'll pick you up tomorrow. I've just really been missing you, and I wanted to spend some time together. If you're up for that?" he raised his eyebrows with his last question, making sure I was feeling the same way.

"Yes, Jude. Of course. I'll see you tomorrow," I answered. He pulled the door closed, and I watched from the window as he drove away.

I turned around to head up to bed, and there was my whole family standing there watching me. They had big smiles on their faces, and I saw in their eyes they were just waiting for the chance to tease me.

"Stop," I warned, unable to keep from smiling, too. Then I ran upstairs, closing my door behind me.

The next day, Jude showed up at my house on a motorcycle. I thought I was smitten before! The motorcycle made me even more enamored. I climbed on behind him, and he sped away from the house, heading up the road that meandered along the river.

I leaned into Jude's back, wrapping my arms around him and holding on tight. He leaned the motorcycle into the turns, crossing the dividing line of the road as if we owned it all. It felt like all of it really was just ours. The trees along the road, the winding river and its endless flowing waters. We didn't come across any other cars or people; we were miles up the river road. The solitude made it feel as though the beauty around us truly was ours alone to relish.

After a long ride, Jude came to a stop at a wide spot in the road. He turned off the engine and parked the motorcycle under a huge tree. The sun was filtering through the branches, its warmth falling on my face. We got off the bike, and he propped it up with the kickstand. I ran my fingers through my hair, trying to put some semblance of order to it after the wind had blown through it and whipped it around with its blustery lashings.

I sat sideways on the seat of the motorcycle, stretching my cramped legs out in front of me.

"It's so amazing out here," Jude commented, looking around at the splendor of our surroundings.

"Yeah, I love coming up the river. It reminds me of when we were kids, building swimming holes to play in," I added.

Jude looked at me, and I glanced away, suddenly a little shy.

"I have to tell you that I honestly have been missing you," he said. I met his gaze now and didn't quite know how to respond.

So, he continued, "I know last year I was kind of a jerk to you, running around with Chrissie, and all that."

"Well," I said, pausing for a second. "Yeah, you could say that. But it seemed like she was the one you wanted to be with, so what could I do?"

"This is really no excuse," Jude said, "but I was just being a stupid kid. You know me better than anyone, and you know I've always struggled with feeling good enough. Good enough for Josh, and good enough for you, too."

I just listened to him. He was right; I did know him better than anyone. And I did know he struggled with his self-esteem and self-image. Ever since we were kids, he struggled with doubting his worth, no matter what we said to him.

"Look, Boot Camp was a wake-up call. It just helped me see what's important to me." He stepped closer to where I was sitting, a little bit into my personal space.

"Jude, this has been a hard summer for me, and a hard year at school so far. With you and Josh gone, I've felt really lost. And now you're home for a split second before you're going to leave again. And this time for a lot longer. Now you're saying I'm important to you?" I wanted him to know how it felt to be left behind, but as soon as that thought crossed my mind, I realized he knew better than anyone how that felt. I was a little ashamed that I hadn't thought of that until now.

"Well...yes. I know; I'm sorry it's lame. All I could think about, though, when I was gone, was seeing you again. And now I'm here, and I'm with you. And I'm just finally – happy." Words were starting to spill out of his mouth, without contemplation or formulation. I liked that he was being honest.

"Jude, you have to know that I've never changed how I've felt about you. You know that, right?" I asked.

"I didn't know for sure. I just figured since I had a girlfriend when you moved back home, you'd probably changed your mind about me," he said a little sheepishly.

"I can't say I was happy about it," I agreed. "But Jude, look at me."

He moved closer still, and we locked eyes. "Listen, I haven't changed how I feel – not since we were little, and we played the summers away together – the three of us. Not since we had to leave you behind when we moved. And not since that moment we had under those African stars."

He kept his gaze on me, looking from one of my eyes to the other, searching my heart for a sign of my sincerity.

"Jude, I've always loved you. You have to know that," I conceded to him, letting every barrier between us fall away and showing him my true feelings.

He reached up to me, and took my face into both of his hands, gently cradling it in front of his gaze. His fingers stretched into my hair and around my ears, and he pulled my face toward him as tenderly as I'd ever felt someone touch me. His lips were millimeters from my own, and I could feel his breath mingle with mine. I reached my chin forward to meet him, but he pulled back, looking into my eyes again, needing me to know how he truly felt.

I closed my eyes inviting him back, and he brushed his lower lip against my top one, lifting it softly so my mouth was slightly open. He still had my face in between his hands, and he pulled me closer, kissing me fully now. I melted into his arms, feeling the passion, but also feeling a sense of what I'd been missing all summer long. I felt at home with him. I felt loved.

We rode home again later, and I kept my hands warm under Jude's jacket, appreciating the muscular torso he had developed over the past couple of months in the Army. He was so attractive, and so romantic. I didn't see how I would survive without him when he went away again in a few days. But that motorcycle ride certainly gave me something to hold on to.

35

1989

"Will you marry me?" Robert was kneeling on one knee in front of me, proposing to me for the third time that day. He held the gum wrapper that he had fashioned into a ring in both hands, offering it to me like my knight in shining armor.

"Yes!" I proclaimed with enthusiasm, also for the third time. Robert smiled wide, his eyes almost disappearing in his joy, and he slid the ring onto my finger before standing up and walking away, already interested in something else.

I was at work; I was on my third job since starting college, and I didn't have any plans on jumping ship from this one. I really loved it. I couldn't stand my previous job as a telemarketer, and then my midnight shift on campus as a janitor didn't last that long either. But this job was amazing, and I actually looked forward to my shifts.

I worked at a day program for adults with developmental disabilities. There were six adults that I was supervising, and I'd take them out to lunch, or bowling, or once in a while to a movie. My job was to make sure they had a meaningful day. I would drive them to these activities, and then assist them in any way they needed while we were there. These amazing people had a variety of disabilities, and some were more independent than others. Two of them at the program were in wheelchairs, and some weren't able to communicate verbally at all.

Robert had Down syndrome, born with an extra 21st chromosome. He charmed me with his incredible personality the first day I met him, and we became fast friends. He loved movies more than anyone I knew, and he quoted them any chance he got. I didn't always understand him at first, since his speech was not very succinct. But the more time I spent around him, I could understand him perfectly – and he was hilarious.

"Jane!" He would say the moment I walked in the door. Of course, this wasn't my name, but he loved to call me Jane, or Mary Jane, or MJ for short. He played the role of Peter Parker from Spiderman, and I was his MJ.

"Peter!" I would play along, and he'd whip off his glasses so that I would be able to recognize him for who he was; Spiderman.

"It's me!" He said, eyes wide, his countenance completely serious.

"Spiderman?" I asked with the most anticipation I could role play.

"Yes!" He'd break into a smile, loving that I'd played along with his game.

Robert and I were the same age, and I felt lucky to have him for a friend.

My job and Robert both gave me an incredible experience, an education that was probably much more valuable than what I was getting out of my classes on statistics or economics. Robert was teaching me lessons I could never learn in a classroom.

We never had any in-depth conversations, because Robert's level of understanding wasn't the same as his typical peers. He didn't know how to philosophize or theorize about abstract and conjectural notions or topics. And I think that's why I loved him. For his innocence, his unassuming modesty, and the way he went about his life without guile.

I grew to love each of my friends at work, but I especially loved Robert. We just had a connection. I loved his hands, his short fingers, the shape of his eyes that truly did almost disappear from sight when he smiled. I loved his enthusiasm, and his playfulness. He would sit for hours and fill notebooks with hand-drawn circles that he would color in with his collection of colored pencils. It was fascinating to me. But that was his routine. It calmed him and put him into his groove. Every single page was filled with those colorful circle montages, and he filled a stack of notebooks, all of which he carried in his backpack.

I introduced Robert to Josh one time when he was on leave, and after that, Robert took a long break from the Peter Parker routine. Now all he wanted to be was a soldier.

"MJ." I was still Jane, even though he wasn't playing Peter Parker.

"Peter!" I tried.

"No, it's me. Joshua," he corrected me. Then he pretended to shoot his enemy and hide behind bunkers like an Army soldier.

I'd seen Josh just this one time since he had been home after Boot Camp, and I saw him off at the airport when he had to leave again. He was going to visit Mom and Dad before he went back to his duty station. I was much more independent now, and although I hated saying goodbye to him, I had a good network of friends to keep me busy, not to mention all of my classes and my job. I missed him, and I missed Jude, but I didn't feel as lost as I did my senior year of high school without them.

At the airport while Josh was waiting to board his plane, he told me that he and Jude worked a lot together, being stationed at the same place just like the recruiter had promised. Josh had been promoted a couple of times and had responsibilities that kept him busy. But the rough side of Jude was being mustered to the surface by Army life; his bravado was emerging and the soft side of him was starting to dissipate as time went on.

"What do you mean?" I asked, concerned by what Josh was describing to me.

"I don't know, every once in a while, I see little glimpses of his dad come out in him," Josh tried to explain. "Especially when he's out drinking with his buddies, and he puts back a few too many."

"Do you guys still hang out?" I asked, trying to probe him for more information.

"Yeah, we hang out, but not like before. I don't think he liked it too much when I got promoted to Corporal," Josh said.

"He's not still hung up on comparing himself to everyone else, is he?" I couldn't imagine that still being an issue after high school.

"Well, I think he kind of is. He might not ever say it, but I feel some tension between us any time I get recognized or rewarded." Josh didn't know what to do about it, though. It wasn't like he was boasting, or anything. In fact, he tried to avoid any sort of special recognition.

"I wish he would get over that, and just realize his own value and potential," I said. "I'm sorry, Josh. I know that must be hard."

"It's fine. Yeah, sometimes it's hard, but I'm still glad to be there with him; I know there's a reason I should be."

"Let me know when you figure out what that reason is," I teased.

"We'll see how things go for the next couple of years, and then maybe I'll get out and settle down. One of these days I'd like to get married, you know. Believe it, or not," he answered. Josh had a couple of girlfriends in high school but was never serious about any of them.

"Well, whoever ends up with you will be a lucky girl," I said. "Please be careful. Please come back to me safely again soon." I had been writing to Jude, and once in a while we'd place a long-distance call to catch up on the phone. But we couldn't afford that too often. The longer we were away from each other, the less frequent his letters would be. I wondered if Jude wanted to settle down, too, like Josh did. I secretly hoped he did.

I hugged Josh tight and watched as he got on his plane and flew away.

36

At the beginning of 1991 my brother went to war. He and Jude both were deployed to Operation Desert Storm and were part of the coalition forces that liberated Kuwait and invaded Iraq. I was scared to hear that they would actually be fighting in an armed conflict, and not just doing drills and working on an Army base somewhere. My parents were nervous, too, and we talked often during that time, anxious for any news from our boys.

We didn't really hear from them directly during the several months of the Gulf War. We saw how things unfolded on television, and before we knew it, the main conflict was over. We got a phone call from Josh after that, and he told us that he and Jude were "tread heads," or part of an armored tank unit. These were M1 Abrams tanks, and were an integral part of the ground battle.

Josh said they would be over there for a while and wasn't sure when he'd be home again, but he'd keep us posted. I asked about Jude, and he just answered with a quick, "Jude's fine. Gotta go, Sis. Talk to you soon. Love you."

That was weird, I thought. I wondered if everything was ok between them, but I put it out of my mind. I was in my last year of college before I would be graduating with my bachelor's degree, and I had a lot on my plate. The busier I kept myself, the less time I had to worry about things like war, and those boys.

I was turning twenty-two, and just when I felt like I had gained a sense of sureness and stability, and felt like I was going in a good direction, my world fell apart all around me.

The phone rang at work as I was about to load up the crew and head out for a fun afternoon of bowling. My coworker answered the call and said it was for me. I took the receiver in my hand and put it up to my ear. It was my Bishop from our old home town. Why would he be calling me at work? And then panic trickled into my heart, and I knew something must be wrong.

"I'm so sorry to have to tell you this over the phone, but you'll need to come home right away. Your parents have had an accident." His voice was so kind and loving, trying to temper the news for me.

"What happened? Are they ok?" I asked, my mind strangely working to remember what my last conversation was with my mother, and attempting to recall the last time I had seen her and my dad.

"Well, no, sweetheart. I'm so sorry, but your parents died this morning." The silence hung in the air over the phone lines, the words not making sense to me. This couldn't be true. I had just talked to my parents on the phone – when was it? Was it last week?

"Are you there?" he asked gently.

I replayed his words in my head. *Your parents died this morning.* And just like that, I was forever changed. My heart broke into a million tiny pieces, spilling out in the form of my tears. I finally let out a distressing sob.

I sunk to the floor and listened as he explained to me that my parents had passed away in their sleep from carbon monoxide poisoning. The regulator from the propane tank outside the old house had frozen, and too much propane was being allowed through the pipes, the flame of their furnace unable to keep up with the volume that was flowing to it. He told me they silently slipped away together into unconsciousness, and then to their joint demise.

I couldn't talk to him anymore. I couldn't talk to anyone.

"I have to go," I managed to say. I opened my hand and let the phone fall from my grip. It slid across the floor, the spiral cord springing and pulling it back toward the receiver.

My coworkers and all of our clients were standing watching me, knowing something was horribly wrong. They didn't know what to do with me, huddled on the floor weeping. Then Robert walked over to me, knelt down, and took me into his arms, hugging me.

"It's ok," he said. "It's ok." He stroked my hair, tears falling down his cheeks in sympathy for me, and he didn't even know why I was upset. He just cared that I was.

I hugged Robert and buried my weeping into his shoulder, letting my sudden and unexpected grief flow out of my body and my heart all at once. But there was no end to it; I felt there was an infinite supply of this sorrow, and that it would never go away. I was in shock, disbelief. My parents were my solid rock, the pillars of my existence that I knew would always be there for me – at least until I was an old woman myself. How could this be happening?

My coworker drove me home. All I could say was, "I need my brother. I need to find Joshua. He needs to be here." I was completely alone without him. How would I find him?

I lay in my bed, lights off and blankets over my head, hiding from the world. How could I ever go on living without my precious mother and father? I couldn't. I didn't want to. I wanted to die and go be with them, wherever they were. Please just let me die. I'd never felt such despair in all my existence, and ironically, in order to be able to bear the burden of this loss, I needed my mother.

But now she was gone. And never coming back.

I spent the next few days shedding thousands of tears, reminiscing over everything my parents had given me, told me, done for me. The experiences they provided me by traveling for my dad's job were alone an amazing gift. I wondered if I had told them enough times that I love them. I cried that they would never see me graduate from college, never see me get married and have children. They would never know their grandchildren! That started a new flood of tears, and my heart was completely destroyed. I would never recover. My life would never be the same.

I needed Josh more than ever. I was empty and use-less, without purpose or desire for living; not without my family. And he was all that was left of it.

He was on his way home for our parents' funeral. The Army allowed him some temporary leave, and he would be arriving tomorrow. We'd travel home together and take care of all of the arrangements. But I simply couldn't face all of that without him.

I thought I was a strong and independent woman. But this cut me to the core. This, I wasn't prepared for at all. I wasn't strong. I was defeated, the legions of anguish having completely razed my sense of security and hap-piness, conquering my very identity. I didn't know who to be anymore.

Joshua, despite his own grief and sorrow, saved me from losing myself in this despair. He comforted me, al-lowing me to lean on his strength. I knew if I stood on the rock of his solid foundation, my frail frame wouldn't be blown away by the turbulence of our tribulation. With Josh, I felt like I might actually be able to get through this.

"I just miss them, Josh," I said through tears as we got ready for our parents' funeral.

"I know you do. Me, too," Josh said. He had tears in his eyes, too.

"I wish I would have called them one more time, and told them how much they mean to me, and that I love them. I wish I would have been able to hug them one last time." I chided myself continually for all the things I could have done or should have done.

"Listen to me," Josh took my shoulders, and squared them in front of him so that he had my full attention. "Mom and Dad both know we love them. They know. Ok? Two children couldn't have adored their parents more.

They know that. I promise you, they do." He looked into my eyes to be sure I believed him.

"Ok," I said, tears rolling down my cheeks. I dabbed at my eyes with tissue for the thousandth time.

"Even though we lost them both, we can take comfort that they are together. Right?" he asked me.

"Yeah, I'm glad they are together. I don't think one of them would do very well without the other," I agreed.

The funeral was a blur, with a lot of crying and hugs from old friends, and a lot of people we didn't really know. My parents were beloved by many people all over the world, and I thought for an instant that Josh and I would somehow have to let Modibo know. That made me start crying again, and Josh just put his arm around me and squeezed me against his side.

Jude had traveled home with Josh, and he seemed to be just as distraught about the loss of my parents as we were. He allowed Josh and I the time we needed together to mourn our parents, but he was so helpful with the arrangements, and his eyes were red and swollen, having shed his share of tears over these dear surrogate parents whom he loved.

37

Josh and Jude were home for two weeks after the funeral, and there just seemed to be something off between the two of them. Something was going on, and I could tell. Things just weren't the same between them, and I wanted to know why.

"What's going on with you and Jude?" I asked Josh while we were at our parents' home, where they raised us and cared for us. It was empty without them; we felt a massive void in the home. How ironic that emptiness can feel so heavy and large.

"What do you mean?" Josh asked me.

"I can tell something's happened between you two. You guys are acting weird. What's going on?" I insisted.

"Jude is just...I don't know. He's just been different lately. You should ask him, I guess," Josh deflected my questions.

"I'm asking you, Josh. You're my brother. What happened?" I was getting impatient.

"I don't really want to go into it, but something happened during our deployment in Iraq. Jude was being stupid, and almost got himself in trouble. I think he might just feel guilty, or something, because I was there when he did it." Josh looked very uncomfortable talking about this, and I knew I should tread lightly, or he'd clam up for good.

"What kind of being stupid?" I asked.

"He was taking off when he shouldn't," Josh offered.

"Like AWOL, you mean?" I was knitting my brows, surprised that Jude would do something like that.

"Yeah, kind of – but I'm pretty sure everything's fine now. I just think Jude didn't appreciate me trying to help him and get him back in line. He doesn't really like the fact that I'm above him in rank. You know how he is with that," Josh said.

"Yeah, I know what you mean," I agreed. "Have you guys talked about it?"

"No, and I don't think he wants to. I just want to let it go and get back to normal." He stood up, and I knew the conversation was over. I guess I'd have to ask Jude about it at some point. I hoped they could work things out, because I knew how much it hurt Josh to have anyone hold a grudge against him. But for that person to be Jude – it was ten times worse for Josh.

The boys headed back to their duty station, and I had no other choice but to finish school. I went through the motions and finished my degree. My parents had left Josh and me some money after they passed away, so I decided to pursue a master's degree right away before starting full-time in the working world. I kept working part-time with my favorite Spiderman, though. I loved that young man. Even through the grief I was experiencing, Robert could always make me smile and warm my heart with his singular personality.

My spirits were lifted even more about a year later when I heard that Jude was being considered for a Silver Star Medal. This was a big deal, because it was awarded for valor and gallantry in action against an enemy of the United States. I was so proud of him. Apparently, Jude had prevented an ambush of a convoy, and had risked his life to do it. I couldn't believe Josh or Jude never mentioned the story, because it happened during Desert Storm. Why wouldn't they have told me? Or Mom and Dad, for goodness sake?

Whatever the reason, I was so happy that something great like this was finally happening for Jude. Now maybe he could move on from that millstone he'd been carrying around his neck his whole life, always insisting that he was never as good as Josh. I couldn't wait to see them again and tell Jude how proud I was – and how proud my parents would have been.

Jude got leave and came home a few months later, this time without Josh. Josh was a Sergeant now, and he had more responsibilities. He would be taking leave a different time, so Jude went home to see his dad. I drove home so I could see him, and to let him know how delighted I was in his accomplishments. I wanted him to know that someone noticed. That someone cared. I doubted that his dad would make a big deal about it, and I felt it was important that *someone* should.

I had finally made it home, and Jude was supposed to be coming over to the old house to see me. So many years had gone by since I'd really spent a lot of time with him – partly because he'd been deployed in the Army, partly because I'd been in school. I was looking forward to maybe reconnecting and getting to know who he was now. The years had surely matured him, and changed him, as they had me. I felt a flutter of anxious energy and went to look at myself in the mirror again before he arrived. A girl in her mid-twenties shouldn't feel as giddy as a teenager, should she?

Jude knocked on the door, and I opened it to let him in.

My smile faded when the stench of alcohol hit me.

"What are you doing, Jude?" I asked, instantly annoyed that he had ruined how I had envisioned our reunion after all this time. I thought maybe we could finally pick up our relationship from where we had left it, safe on a shelf for when we finally had some time to devote to it. We were more mature now, and ready for something more serious. Or so I thought.

He had obviously come to my house straight from a bar.

"What do you mean?" he was defensive. "Come on, don't be such a prude. I've just had a few drinks, no big deal." He came in and made himself at home on the couch.

"A prude? You can go home if you think I'm being a prude. There's the door." I wasn't going to take his snide comments.

"Ok, ok...I'm sorry. That's not what I meant. You're not a prude," he corrected himself, sensing he was already off on the wrong foot.

"Gosh, Jude, I was looking forward to you coming over, and telling you how proud I am of you for your medal." My feelings were started to get hurt. Why couldn't he have come over without numbing himself with whiskey first?

"I'm sorry. Come sit down over here," he patted the spot next to him on the couch.

I reluctantly went over and sat down, looking at the man sitting next to me.

"Look, I'm sorry – I shouldn't have gone to the bar first," he apologized again.

"Jude, it's not about the bar, or just a few drinks. I just wanted to see you, with all your senses and all of your attention. I've missed you. And this isn't who I wanted to see," I explained.

"Ok, ok, you're right." He tried his best to sober up and be attentive. "Can we please start over?" He stood up and walked back outside, closing the door behind him. After a second, he knocked on the door again.

How did he know how to make me stop being mad at him? I opened the door, and he stood there, more poised and serious than before.

"Hi, can I come in?" he asked.

I couldn't help but smile, and I let him in. He gave me a big hug, which melted me even more, and I started to let my guard down again.

"You look great, you know that?" he said, and it sounded like he really meant it.

"You don't look bad yourself," I replied. "Congratulations on your medal, Jude. I'm *really* proud of you. And Mom and Dad would have been proud, too."

The mention of my parents made him cast his eyes down for a second, almost as if he felt some regret. Or maybe it was shame...? I couldn't tell before he looked up at me again.

"Let's sit down," he suggested.

We sat down on the couch for the second time now, his eyes again retreating to the floor.

"Jude, I'm proud of you," I repeated. He didn't reply, and I felt so confused, wondering what I was missing.

"What's going on, Jude? I feel like I'm in the dark here. There's been something off between you and Josh for a while now, and it's like a huge elephant in the room that nobody's talking about." I wanted to look into his eyes to see if I could discern something – anything – but he wouldn't look at me.

"Jude, you just got an amazing medal. You should be proud of yourself!" I wanted to shake him, and wake him up from this lifelong trance he was mired in.

"I know I should be proud," Jude started. He raised his eyes to me, and added, "But I'm not, ok?"

"What?" I was confused, and it showed visibly on my face. "Why?"

"Things aren't right between me and Josh because I screwed up," Jude explained. But there weren't enough details, and his thought process was a little muddled by the buzz he was feeling. I needed the information that would put the puzzle together for me, so I pressed on.

"Jude, what happened?" I insisted he tell me the whole story.

It started when the two of them were in Iraq during the invasion of Desert Storm. They were in a convoy of tanks, and once in a while they would stop in little settlements or villages. Jude was always off talking to the locals whenever he had the chance. He would sell things to them to make some extra money – things that weren't exactly legal. He told me he used to sell alcohol whenever he had the chance. It was in such high demand, but he would get into some real trouble if he got caught. Alcohol was technically prohibited in Iraq.

I listened as he told me the story, and he seemed lost in the trance of his memories, having never recounted the story to anyone else since it had occurred.

"One day I wanted to make a sale – the biggest I had made yet. But I was dealing with some of the bigger players in the black market, and it was starting to feel a little dangerous. I didn't care, though; I wanted the money. Plus, it was an adrenaline rush." He looked down again, embarrassed to tell me, but also wanting to finally get it all out. He seemed relieved to divest himself of this arduous secret, a weighty and taxing burden that he was shedding as he told its tale.

"This deal was so important to me that I skipped out on my duty post." He looked at me, waiting for a reaction to his confession, but I just listened.

"That's AWOL, you know. That's no minor thing." He was driving the point home to me, trying to emphasize how serious this was.

"Ok, I understand," I answered, wanting him to continue with the story.

"Well, that's a huge deal – I could have gotten into some major trouble if it weren't for..." He looked down again.

"For what?" I urged.

"If it weren't for Josh," he reluctantly admitted.

"Josh? He was AWOL with you?" I was surprised at this idea.

"No, he wasn't AWOL with me." He stopped for a second to contemplate Josh doing something of the sort, and he laughed. "No, but he noticed that I was missing, and he came after me," Jude clarified, and then continued with the story.

Josh had noticed that Jude wasn't at his duty post, and he knew that he had been doing some trading on the side. He followed Jude's trail by asking around to see who had seen him last, and where he was headed to next. Soon enough, Josh came upon three men who were standing guard at the door of an empty store in a small nearby village, where Jude's deal was going down. Josh told the men he was looking for Jude, and that he just wanted to talk to his friend. He didn't want any trouble.

"I was standing there, negotiating my deal with the head honcho, and these guys drag Josh into the room. They had beat him up a bit," he said, looking at me with regret written on his expression. I covered my mouth, worried. I knew Josh was ok – I'd seen him several times since this had happened. But it still concerned me to hear that he had been hurt.

"They asked me if I knew who he was." He looked at me, and his eyes moistened with a few mounting tears. "Josh said to me, 'Jude, tell them. Tell them we're brothers. We need to get back to our post.'" He described the scene to me, and then paused his narration, hesitant to tell me the next part. Finally, he confessed his act of betrayal, "I just looked at him and didn't say anything."

Jude sat still next to me, remembering. He put his face into his hands and rubbed his eyes like he was trying to wake himself up – maybe from a bad dream. He rubbed his hands brusquely through his hair two or three times, and then looked at me, shameful of his next admission.

"Finally I told them I didn't know who he was. Can you believe that? What a coward I was! All I cared about was the money. That, and I was so mad that Josh would follow me and try to show me what an upstanding soldier he was." Those last words were said with feigned arrogance.

"I didn't need him to save me. You know? I thought he was being self-righteous." A determined tear escaped Jude's eye, and coursed down his face.

"I'm so sorry," he said after a brief pause, looking at me with contrition, his voice almost a whisper.

I smelled the liquor on his breath again, certain that it heightened the courage he needed to tell his terrible tale.

I wiped his tear away. Even though I didn't like what he had done to my brother, I still felt compassion for Jude because I loved him. I didn't say anything, but kept listening, hoping he'd tell me more.

"You should have seen the look in Josh's eyes when I denied even knowing him. It was like I'd crushed him. My best friend. The closest thing I've ever had to a brother." Jude was holding the coin Josh had made for him between his thumb and forefinger. It was still attached to his dog tag chain just like it was when they came home from Basic Training. He rubbed it, polishing it with his worry and guilt.

He continued, "They took him outside, and I didn't know what they did with him, but I had a good idea that they'd probably knock him around a bit. I got my cash, and I headed back out, hoping to get back to my post before anyone else noticed."

He was silent for a minute, like he was done with his story. He'd held it in and hid it from everyone for so long, and now he was feeling liberation from its revelation from darkness into the light. But I didn't want it to be done; I wanted to hear more so I pressed him further, "Then what?"

The hair on every inch of my skin started to stand on end the more I heard, tiny follicle soldiers standing at attention, focusing on Jude's story and eager to hear the rest. It seemed I was there in Desert Storm myself as he unfolded the rest of his account; I could see the scene play out in my mind as it was retold.

Jude planned to meet back up with his team as they came through the town, hoping no one would notice he'd ever been gone. He could feel the money in his pocket and the adrenaline in his veins as he stepped into the street. His rush swiftly fell flat, though, when he saw Josh step out of the shadows on the other side of the dirt road. He had been waiting for Jude behind the corner of a house where he could watch for him. But the absolute last thing Jude wanted right now was to face Josh after he had left him with such a brazen betrayal. So, when he saw him, Jude turned and started walking the other way.

"Jude, listen – I'm here to help you ok?" Josh called after him.

"I don't need your help, Josh," he seethed. "For once, I need to do something on my own!"

Josh already felt hurt by what had just transpired a few minutes before, and these words just made the feeling worse. But he pushed them aside, burying them away for now, and tried to get Jude to listen to him for just a second.

"Fine. We can talk about that stuff later. Right now, you need to listen to me," Josh instructed.

"Is that an order, Corporal, Sir?" Jude said with dripping sarcasm. He snapped to attention and saluted Josh in mockery.

"Jude, stop. I'm serious – there's something going down over there across the road. We need to forget the stuff between us right now and handle this situation." Josh's words finally gave pause to Jude's resentment, and he stopped talking long enough to listen further.

"As soon as I came out into the street and headed back to my Hummer, I noticed something strange on the top of those buildings over there." Josh pulled Jude behind the corner where he had been waiting so they wouldn't be noticed. "Take a quick turkey peek around the corner," he told Jude, who did as he was told and poked his head quickly around the edge of the building. Josh described a location across the street and down a couple hundred feet or so where he saw a two-story building. He directed Jude's attention to the flat rooftop. There was a two-foot wall around the roof that blocked their view, but Jude suddenly noticed a red checkered head scarf pop up over the wall for a brief couple of seconds before disappearing again.

The two friends ducked behind the corner again and looked at each other with widened eyes. Someone was hiding behind the short wall on the roof. They had to be lying down up there, or maybe sitting; if they were standing, they would be clearly visible. They were definitely hiding, and that couldn't be good.

"There's another building just like it kitty-corner to that one, and there are some guys on top of its roof, too," Josh informed Jude. Josh was a cavalry scout in his squad and was skilled at forward reconnaissance. He would go ahead of convoys and determine potential threats, radioing back to them with any pertinent information.

"Our convoy is coming this way and will probably be here within thirty minutes," Jude said, concern visible now on his face, putting together what Josh was trying to convey. "I was going to rejoin them as soon as they rolled through here. Do you think those guys on the roof are Ali Baba planning an ambush?" He used the Army slang for enemy forces.

"That's exactly what I think," Josh answered.

"Get your radio and warn them!" Jude said.

"I wish I could. I left it in the Humvee," Josh said disappointingly.

Their own battle had to wait for this new one – theirs was more a battle of honor and friendship and brotherhood that would be waged another day. But this one had to be fought at this very moment. It could mean life or death for the American convoy that was headed their way.

Josh and Jude huddled together and formulated a quick plan. They had maybe fifteen minutes to carry it out before the convoy would be close enough for the enemy to ambush. They had to move quickly.

"Ok, I'll take this building, and you take the other one. We're going to have to divide and conquer," Josh instructed.

"Yeah, you're right. There's no time to go together. We have to take them out at the same time," Jude agreed.

Their plan was unsophisticated at best. It probably wouldn't be used in textbooks later as an example of how to plan and carry out an attack. But it would have to do, because that's all they had right now. Each of them was armed with their M-16 rifle and two extra clips of ammunition. Josh had one grenade, but Jude didn't have any with him; he hadn't planned on engaging with the enemy like this when he first set out on his lucrative transactional detour. The two of them knew they were short on munitions, but they also knew they didn't have a choice. They had to try anything they could to stop the imminent assault on their approaching unit.

Josh would sneak onto the first roof where some of the saboteurs were waiting. He'd get there from the adjacent building's roof. They were close enough together that he could jump across and hide behind the little stairway covering that gave access to the roof. It looked like a tiny hut that covered the stairwell from the inside of the house. He would assess the number of people and weapons and try to take them out with his grenade. They were hoping that this would provide a distraction, drawing the attention of the other group of radicals on the building kitty-corner to it, so that Jude could pick them off one by one, hopefully eliminating them and their threat.

"This is going to be dangerous, Jude," Josh cautioned. "You don't have to do it if you don't want to. Maybe the grenade explosion will be enough warning to the convoy." He knew this could be a futile mission, one that was most likely impossible to pull off. But he felt he had to try. There was no time to go back for the radio. This had to happen now.

"If you think I'm going to miss out on this, you're crazier than I thought," Jude said, clearly eager to be part of the plan. "If you're in, I'm in." He reached his hand out and Josh took it, shaking on their commitment to the plan.

An image flashed into Josh's mind of the two of them, just young boys, clasping hands in Joshua's Tree, swearing brotherhood. The bittersweet image was gone just as fast, as they broke their grip and readied themselves to carry out their plan.

As they took off in different directions, crouching low so they wouldn't be seen, the thought crossed their minds that they had probably just exchanged their last goodbye. The hard feelings were temporarily forgotten and put aside for this shared duty. They were a team again like they had been their entire lives, and it felt right again. This might be a crazy plan, but at least they were in it together, live or die.

Josh went through the gate of the house next door to the first building and stealthily opened the front door, weapon ready to fire. The living area was empty, so he located the staircase going up and started climbing. He tried to be quick, but also quiet. He abruptly came face to face with a woman coming down the stairs. When she saw Josh, she covered her mouth with her hands and let out a muffled scream. Josh lowered his weapon and told her it would be ok, that he wasn't there to hurt her. He didn't have time for this, he thought; he had to hurry.

He scurried past the woman, who was melting into the wall with fear. He passed a little boy, too, who just stared up at him with his big round eyes. Finally, Josh made it to the rooftop. He scurried over to the edge near the other building and leaped across the gap, landing as quietly as he could so he wouldn't tip off the terrorists on the other side of the roof. He quickly hid behind the little building that covered the stairs, just a few feet away.

Meanwhile, Jude was making similar progress at his location. He broke into the front door of the house, trying not to make any noise, but ready with his weapon in case he accidentally alerted the occupants to his presence. He was relieved to find the house empty, so he climbed the staircase three steps per stride. When he got to the top level of the home, he found that he had a great vantage point of the building next door from one of the bedrooms. The window was open, curtains moving in the breeze, completely oblivious of the thick danger fluttering through their dark green fabric.

He crouched beside the window and slowly peered out to where the men were hiding. He didn't want to catch their attention with any quick or sudden jerks, so he was careful and measured in his movements. He was behind them now and could count four men lying behind the short wall, one of them keeping a look-out for the convoy. Jude followed the direction in which the man was looking, and in the distance, he saw the dust blowing in a thin line behind the convoy.

"Hurry up, Josh," he said in a hushed tone, more to himself than to anyone. He crouched there, waiting for the sound of Josh's grenade, ready to take quick aim and eliminate the four men in his sights.

Josh had quietly lifted himself to the top of the little building and crawled on his stomach to the edge where he could see the five men on the far side of the rooftop, readying their weapons. They could see the convoy coming their way and were beginning their preparations. Josh saw a rocket launcher being loaded, and several guns lying around at the ready. This was it. Now or never.

Josh put his M-16 down next to him, rolled onto his back, and grabbed his grenade. He clamped the spoon of the little bomb with one hand and pulled the pin with the other. If he let go of the live grenade now, it would explode in mere seconds sending fragments of death in every direction from its core. He said a silent prayer, flipped over, and lobbed the grenade into the little nest of terrorists.

Jude heard the anticipated explosion, and it made him jump. He quickly turned and knelt on one knee, resting his rifle on the sill of the open window. He could see the four men looking over at the cloud of smoke from the grenade blast. The distraction had worked! He aimed at the head of the first man and pulled the trigger.

He managed to quickly kill three of the four men, but the fourth one ran off and hid when he saw his friends dropping, and Jude couldn't see him anymore. It was time for him to run and meet Josh at the rally point: Josh's Hummer.

Josh had killed all but one of the men with his grenade, and the fifth one was running for the stairwell, completely unaware that he was heading straight for Josh. Josh aimed and fired, killing the last enemy before jumping down from his perch and running down to the street.

Jude suddenly stopped telling the story and was silent. I woke up from the trance of his narrative, wondering why he was pausing.

"I was walking along the wall of the buildings in the shadows, heading toward the vehicle. I was trying to keep out view and get back to where I was supposed to meet Josh. But suddenly a shot rang out and I instinctively ducked," Jude said. I could tell he was back in the moment, seeing it happen all over again, because he ducked a little sitting there beside me.

"It was Josh. He spotted that fourth Haji that was hiding from me that I didn't have a chance to kill before he got away. Turns out he was still up on the roof and had me in his sights about to take me out when Josh shot him from across the street." Jude was quiet, talking in reverent tones, reliving again how close he had come to death.

"He saved me." Jude looked into my eyes as he said these last words, and then he looked away.

After a moment, I said, "That's really amazing. I can't believe that happened to you guys."

He still didn't say anything. I could see he was weary from disclosing his story, from the alcohol, and from the feelings of shame that I still didn't comprehend.

"Jude, what's wrong? I'm proud of you for what you did. No wonder you got the medal." I still didn't see what he was so troubled about.

"Don't you see?" he asked me. "When the Army investigated the events of that day, Josh just sat back and let me take all the credit for it. I was caught up in the spotlight, and the moment of my greedy glory. And I took all the credit. All of it."

He hung his head, resting his elbows on his knees as if to catch his breath from the exertion of his confession.

"That's why I got that stupid medal. I don't deserve it. It was Josh's idea. He saw the ambush, he convinced me to stay, and he saved my life! It was mostly him, you know. Yeah, I helped him. But I took every ounce of the credit, just to make myself look good. And he didn't say a word. Not about that, not about my black-market deals, not about pretending I didn't know him. None of it."

Now he was crying. I knew he'd been keeping all of this bottled up inside for a while now, and I finally understood the cause of all that angst between the two of them that I was sensing these past couple of years. No wonder, I thought. The pieces were finally falling into place, meshing into a more complete picture of what had happened.

I put my arm around him and waited while he regained his composure.

"I'm such a coward," Jude said, elbows still on his knees. He buried his face in his hands.

"Jude," I put my hand on his back, trying to comfort him.

"Jude," I repeated, "I know Josh. I know him best. And I know he wouldn't want you to torture yourself over this. I know he'd want to just mend things with you and move on," I tried to reason with him.

He didn't answer me, and I tried to think of what else I could say.

"Let's just all sit down and talk about it together and work it out. Ok? I know Josh will just want things to be good between you two again," I reassured him.

Jude looked at me, his face red and eyes starting to swell from trying to rub them dry. I saw the vulnerable boy inside of him that I knew from our childhood. The one who got beaten up by his dad. The one who cried on my shoulder when he knew we were moving and he was being left behind. My heart surrendered to his pain.

I took his head and laid it against my shoulder, and he buried his face in my neck. I just held him for a few moments, stroking his hair and remembering those innocent and simple days of our childhood.

I was pulled from my ruminations when Jude abruptly lifted his head and looked straight into my eyes. Without warning, he kissed me. It was completely unexpected. I'd always held a place for Jude in my heart, though, secretly wishing that he still loved me during all of these years that we'd been apart. I never allowed myself to get too close to other men, always putting up walls for one reason or another. The real reason, I had to admit deep within myself, was Jude. I still loved him.

And so, I kissed him back. I wanted to heal this broken man. Rescue him. Save him from himself. I wanted him to become whole, and then he could perhaps take care of me, too. I needed him to be strong enough to take care of me.

Could someone please take care of me?

I could taste the alcohol in his mouth and thought he must have had more than just a couple of drinks. He started kissing me harder, his emotions extraordinarily raw from the confessions he had just divulged. I wished he would be gentler, though. My heart was overflowing with emotions, too, but we seemed to be on opposite sides of the spectrum when it came to how we wanted to express them.

He was passionate but frantic; impulsive and desperate. I backed off, trying to show him I wanted his tender side. I wanted to feel his heart and his love for me through his delicate and measured touch.

He grabbed the back of my neck, and pulled my face roughly toward him, forcing me to my back on the couch.

"Jude!" I protested. "I'm not going anywhere," I tried to reassure him. Then I whispered into his ear softly and tenderly, so he knew I wanted him, but just not in such a harsh and abrasive way, "I'm here." I wanted him to cherish me and treat me like something of significance in this hour of our overdue reunion, not just an object to exploit in the heat of the moment.

But he was past the emotions now – past listening.

He grabbed my wrist, and he kissed me almost angrily. My mind all at once flashed back to Mount Moorosi, and Datu pinning my arms to his bed. I remembered how petrified I felt in that moment so many years before. Somehow, it seemed like I was there again, even though I knew logically I wasn't. I was here with this man that I'd been waiting for all my life. Waiting for him to notice me when we were just kids. Waiting for him to write me a letter when I lived across the ocean. Waiting for him to take me to the prom. Waiting for him to miss me while he was in the Army. Waiting beyond reason for more.

I was always waiting.

When would he realize we were meant for each other? I've known it from the genesis of our memories, and its truth has always withstood the trials of my perseverance. Couldn't he just this once come through as the man I knew he could be, and make this much-anticipated connection the perfect moment I always knew we both wanted and deserved?

This – whatever this was that was happening right now – this was not what I wanted with Jude. Maybe it was the alcohol, maybe it was something else – I didn't care the reason. He was making me feel uncomfortable, and I wanted some tenderness and affection from him. Not this.

"Jude, please," I said, pushing him back. "Let's let the liquor wear off of you for a while, ok? This wasn't what I had in mind. I mean – not like this." Of course, I wanted to be close to him. I just didn't like this transformation into Mr. Hyde that I was witnessing.

Jude sat up with a bolt, his face livid and foul. "You know what? I just poured out my soul to you. I freaking cried in front of you! And this is how you treat me?" He was yelling now.

I was shocked. And hurt. I didn't know what to say. Who was he? Where did my Jude go?

"I was right the first time I came in," he said, as he climbed off of me and off of my couch. "You're just a self-righteous frigid prude. You're just like your brother. You know that? You both think you're so much better than I am."

I was stunned; stupefied. My mouth was open, but nothing was coming out. I was crushed and confused by his injurious assertions, my heart heavy with the weight of his cruel words, swift and deep lacerations to my soul.

"Whatever. I'm out of here," he announced.

He stood up and walked out of my front door. And out of my life.

38

1995

I had just defended my master's thesis toward the end of the previous year. I had completely immersed myself in the continuous stream of school and work. Without the trickling flow of school assignments or the daily tidal pull to and from my job to fill the empty hours of my days, I knew I would start to feel anxious. Any idle time would turn into worry and disquiet. I would start to miss my parents and Josh. Even worse, I would start to think about Jude, and that wasn't good for me.

So, I filled my days with something – anything – that would keep me engaged. Any pursuit that would make for an occupied mind, too busy to dwell on former re-membrances and the bliss of years gone by.

Then I got a phone call. I had developed an aversion to any phone calls that I wasn't expecting, and this one wasn't good news, either. It was Josh.

"Hi, Sis. Listen, I need your help," he started.

Josh and I talked for ten minutes, and then he had to go. He was calling me from "The Brig" – that's what the military calls their jail. He had been there for two weeks already, and he had another twenty-six days to go before his forty-day sentence would be up.

I tried to find out as many details as I could about why he would possibly be in jail. He didn't really want to tell me over the phone but promised to give me all the details if I could just please fly out there to see him. He was having a really hard time and needed to see someone he knew. He just wanted a friendly face, and then he knew he'd be able to make it the rest of his time there.

Of course, I dropped everything and flew out there, knowing that I'd get the full story when I arrived and could finally see him face-to-face.

"I can't believe you're in here, Josh," I told him, once we sat down for his visiting time. He didn't look very good. He seemed down, even depressed. That was not like the Josh I knew, and I was worried for him.

"I know," he answered. "It's such a long story; I don't even know where to begin."

"I'm not in a hurry, so take your time. Are you eating enough?" I asked.

"Yeah, I'm just having a hard time, that's all. But seeing you is just what I needed. Thanks for coming," he answered, hugging me tight before we sat down together.

Josh told me what the last two weeks had been like. "It's actually a little easier than Boot Camp," he said, smiling. "At least we don't have to do all the PT drills." The worst part, he told me, was just waiting for time to happen. He didn't like going to sleep at night, because he knew when he opened his eyes, he'd have to face a new day again. But he knew deep down he would make it. It was only forty days, after all. Not a year, or two years, or even more, like some guys had to face. He couldn't fathom how anyone could be locked up for that long, and he'd only been here for two weeks.

"I can get through twenty-six days," he said, trying to convince himself, I think, more than to reassure me.

"I know you can. I have all the faith in the world in you," I told him. I was anxious to hear the details of why he was in here, though, so I prodded him along. "So...tell me what happened, and don't leave anything out."

Josh told me that the Army had been getting some complaints from the press concerning soldiers participating in illegal activities during Desert Storm. He wasn't sure why they were bringing this up now, other than some other more widely broadcast stories that were going around regarding the war that portrayed the Army in a very unflattering light.

They had been getting a lot of bad press, including some major controversies from the war, such as the "Highway of Death" where the coalition had been accused of attacking and killing a retreating army. Also, the "Bulldozer Assault," where our forces were accused of burying the enemy alive in long sandy trenches in the deserts of Iraq. Because of these controversial issues, it seemed like the Army was extremely sensitive to any bad press over the last several months. So, when a reporter had contacted their PR people about some illegal sales of alcohol to Muslim villagers, they opened an investigation.

The Army made their inquiries and found that Josh and Jude had been away from their duty posts without leave during the time period in question. This little fact had been pushed aside during the war itself, since the two soldiers had saved the Convoy from attack. But now, someone had to take the blame. The Army wasn't going to be accountable for insulting the Islamic people by pushing the evil of the West upon them through illegal substances. Alcohol was against their religious health code and wasn't permitted for sale among their people. If American servicemen had been involved in the black market providing this substance to the Muslim people, the Army wasn't going to stand culpable, and would definitely avoid the bad press.

Since they had decorated Jude with the Silver Star, it wouldn't be prudent for the Army to single him out for wrongdoing. In fact, that might look worse for them to incarcerate a decorated war hero. So instead, they looked to Josh as the fall guy to feed to the hungry reporters.

"Didn't you tell them you were out there to get Jude back to his post? Didn't you tell them you were the one who prevented that ambush?" I asked him, incredulous that he would take the fall for Jude yet again. This was starting to become an endless expiation for Jude, always at Josh's expense, and I couldn't bear it anymore.

"Jude prevented that ambush right there along with me," Josh insisted.

"Josh. Now is not the time for modesty." I chided. "Jude threw you under the bus like I've never seen anyone do before." I was getting mad now.

"It's ok. Please just listen to me," he said with an even tone. "I didn't say anything because I didn't want Jude to have to come here to the Brig. You know as well as I do, it would have broken him completely."

"Josh, he denied even knowing you! Don't you remember that? After everything you've done for him our entire lives, he betrayed you!" My blood was starting to roil with the heat of my anger, bubbling out through my fiery tone.

"I'm over that, ok?" His manner was curt and abrupt, and I knew I needed to check myself. Josh was handling this better than I was. That much was clear.

He continued with an almost soothing tone, trying to ease my ire and lull my indignation.

"Look, I just needed to see your face and know that you're here with me. I just needed a little pick-me-up so that I can make it for twenty-six more days," he said, trying to change the subject.

I backed off a little, realizing that I was making his situation worse.

We sat in silence for a few seconds, and I could see on his face that he was happy to have me with him – even if it was just for a couple of hours.

"I'm here for you, Josh. Always. You know that," I promised.

He smiled at me and held my hand. He nodded.

"Does Jude know you're in here?" I asked him.

"No, I don't think so. I don't want to add to his load, though, so let's not tell him if he doesn't already know, ok? He's going through a rough time of his own," he added.

"What do you mean?" I asked. I hadn't heard anything about Jude in a long time, and I was completely ok with that. I couldn't help a little curiosity, though.

"Well, he just got married," Josh said, looking sideways at me to gauge my reaction.

I felt a stab through my heart. I was moving on from Jude, but this bit of news took me by surprise, and admittedly hurt.

"Wow. Really?" I asked. "How long have you known about that?" I asked almost accusingly. I shouldn't project my emotions for Jude onto Josh, but in my weakness, it just came out.

"Well...I guess I've known a little of it for just a few weeks or so." He tried to minimize the blow for me. "He got a girl pregnant, and so they got married. I think they're going to have their baby early next year."

This news hit me even harder. A baby? This wasn't just a stab to the heart; it was a blow to the gut. I couldn't find my breath; the wind having been knocked from me by the force of this news. It was so – *permanent*.

I sat in silence for just a moment or two, feeling my loss all over again. I had lost Jude once. Not to mention losing my parents prior to that. And now I was losing him all over again. I was a powerless observer, watching the wreckage of my life from a distance. Over time I had managed to staunch my wounds with gauzes and dressings of diversions, salves of new pursuits and distractions, wrapping and concealing the lacerations so they could begin to heal and hopefully scab over.

But this.

I could feel the blood seeping through my figurative bandages, streaming anew. I wasn't sure the lesions could be bound up sufficiently anymore.

"Last time I talked to him, he was trying to make the best of the situation. He said they're going to have a girl." Josh tried to be gentle with the news. He knew how I felt about Jude.

I tried to imagine Jude married. That part wasn't hard. I'd imagined him being married to me ever since I was a little girl. It was imaging him married to someone else that was the hard part.

"Well, good for him," I tried to sound positive, shoving my feelings away as best I could for now, trying to focus again on Josh and his current ordeal. I'd cry later when I was by myself. Right now, Josh needed me.

We spent the rest of our time together talking about Mom and Dad, and all of the wonderful times we had together as a family. We missed them so much.

Josh said, "At least they don't have to see me in jail."

After Josh paid for Jude's offenses, the Army discharged him with dishonor. Josh was dismayed to know that his Army career would end this way, but, as ever, he felt a sense of duty and responsibility for Jude. Josh didn't want him to end up a broken man like his father was – he wanted Jude to be able to raise his new daughter better than he had been raised. And maybe this would give him that chance.

I wished Jude could know all of the things that Josh had done for him. When they cut their palms up in that Joshua tree all those years ago and promised each other they would remain brothers to the end, Josh really meant it.

39

Seven years had slipped away when Josh and I decided we wanted to visit our hometown again. It had been even longer than that since we'd been back home - to the house where our parents first started molding our little minds and souls. To our farm, where we fled from our hostile geese and cultivated all of that corn. To Joshua's Tree.

We wanted to sit up on the platform of that favorite tree of his, and reminisce about our childhood, and about our parents. This year made it ten years ago since our parents had died, and we wanted to pay tribute to them just between the two of us. In the place where we first knew them; on our farm in that small town where the adventures of our childhood all began.

So, we took a road trip, and braved the snowy roads, winding along the river where we had played as children.

Josh had gone to college and graduated and was well into his new career now. He felt like he had a new lease on life. He never regretted his decision to sacrifice his own success and reputation for his beloved brother, though. He would make the same decisions today if he had to do it all over again.

Josh was just that way; he simply forged ahead, not looking back. My heart was more reluctant than that. It concealed itself over the years, hiding its susceptibility away in shyness like it was five years old, burying its face in my mother's neck.

I looked over at Josh, who had his hand on the wheel, looking from time to time out his window at the scenery. He'd point out all of the things that were different from when we were kids; new buildings, paved roads. I was glad to just spend time with my brother, trying to give reverence and memorial to the heritage and legacy our parents left us. And that's when we came upon the bus.

The school bus.

Suddenly I was in the water again – the profoundly cold liquid surrounding me. I could feel Josh pulling on my wrist to save me, dragging me from the depths of that river up to the surface. Pulling...pulling...

"Wake up," Josh said, pulling on my wrist where I was sleeping next to his hospital bed.

I jerked awake, and sat up next to him, realizing that he was conscious!

"Josh, you're awake!" I said, looking at the clock, and wondering how long I had been asleep.

"Yeah, I'm awake," he said groggily. Tears started pouring down my face from sheer joy. Thank you, Father in Heaven, I prayed silently. Thank you for not taking him from me, too.

I leaned over and hugged him, kissing his forehead, and bathing his cheeks with my tears.

I told him how happy I was and let him know that he had been in a coma for three days. I was starting to worry that he wasn't ever going to wake up.

"Oh, you know me. I'm a fighter." He was teasing with me, even though I could see that he was a bit bleary and weak.

"Josh, you saved my life. And so many little kids' lives, too. Do you remember?" I asked him.

"Yeah, I remember the bus going into the river, and then trying to save all those kids," he said. "You helped me, too, you know."

"I tried, but you had to save me, too," I said. "I'm so glad you're ok." I hugged him again and held his hand tight.

We sat there talking for a while, between doctors and nurses checking him out. I told him that I practically dreamed our entire lives while I was asleep. I told him I dreamed of Kuntigi, and Modibo. And even Kéta. He smiled. He was the only other person on earth to share those seminal and shaping experiences, now just recollections, and to know them exactly as thoroughly as I did.

"I wish I could have dreamed that, too. I would love to relive all those memories. Well, most of them," he smiled.

"Remember our mango tree?" he asked.

"Yes, I remember," I said, seeing again the young versions of ourselves ready to leap into our pool from the mango tree's proffering branches.

"I wish we could have sat together in my tree one more time," he said.

"What do you mean?" I was quick to reply. I didn't like the way he was talking. "We still can. When you get better, that's the first thing we'll do."

He paused for a few moments, and then appeased me saying, "Ok, we'll do that first thing."

My heart was healing quickly from the last three days of worry and concern for my brother. It had been draining for me, and I felt such a relief as the weight started to lift from my shoulders. After a couple of hours, Josh told me I should go down to the cafeteria and get something to eat. I was getting an appetite again, so I readily agreed and headed downstairs.

I got a bagel with some cream cheese and grabbed a Diet Coke. I didn't want to take too long because I was uneasy being anywhere other than right by Josh's side. I didn't like being away from him for even five minutes. I took the elevator and walked toward his room, relief flowing over me the closer I got to him.

I walked through the open door and at once stopped in my tracks. I was shocked to see Jude standing there next to Josh's bed. What was he doing here after all these years?

Jude saw me, too, and turned to look at me with that unforgettable face. He seemed a little older and more mature, perhaps filled out a bit from almost ten years ago.

"Hi," he said, unsure what else to say.

"Hi," I responded. "Wow, it's been a long time."

"Yes, much too long." He seemed more peaceful and composed than the Jude I had last seen. He appeared a little more confident and happy with himself. I could already see it in him just in these few seconds.

"It's so good to see you again," he smiled at me genuinely.

So many years had gone by; many of them spent trying to move on from this man who had made such an indelible imprint on my life. I had rehearsed countless times what I would say to Jude if I ever saw him again. But the moment I walked into the room, I couldn't remember a word of any of it.

I wasn't prepared for this.

"I want to introduce you to my daughter, Kay," he said, pointing to the little girl whose hand he was holding.

My heart stopped beating for a couple of seconds before it remembered its usual pace again. And then it swelled with such feeling, I thought it might erupt with flowing streams of molten emotion. It was different than what I'd felt any time before; it wasn't the sorrow I'd felt at losing my parents. It wasn't the love I'd felt for Jude. But it *was* love.

It was definitely love.

I had seen this little girl just a few days before. She had been reaching out to me in the back of the drowning bus, her terrified eyes pleading with me to save her. This was the little girl who wrapped her arms around my neck so tight while we swam to the shore and didn't want to let me go once we got there.

Tears ran down my face and I said, "*This* is your little girl, Jude?"

"Yes," he said, looking at Kay and wondering why I was reacting like this. "Do you know her?"

"Yes," I said, crouching down to the floor, and opening my arms. "We met when the bus was in the river." Kay recognized me, too, and she ran into my arms, hugging me tight.

I thought that my connection with Kay in the bus was because of how much I loved Robert from my job at the adult day program during my college years. They both had Down syndrome, and I just figured when I saw her in the bus, that was the reason I felt an immediate connection with her the way I did. Now, I knew it had to be more than that. I had to wonder if it was also because she was Jude's.

"Kay Kay, do you want to go for a walk with your friend?" Jude asked his daughter.

"Yes!" she answered, grabbing my hand.

"Do you mind?" Jude asked me. "I was hoping to talk with Josh for a minute."

"I don't mind at all," I smiled.

While Kay and I walked down the hallways of the hospital, Josh and Jude had some time to talk. I looked at Kay beside me, holding my hand as we ambled along. I can't believe this is Jude's daughter, I thought to myself. I just can't believe it! I couldn't wait to catch up with Jude – it had been so long.

Kay wanted to walk faster and pulled at my hand. "C'mon!"

In Josh's hospital room, Jude sat on the edge of the bed and looked at his old friend.

"I guess along with everything else you've done for me, I hear you're the one responsible for saving my daughter's life," Jude started.

"Actually, you have my sister to thank for that," Josh said.

Jude raised his eyebrows. "Really? I thought it was you."

"We were both there. It wasn't just me." Josh was getting tired and found it a little arduous to breathe.

"Well, thank you. Thank you for your part in saving my little Kay Kay." Jude didn't want to consider what would have happened to his sweet little girl if Josh hadn't been there. The news that I had seen her safely to shore was something new for him to consider.

But let's be honest; I only jumped off that bridge because Josh did.

Jude wanted to make things right with Josh and begged his forgiveness for the way he had treated him those many years ago. Josh tried to play it off, but Jude was determined to say everything that needed to be said.

"I hope you can find it in your heart to somehow forgive me, Josh," Jude said, his voice soft and full of humility.

"There's nothing to forgive, brother," Josh granted him absolution.

"I flat out denied knowing you, Josh. And I'll forever be sorry for that," Jude insisted.

He apologized for each one of his wrongs, admitting his selfishness and culpability. Josh listened as he sat propped up in his hospital bed against a few pillows.

"I don't know why it took me so long to change. I was so jealous of you, and I just never felt like I could measure up. Not when we were little, not in high school, and I held onto that even when we went into the Army. It's like I was looking for a reason to resent you – holding on to the envy and bitterness as an excuse for my inevitable failures. Like a self-fulfilling prophecy or something," Jude confessed.

"You were never a failure in my eyes, Jude. Never. The only thing I regret was that you could never fully trust me. You always doubted," Josh said, lamenting.

"I know," Jude admitted, his eyes cast down, wishing he could redo so many things from his past. He knew that Josh wasn't perfect and that he was living the human experience just as much as anyone else. But Josh was just so different from the rest of us, Jude thought. He was everything that was good about life. He was so thoroughly and unequivocally good.

"I want you to know *I believe in you.* You're my brother, remember?" Josh asked. There was a pause, and Jude just listened. "I've always believed in you. I want you to believe in *yourself.*"

"I believe in myself," Jude said with a little hesitation, clasping hands with Josh. Then after some reflection he implored, "Will you help me believe?"

Josh smiled and pulled his brother close to hug him, and then let him go again. He was tired and felt depleted.

Jude remembered something he had brought with him and he reached into his jacket pocket, producing his Silver Star.

"This really belongs to you, Josh," Jude said, putting the medal into Josh's hand.

"No, Jude – that's yours. You need to keep that," Josh answered.

"Please – for me. Take it. I haven't ever deserved it, and I don't deserve it now. *You* are my hero, Josh, and you always have been. I want you to have it," Jude was pleading with him now.

Josh reluctantly held the medal in his hand. Jude let his tears flow freely.

"I'm so sorry, Josh," he said again.

"Jude, I don't want you to spend another moment worrying about this. It's over now. We're brothers, and we have our future ahead of us," Josh said.

Jude contemplated those words for a second, remembering the time they cut their palms up in Joshua's Tree. With that vision from his past lingering in his mind, he suddenly recalled his cherished keepsake and pulled his keys from his pocket. Hanging from the key ring was his little metal disc, one side displaying the two J's, and the other side with the tree.

He showed it to Josh, and now they both had tears streaming from their eyes. "You're right, we're brothers. Forever," Jude said.

Later that night, Josh took a turn for the worse, and he quietly passed away in his sleep while I held his hand. The doctors said he died from complications related to pneumonia.

I wondered if my parents were waiting for him when he joined them in the next life. I imagined their joyful reunion, my mother and father welcoming Josh into their outstretched arms. My heart bruised with envy at that vision, and I was suddenly overcome with hunger for that delicious savor that was certainly theirs in being reunited.

I won't lie and say that it was the same as when my parents died. To be truthful, in some ways it was worse. When they died, I still had Josh with me, and he was suffering everything I was – we were companions in our consternation and grief. Now, I was completely alone in the world. I had no more living relatives, and that was an emotionally daunting reality to face.

My heart was already fractured with deep rifts from my parents' passing. These were fissures that would never be fully healed; it was just the new form and figure of my heart, scarred and broken. I learned to live a new existence without them, leaving behind the old version of me, buried together with them and their memories, a new me emerging from necessity, different than before.

Now, with Josh leaving me, my heart was splintered into infinite and limitless fragments.

I was heartbroken. Again. Still.

Through the misery of losing my brother and amidst the despair of my heartache, I couldn't help but realize that Josh had died in a way that I couldn't envision being more "him." Just as he told Modibo on top of that big canoe in the middle of the Sahara, Josh always thought he had some sort of purpose. He felt he wanted to make a difference to other people. And that's exactly what he did. He always put himself after others, he kept his promises, and he was kind and loving.

All of this culminated in his last act of heroism and selflessness. He didn't think twice before jumping off that bridge into the icy waters below.

I understood as I sat there with him, holding his lifeless hand, that this was the Providence that Modibo was talking about. This was the plan for Josh's life. It would happen, no matter what. Not because it was destiny, but because of who Joshua was, and because no matter which of many paths he could have chosen, whichever one he took would ultimately lead to this outcome.

It was self-determination.

He couldn't choose any other way – it just wasn't in him. It never was, even from the time we were kids and he insisted on making peace and becoming friends with Kuntigi.

Yes, this was Josh's purpose. I knew it. I felt it. In my gut, in my heart, and in my soul. He was remarkable.

40

My legs were swinging back and forth as they hung over the platform in Joshua's Tree. Jude was swinging his legs the same way sitting next to me. Every now and then, the tempo of our swinging feet melded into unison, disappearing underneath the platform at the same time, and reappearing into our view in perfect harmony. My shorter legs would soon break from the rhythm and swing underneath us a little faster than his, breaking the cadence again into dissonance; a mesmerizing duet.

We watched Kay running on the ground below us, examining anything that poked out from the snow, and running with her arms stuck straight out behind her back, her head leading the way. I loved watching her play. She was beautiful, and I was falling in love with her little spirit more and more as each moment passed.

"She's amazing," I said. "She looks like you, too."

"Thank you," Jude answered. "I love her more than anything."

"I'm sure you do. I'm a little jealous, actually," I admitted. "I always thought I'd have some kids of my own by now."

"You will - you've got lots of time," Jude said. "Don't rush it."

"I actually wanted to adopt a couple of kids from Africa, you know," I told him. I often thought of the kids we knew down the alley from our house in Bamako, and in my heart, I always longed to bring two kids just like them into my home, into my family. I wondered if that idea would make Kuntigi smile.

"Really? Well, I'm not surprised. That would be amazing, actually," he admitted.

"Well, your little Kay is just a sweetheart," I emphasized again.

"Yes, she is. Her mom left us when Kay was just about a year old. She couldn't handle having a kid with any challenges, you know. The Down syndrome was too much for her. I don't think she was ready for kids at all, actually."

"I'm sorry to hear that," I said with sincerity. "I'm sure that wasn't an easy time."

"No, it wasn't. Kay was completely unexpected as it was. Not a mistake, mind you. She's perfect, and I wouldn't be who I am today without her. Just unexpected," he clarified.

"You're lucky to have her," I said. And I truly meant it. If she were mine, I'd be overjoyed.

We sat for a while, following Kay with our gaze everywhere she roamed. She was chattering to herself, and it reminded me of Robert who used to do the same thing even as an adult.

"Yeah, Kay really changed me. It's hard to explain, but when she was born, all I wanted to do was protect her and take care of her. Especially when they told me she would be different from other kids. I almost resented that, like how dare they insinuate that she wouldn't be just as amazing as any other kid, you know?" He looked at me for my understanding.

"Yes, I understand," I acknowledged.

"Well, I loved her even more when I saw her little face – that tiny little nose, the stunning sparkles in her eyes, her precious little hands. Oh, her hands," he said, looking over at me to emphasize just how much he meant it. "My heart just fell in love with her even more, if that's possible. Maybe I just felt more protective and wanted to be the best dad she could possibly have," he explained.

"I'm sure you've been a great dad," I said.

"Well, I try to be. I had to do some major growing up, and act like a man instead of the selfish jerk that I'd become," he said. "I learned a lot of hard lessons in a really short period of time. But Kay and I got through it, and now we have each other." He smiled down at her from our perch in the tree.

Kay tripped and fell in the snow but picked herself back up without batting an eye and kept running. "I'm OK, Daddy!" She yelled without looking up at us, already running off to see what else she could find.

"She has an amazing personality. She's so independent, and she lights up any room she's in. She's so clever, too. So smart." He was watching her play, and I loved hearing him talk about his little girl with such love in his voice.

Jude and I didn't have to say anything, comfortable in the silence and enjoying the scenery of the old farm. We'd talk when we had something to say, but were completely contented to just sit next to one another without having to fill the quiet. Now Kay was eating some snow, her little hands turning red from the cold.

"This is where it all started, you know," Jude said.

"Where what all started?" I asked.

"Our story." He looked over at me, and I looked back into his dark brown eyes, the ones I'd known since I started remembering anything in my life at all.

"Yes, I guess you're right," I agreed. "It's quite a story, too. Ups and downs."

"Most of the downs are because of me," he admitted.

"At least some of them," I said, smiling at him in agreement.

He paused before he made his next assertion.

"I want you to know I've changed. Really changed," Jude said.

"Ok," I acknowledged what he had said. I was feeling cautious, but I was also starting to believe him.

"I should have changed before Kay was born. I told Josh the same thing in the hospital. I wish I would have changed a long time ago. But I can't alter the past." He was being as earnest as he could with me, really trying to convey his sincerity.

"All of us have done things we wish we could change," I said, trying to make this easier on him. I could tell it had been a lengthy struggle.

"Yeah, but some of our things are much worse than others'," he smiled again. That smile! So charming, as always.

"At some point, though," he continued, "I had to decide to look forward and change my future, since I can't change the past. I can beg for forgiveness, which I did with Josh, by the way."

"You did? What did he say, if you don't mind my asking?" I longed to hear something about my brother.

Anything. My heart ached just hearing his name. I missed him so much already.

"He was just as gracious as he always is – he told me not to think about it for another second. He said I need to let it go, and forgive myself, because he forgave me a long time ago." Jude's voice cracked a little with emotion, obviously touched by Josh's gracious nature.

"That sounds like him," I smiled at the thought of my brother, and my emotions welled up inside of me, tears instantly springing to my eyes.

"Anyway," Jude continued, "I feel like I've woken up from some sort of deep slumber, and now I'm wide awake, ready to focus on the important things in life."

"I can tell," I said, genuinely seeing a change in Jude.

He turned his head and looked at me with a wry smile.

"What?" I asked, smiling back.

"Oh, nothing. I'm just remembering when I went with you and Josh on that trip when we were all in Lesotho," he said. "That was quite a moment in time, wasn't it? Out there under the stars?"

I smiled, remembering too. "Yes, it really was."

"I'm glad we have that memory together. I'm glad it was with you," he confided.

"I wouldn't want that memory with anyone else," I agreed.

He smiled bigger, and added, "And then there was that fire you started out there in the grasslands of Africa!" The air filled with his laugh, and I hit him playfully on his shoulder. He looked at me, still smiling widely, and we both broke out laughing at the memory.

Laughter. I needed it. It was a healing balm; a palliative salve for my bruised heart in that moment.

We watched Kay for a few more minutes, and then Jude grabbed the rope that was hanging from the branch and asked, "Should we swing down from here for old times' sake?"

"Are you kidding? I'm thirty-two years old, Jude! I'm too old for that kind of thing," I protested.

"You can never be too old for this," he smiled, and swung from the platform into the snowy ground below. He ran over and gathered Kay into his arms, and they started making snow angels, tiny particles of snowflakes swirling all around them in the cold, brisk air.

Kay got up from the ground and looked up at me sitting in Joshua's Tree. She smiled with those gorgeous unassuming eyes and called to me, "Come play!"

I grabbed the rope and followed Jude, sliding from my perch and swinging into the open air.

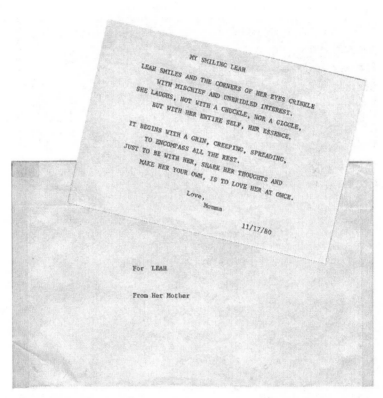

The poem my mother wrote for me on my 10th birthday.

Growing up on our farm.

Playing in the creek.

Rope swinging into the creek.

Swimming in our pool in Bamako, Mali.

My brother jumping into the pool from the mango tree.

Kéta roasting his rat.

The boat we took to Timbuktu.

One of the stops along the way – the pinasse behind us.

Staying warm with Modibo.

Group of villagers gathering around.

Little girl on our boat with her new Mrs. Beasley.

Trading babies; I'm holding the real one.

Two kids, a rooster and a hungry cow.

Modibo with our dog, Rahtchy.

Malian woman with mortar and pestle.

Modibo

ABOUT THE AUTHOR

Leah Martin is co-owner of A Brighter Community, a day program for adults with developmental disabilities in Arvada, Colorado. She recently retired from her twenty-three year career in remote sensing and satellite imagery to focus full-time on her business. She is currently pursuing her PhD in Psychology. Joshua's Tree is her first novel.

BOOK CLUB QUESTIONS

1. People from various faiths, as well as those without a background of faith, have been touched by this book; one does not need to embrace a Christian view to gain insight from the story and its parallels. Either despite or because of your own personal worldview, did you notice on your own that there is an allegory embedded within the story? At what point did you first see the parallels?

2. What was your favorite allegorical inference? Why did that one stand out to you?

3. There are some fictional threads throughout the book (for example, the author used the name Joshua instead of her brother's real name for the sake of the allegory), but many of the stories are true from the author's own life. What are your thoughts regarding this *fictional memoire* genre?

4. What were your impressions when you found out that Jude's daughter was the little girl from the bus crash?

5. Why did Jude struggle with his sense of self-worth? How did his struggle affect each of his relationships?

6. Discuss how each of the three main characters experienced betrayal, and how it affected them.

7. How do you feel about her ending up with Jude in the end?

8. The protagonist is a strong female. What experiences in her untamed and abundant childhood formulated her independent and fearless character, and allowed her to discover herself?

9. What in her childhood prepared her to embrace diversity as an adult?

10. The protagonist's name is not mentioned in the story at all. Why do you think the author would omit her first name from her own story?

ALLEGORICAL INFERENCES

The Book	The Allegory
The name Joshua.	Joshua is the Hebrew equivalent to the Greek-derived name *Jesus*.
Joshua was born in a year by which all time seems to be measured (lunar landing).	Jesus was born in the Meridian of Time. *Anno Domini* (AD) and before Christ (BC) are used to number years in the Julian and Gregorian calendars.
Joshua had a kind heart and generous disposition.	Jesus is the definition of charity – the pure love of Christ.
Following in the footsteps of my dad through the fields on our farm.	Figurative of following God and following the example of Jesus Christ.
The Joshua Tree.	Jesus was crucified on a wooden cross – a "tree."
Joshua went to the tree for solitude.	Jesus spent some time in solitude – in fasting and prayer.
The tree was his hiding place and his refuge.	This is from The Psalms.
Joshua and Jude were blood brothers.	Christ spilled his blood for us – as our Eldest Brother, the Son of God. It was an atonement for our sins.

Josh felt responsibility for Jude, a concern for his well-being, etc.	We are invited in 1 Peter to cast our cares on Jesus because he cares for us.
The protagonist said, *The very notion that I could be like my brother fueled my abilities and gave me strength to rise up to the challenge with wings as eagles.*	Aspiring to be Christlike gives us strength to overcome challenges. See Isaiah 40:31.
Joshua wanted to make peace with our enemies.	Jesus said, "love thine enemies." He is the Prince of Peace.
Josh's dad had a dream before he was born. He saw Joshua and heard his name.	Joseph had a dream and was told to stay married to Mary. He was told that the name of her son would be Jesus.
Josh had a group of "disciples" and was like a shepherd to his flock of little kids.	Jesus had disciples. Jesus is the Good Shepherd. He knows us, his sheep.
Josh taught Modibo about Christianity when he was 12 years old.	Jesus taught his gospel in the Temple at the age of 12.
Josh felt he had a purpose in life.	Jesus had a foreordained and defined purpose in life.
Imagery of baptism: the end of my childhood, beginning of life as a young woman.	Jesus was baptized and asked us to also be baptized, to put away our old life and begin a new life as His followers.

Josh suggested we give away our things to the poor.	Jesus said we should give of our temporal things.
Josh told Jude to trust him.	Jesus asked us to believe in Him and have faith in Him.
Josh gave up college to enlist with Jude.	Jesus didn't seek after fame or fortune. He gave everything up for the good of each of us.
Jude was jealous of Josh. He resented his success and ease of rising to the top.	The Deceiver is jealous and envious of Jesus.
Jude denied knowing Josh.	Peter denied knowing Jesus.
Jude "sold Josh out" so that he can get the money from his black-market deals. Jude betrayed Josh.	Judas betrayed Jesus for thirty pieces of silver.
Jude took the credit for preventing the ambush on the convoy. Another betrayal.	Christ was betrayed many times. He did not receive credit for many things He did. Barabas was released instead of Jesus.
Josh went to prison for something Jude did.	Jesus paid for the sins of everyone else. He was sinless.
Josh was dishonorably discharged from the Army. He took his oath of	Jesus was given lashes; a crown of thorns was placed on his head. He was dishonored without

brotherhood to great lengths.	cause and spat upon. Jesus took his oath to the ultimate extent: his oath of salvation for us.
Josh woke up from his coma after three days.	Jesus was resurrected and broke the bonds of death after three days.
Jude asked forgiveness and Josh willingly gave it.	We ask forgiveness from Jesus, and He willingly forgives the penitent soul.
Josh said to Jude, *I wish you would have trusted me more. I wish you would have believed in yourself.* Jude said that he does believe in himself, and then asked Josh – *help me believe.*	Jesus told a man, "If thou canst believe, all things are possible to him that believeth." And the man said with tears, "Lord, I believe; help thou mine unbelief."
Josh and Jude were committed to their brotherhood forever.	Jesus is our eternal brother.
Joshua died because he saved the lives of others.	Jesus died to save our spiritual and temporal lives through the atonement and the resurrection.
Josh died at age 33.	Jesus died at age 33.
Joshua's life wouldn't have led to any other outcome, because of who he was; it was his purpose.	Jesus' life would not have led to any other outcome, because He is perfect, it was the purpose of His life, and He was willing.

JOSHUA'S TREE

Made in the USA
San Bernardino, CA
06 October 2018